Caroline Seton Ledlie

Peaches
A Southern girl grows up

Caroline Seton Ledlie

Pibbtown Publishing
Atlanta

This is a work of fiction, and all the character, incidents and dialogues are products of the author's imagination and are not construed as real. Any resemblance to actual persons, living or dead, is entirely coincidental.

Version 1.2

For information, please contact
joe.ledlie@theledliegroup.com.

ISBN: 1511928670

Pibbtown Publishing
Buckhead Centre
2970 Peachtree Road, Suite 805
Atlanta, Georgia 30305

Southern Genesis

As a new day of days began from the South to the North, minute hands slipped past midnight on timepieces up and down the eastern coast. In the dark before dawn, heaving presses churned out daily newspapers for the big cities, small towns, and the unseen counties in between.

In each newspaper's local section were printed the area's death notices. Each was a testament to a day that had turned remarkably and malignantly special, changing from all the colors of life to stark, sudden black-and-white. In time, the paper would yellow and tear, but for now the dark print was homage to a life somehow lived, capturing the ageless and painless last breath of air from a new corpse, like a handful of gray dust scattered in a final wind.

Deep down South, morning found its way in the glory of first light, blazing, and burning away the guileful shadows hanging close to the ground. In a small town that lay within the last and luckiest colony, the land, though the calendar said Tuesday, was dressed in its Sunday best of yellow, blue, and green. The weekend was still as far off as winter, that autumnal afterthought in the South even in the coldest years. No, now, at this moment, spring was sovereign across the Southern land.

In a cul-de-sac of the town, a red toy wagon shone with buckle-shoe brightness. In a sun-drenched backyard, clean, white sheets stenciled with blue swirls flapped on a clothesline, which had been roped around an old oak and a flowering peach tree. Both trees threw shade over green grass growing immortal from the rich black Georgia soil. Primary tones shone in their full vibrancy, and a breeze blessed by springtime floated memories through the screened windows of an old house.

Mama appeared downstairs. Sunlight overcame her eyes and seeped into her skull. The buzz of warmth was pleasant, proceeding slowly from the inside out. The baby within her napped contentedly across her pelvis as if it were a hammock, not quite asleep or awake as Mama breathed easily for both of them.

In the front room the light dribbling of fingers across piano keys sounded an old blues melody. Mama pushed through the swinging kitchen door to smile at her favorite husband as he stepped from the piano. The two joined together at the front door like paper dolls, and Mama stood on tiptoe to kiss her seersuckered man goodbye. He patted the baby under the tied sea green sash of her cotton robe where his wife swelled like a full moon.

Mama opened the door, and her soulmate paused to breathe in the fresh, tart air deep down. A train whistle sounded from the center of town. "Today's going to be one of those days, I think," he said.

He smiled at his young wife and took a last sip of coffee. Then he handed her the slick sky blue mug as he stepped over the threshold to the outside. Mama was reminded of a virginal Norman Rockwell boy brimming with energy and exhilaration. Her husband's excitement was infectious, and Mama felt a deluge of bouncing coming from the child within her.

"What do you mean by that?" she asked him sweetly, adjusting his tie and smoothing him over, his light hair damply clean and slicked back like a movie star from filmdom's glory days. In her mind, his appearance was her looking glass, and his handsome freshness made her existence seem pleasant and right.

"One of those days that makes you feel full of life," he grinned. He pointed at a flowering peach tree with fat buds in bloom that hung an umbrella of cool shade over the front porch. "Soon we'll have peaches!"

He kissed Mama on a soft eyelid, and then strode down the driveway. Mama headed back through the living room towards the heart of the house. The kitchen smelled of waking humans and of frying meat. Mama stood at the doorway, enjoying the slow moving moments of morning as she watched her mother cook breakfast. Gram found a stove every sunrise like a crowing rooster finds a picket fence. She had arrived the day before after sensing the baby's emerging presence and packing her bags to head down from Atlanta.

Gram smiled warmly at her daughter as she napped thick strips of bacon and stirred smooth grits creamed with salty lumps of yellow butter. She turned to look at the distended belly that held her grandchild, and remembered a time when she had held her own daughter that close.

Weighted footsteps on the front stairs and the kitchen door swung open as though from a black-hatted cowboy itching for a fight. A small pit bull of a woman with looping, poufing hair entered the kitchen. Granny Fanny grunted an indecipherable greeting that fell slowly in viscous clumps from her mouth. Mama felt a sham portrait of a charming smile etch across her face. Her mother-in-law had been in town for weeks, driving Mama mad by stalking her like an angry hen in search of stolen eggs. The old woman was impatient, waiting to find out whether the family name was climbing into its

3

deathbed with the arrival of a girl, or if a son and heir would claim the name for a new generation.

Mama sipped the remains in her coffee cup, the little bit that her husband had left behind. The coffee was grayish and sweet like chocolate, a breakfast dessert. She held its taste in her mouth and watched a mockingbird land in the tangled branches of the blooming peach tree. Its copycat melody came through the window, and Mama decided today was as good a day as any to have her child. The due date was many days ago, and she thought it was discourteous to keep others waiting so long, especially Madame Fanny, whom Mama was desperate to send back across the border to Pickrick, Alabama. She dialed her doctor, who heartily agreed to induce labor. Mama hung up and announced her intentions to those in the kitchen, and a smile planted itself firmly on the lower half of her face.

Gram warned Mama from over the stove's cracking and popping din: inducing labor was sometimes valued for its convenience, without proper regard for its effects. She prophesied the child would move around from place to place during life, as if pushed by an unseen force. "Everything costs something, my dear."

Granny Fanny snorted at Gram's comment as she sat knitting the latest in an endless chain of baby blue talismans. She turned to Mama, asking a question that was tangled up in its own offbeat rhythm. "Is my boy at work?"

"Yes, ma'am, he's at work."

The tatting spider lady gestured towards a one-pound bag of white clay on the corner of the counter. "Did you eat that dirt, girl?"

4

Mama knew of homemade jam and jellies, but she never believed dirt could be promoted as edible fare.

"Tha's the good kind. They import it from Georgia." Granny Fanny forgot that she had crossed the state line and was now solidly within Georgia's boundaries. "The 'Bama clay has some grit in it. It's not as good." Granny Fanny pointed towards Mama's abounding belly with an obvious discreetness. "Women in your condition back home just crave it."

Her articulation of the word "crave" was grotesque, stirring Mama to imagine unkempt, big-bellied women growling and tearing into bags of dirt with their teeth, like squabbling alley cats.

At that moment, the female populace in the kitchen shifted as a miniature man rocketed through the door. Mama bent to kiss her son on the forehead and told him that today was the new baby's birthday.

He frowned. His shoulders dropped. For a moment he looked as though he was drowning. He stood glowering by the stove with Gram's hands on his shoulders.

"Mama, I don't want a brother or a sister, I'll be good!" He looked like a pubescent god at a crop burning, smiling, with his sharp milk teeth exposed.

"Hush, child." Mama spoke softly, searching for a glimmer of how to ease the newness for him. She tried a new tack, one as misguided as a desperate sailor in twisted storm waters. "Now that the baby's coming, how about we call you Brother from now on?"

Brother's face scrunched up and he kicked the wall hard. Refusing the glistening breakfast Gram had cooked up, he purposely splayed his juice across the floor.

Mama bent low to clean the puddle, struggling to reach the area beneath her feet. A part of the floor remained stained with a sticky patch that didn't get mopped that day. Lint and fibers soon grew from the stickiness. (Much later, Brother would touch it with his tongue when it was dry and fuzzy to see if it still tasted orange.)

The three women made arrangements for the birthing day, trying to decide who would watch the boy and who would tend to the great event. When Mama realized Granny Fanny would accompany her to the hospital, she sped through a loop of prayers in penance for her past sins.

Granny Fanny prepared herself by raiding the fridge to construct a half-dozen thin ham sandwiches. She carved slim slices from the spiral of rosy meat, laying the salty pork strips down on freshly baked white bread, one side coated in butter and the other thick with mayonnaise. She packed her day's rations within the cavernous depths of her knitting bag as Mama changed into a proper dress for a trip into town.

Brother lay in wait under the porch for the two women to exit the house. He spat in the powdery red clay, then dabbed his fingers in the wetness to draw stripes under his eyes with the blood-colored mud. He heard the screen door squeak open, then slam shut. His heart thumped an excited rhythm as the steps creaked from weighted feet. Brother waited as long as he could before popping out and scratching the dirt, howling like a wild boy.

Granny Fanny drew back in fright, holding her bag close like body armor. She kicked at the growling boy. "Scat, you pup." She turned to Mama and spoke shrilly, "Yer boy's a damn animal."

Brother screwed up his face and bared his teeth. Mama patted him on the top of his head at the cowlick, a gift from her first husband. Brother smiled sarcastically at the older woman like a little prince.

He scampered beside Mama, showing off his muscles and singing a backwards version of his ABCs. It was his final, desperate attempt to convince Mama that he was the only one she needed.

She paused to kiss her son goodbye, taking his hand and slipping it over the buttons of her jacket where the baby lay. Brother felt a light push on his balled-up fist and had only mean thoughts for the little person who had just nudged him. He scampered up a green-leafed dogwood tree, where he hung upside down like a possum. As they moved down the street, he dropped down from the tree to go eat the breakfast he had disdained earlier. On the way, he made up a song about bacon that featured a repetitive chorus of raucous squeals, laughing heartily at his own cleverness.

Mama walked the main avenue of the town towards the hospital with her mother-in-law. Each minute with her was a slow decade in purgatory. The old lady cussed as they passed black children in a park, and the young mother and her unborn baby shifted uncomfortably at the noise.

"This one better be another boy to make up for that one you got already." Granny Fanny spat into the innocent grass on the edge of the sidewalk.

Mama ignored the poke at her son. "I would be quite happy with a girl," she replied. After all, the world had changed its mind about children since she was young.

"Girls are just useless." Granny Fanny grimaced. "Can't carry the name."

"Shh." Mama chided as she shielded the curving lump of her body with her arms. She wished she could cover the baby's ears. Granny Fanny muttered more words from a dark yesterday, and Mama felt stuck.

Even in these youthful hours of morning, the humidity was oppressive and the sun burned deep, stifling any breeze. God's plague for every Southern state.

At the hospital, Mama found the child had quite a grip. Coaxing it out was a Herculean task that neither she nor the doctor could manage. The remnants of morning and a fistful of afternoon had passed. Long after she had drunk the last sip of her husband's coffee, she lay in the gray-green delivery room with ankles tied uselessly in stirrups, her belly still full of child.

A terrible song of pain popped and whirred in Mama, as if her physical agony was sound that filled her body and flowed through her mind. She repeated the refrain mutely. No one was listening to her anymore. The epidural had worn off, and the doctor wouldn't allow more. "Water," she moaned.

Sweat glistened from his brow as the doctor struggled to release the new life from within her. Mama watched new dew appear on his temples each time he voiced another rejection. "No water now." Her sudden hatred for him grew thick, and she wished him in hell or anywhere else but here.

Thirst was Mama's desperate need, and her anger turned to the nurses who offered chips of ice, slim needles of freeze that were drops of nothing inside her parched mouth. Mama's humor grew dark and bitter like beech trees in the Yankee winter. She stared at the doctor and nurses through exhausted cobalt slits.

Granny Fanny sat in the corner of the labor room, knitting and grunting indiscriminately so she would not go unheeded. "We been here a long time, girl."

Mama wished desperately that her own mother had come with her, but she knew that would have meant either Brother or Granny Fanny, one or the other, would have been maimed or dead before sundown.

Mama gripped a nurse, pinching her wrists like handcuffs. "Can't I have some water, please?"

The nurse voiced another weak rejection. "I'm sorry, just ice chips."

Mama slumped back, her strung-up legs aching as the ugly metal claws bit into her feet. She felt shamed and tortured as she struggled to push the painful chunk of life from within her. Her womb was a still desert where a creature bided its time beneath the sand.

Granny Fanny raised her head to study the situation. "It's like a chicken trying to swallow a watermelon!" She crowed at the backwards analogy.

The doctor paused his tussle with Mama's insides to stare at her. "What?!" The whole room turned towards the old crone.

"You know, like a little chicken gullet trying to get a big old greasy watermelon down." Granny Fanny laughed. Baby garments grew like weeds from her gnarled thumbs. The doctor and nurses went back to work after the garbled banjo-speak.

The image of cool, sweet watermelon danced through Mama's head. She painted a grimacing, desperate smile with her last, rounded drop of patience. "Watermelon is like ice. Please find me some watermelon."

"But ma'am, where can I get watermelon?"

"It's nearly summertime," Mama hissed. "Go trip over one."

The nurse scuttled away and returned, holding the pink slices out of the doctor's view. Mama's heart rolled like a summer twister at the sight of the rosy pink wedges on the plastic plate.

Mama plucked a chunk of juicy, packed pulp from the plate, nearly biting off a finger in her haste. She swallowed the sliver whole.

The nurse popped another piece of watermelon in her mouth as Mama lay back and stared heavenward at the intense lights. She felt soothed and inspired. With precise suddenness, Mama birthed her child in one fluid motion. It came headfirst into waiting arms. The doctor nearly dropped it, as surprised as if world peace had just fallen into his grasp.

The baby seemed perplexed upon emerging from her cavernous, comfy home. She moved her arms and legs in a swimming motion towards the bright lights above her. The nurses wiped her down and patted her dry. Then they handed her back to the mother whose epic struggle had finally ceased. Mama thought her baby looked like a white peach, newly plucked off the tree and rinsed clean. She could barely wait for her husband to see their child.

Granny Fanny came close to determine the child's paternity, noting her son's evergreen eyes in the baby girl's face. Then she soured, tossed her blue knitting in a pail and muttered curses at her daughter-in-law's inability to bring forth a male child.

Outside, she called her own boy with the news. He hung up the phone and whooped foolishly as he sped from work over a shortcut across the railroad tracks. By some strangeness, just about the terrible moment that her father exploded upon the passing train, the newborn child's face ran red and wet.

Minutes later when his awful news came, the nurses tried in vain to whisk the baby away. Mama held the crying baby to her like a shield, weeping herself as if she had been torn apart. Granny Fanny cried out her agony like a swamp boar.

Despite his bloodline, he had been an artist, a poet, and the only Southern boy with sensitivity Mama had ever met who liked girls. She wondered why God came down so hard sometimes.

Then she looked closely at what he had left behind. The baby stared back with green-black eyes, a gift that was sorrow, and beauty, and vision for a lifetime. Mama named her Peaches, hoping that her husband would watch her grow and bloom, like his beloved tree in the yard of the house that was now only hers.

After Birth

Peaches lay on her tiny back in a cradle inside the hospital's baby garden. A wristlet marked her as the living chattel of a dead man.

She gazed around the new world she had dropped into quite suddenly after making a south turn down the proper canal. The babies around her cried, whined, and noisily drooled from inside their clear plastic boxes. Unlike her peers, Peaches remained calm and quiet in her crib, as content as a well-petted dog. Her womb eyes delicately filtered brightness into colors and her soul lay lightly atop her, like the soft pink blanket that lightly wrapped her living body like a shroud.

Floors below, the remains of her father arrived, wrapped messily in a sheet to be tucked away in a corner of the hospital's small morgue. Meanwhile, his spirit, whole and entire, paused to gaze upon his daughter as he rose through the building on his journey up and out of this particular world. Peaches saw the breath of aquamarine threaded with silver hover above her, then slip through a crack in the windowpane and wisp towards heaven.

Faces materialized fuzzily behind the small window. As time passed, more came then went. None seemed to matter until one tear-swept face smiled and waved through the glass. Peaches felt chosen, and she watched the graying lady point to herself and mouth, "Gram," then pick up a little boy and mouth, "Brother."

The boy was a different story. He pressed his face against the glass, staring at his half-sister blankly, waiting until her eyes were hooked in his. Then his face screwed up angrily. He flailed his arm to the side and struck Gram's cheek with the palm of his hand. Gram cried out, holding her face in pain and surprise as Brother grinned meanly through the glass. Peaches' womb eyes melted away, and she cried for the second time in her day-long life.

Back downstairs, Granny Fanny cajoled the morgue attendant with a choke of palmed greenbacks. Then the trifling old woman made haste for the state line with the remnants of her son. The baby girl was something to be left behind.

The First Odd Year

The infant Peaches lay toothless and a little hungry. Her eyes these days were nearly always open, peeled back like fresh, dark wine grapes. The world was still blurred hues and textures, but Peaches still tried to swallow it whole. Much of her first year she spent in her bedroom, within the bars of an old wooden crib. Mama always shut the curtains tightly so the room was cool and gray with shadows, like the hallway of a haunted house or the inside of an old brass trunk. Peaches would often stare at the electric square of bright sunshine around the edges of the drawn blinds until her sleepy eyes drooped shut. As she dreamed, a purple outline traced itself across the darkness under her eyelids. Doorways opened into places she hadn't yet been.

One day Peaches grew tired of lying there in the dark. She was desperate for noise, anything to end the dead silence. The squeak of her stuffed rabbit, the dangling mobile, and her own deep gurgle—they were not enough. She lay on her back, staring at the paint on the wall as she focused on the tiny single drops making up each long stroke. She found the wall was thick teardrops of color sliding down, little pocked bubbles of air created from the contact of rough on smooth.

The baby rolled onto her stomach, propping herself on fat elbows to look through the bars of the crib. She stared at the door, her unreachable exit from this monotony. Today it opened ever so slightly, and Brother peeked in.

Peaches stood and held her arms out, pleading to be saved. Brother goaded her. "C'mere, sweet Peaches, baby." And he held out his own arms from the doorway.

Peaches yearned to be out of the crib so bad that her head hurt. Brother danced in place at the doorway to show how much fun his freedom was. The little girl grabbed hold of the pole supporting the crib's canopy and defiantly slung her chubby, sleeper-clad leg over the side. Her fat diaper balanced her as she straddled the bar, pondering her dismount. Oh, of course. She imagined she was a bird and stuck her fat, soft arms out like plane wings, and dropped like a rock, landing softly on the carpet below, just fat enough to bounce. But her fall tilted her and her forehead met a metal screw on the side of the crib which etched her temple with a jagged cut. Blood flowed freely from her soft baby skin.

Brother laughed when Peaches landed, but his child-conscience burned when he saw the blood. He called for Mama, who came at a run, fear shooting from her long, black braids. She scooped up the shocked, silent Peaches and held her close, as if rescuing a baby cub chased by hunters.

Peaches didn't cry, even when Mama dabbed at the wound with a wet cloth. Blood trickled down her face, and Mama hemmed and hawed about the need for stitches. On the car ride to the emergency room, Brother fed her M&Ms one at a time. Peaches nibbled the soft-shelled candy, distracted from the throbbing pain as her teeth, tiny and few, cracked through the thin shell to the chocolate inside.

The M&M's were all gone when the long point of the needle headed towards Peaches' head. She screamed like a baby banshee as the needle plunged into numb her face from forehead to chin. The doctor knitted tiny black crosses across her forehead, hemming the skin that had been drawn by the sharp metal screw. It was dark when Peaches fell asleep on the way home.

The next morning at breakfast, Brother stared across the kitchen table at the black caterpillar bunched across Peaches' forehead. While Mama wasn't looking, he reached out to trace it lightly with his fingers. Peaches whimpered and arched back in her high chair, but Brother stuck out his fat, little-boy fingers to flick the knotted line. Peaches cried out as a drop of bright red oozed from the ugly, angry rosebuds of thread.

Brother feigned innocence, like a wide-eyed choirboy. "I don't know why she's crying, Mama."

Mama rushed to dab the blood with her apron, trying to soothe her with soft words. Peaches' head buzzed with the strumming of a tightly strung guitar. Her gaze fixed on Brother, who sat silently finishing his bowl of cereal.

In time, the wound healed and faded into a timid white scar, a thin strip of smile on Peaches' forehead. Soon, it grew invisible, and Peaches' mind erased the event, though Mama remembered and Brother never forgot.

At Three

Peaches was standing in front of her closet mirror, dressed in her Sunday best. Staring back from the glass was a discomfited young veteran of the aesthetic wars. White Mary Jane shoes buckled into monochrome tights that rose towards a crocheted, pastel dress. Peaches, Crown Princess of Primaverdi. Why not a kilt? Or even a sailor dress? Something she could play in! For a brief moment she wondered if Mama would notice that she had put on a pair of shorts underneath.

Her pigtailed head still throbbed from the night before when Mama had twisted plastic clips of spongy, pink curlers that pressed imprints into her skull before dawn. It was a painful effort for curled hair, and Peaches wasn't sure she had the heart for the sacrifice. As long as Mama embraced Beauty as a second religion, the image of a wee goddess topped with curly locks would continue to frown back from Peaches' looking glass.

As a once-divorced, once-widowed woman in a small town, Mama had no choice but to paint her children up like portraits for the weekly event called church. Her children were her sole shield from whispers. Peaches never heard the talk, though she sometimes wondered why her mother didn't always get along.

Maybe Mama was different from the town women. She didn't cake on makeup, which many slapped on like they were paving a road. Her hair was uncoiffed, unfashionably long with a silver-gray stripe, as if there might be a Spanish tinge to her blood. Only her mother herself knew it was a stress mark from single motherhood, the sole winnings of a poor gambler at love, beaten in the first game and broken in the second. In any case, Mama wouldn't let her children change clothes until late Sunday afternoon, so neighbors of every denomination could take note of them as they passed by the cul-de-sac; kindly, as it turned out.

The town's consensus was that Brother might be a bit of a hellion, but that was natural for a boy, especially one from his line. When spiffed up, he seemed a handsome, black-haired, blue-eyed little chap. Peaches was a cooed-over doll who knew most everyone in town by name, addressing them as "Miz" or "Mr." as Mama had taught her. Peaches didn't quite fit their definition of a little lady, since her clothes rarely matched when she dressed herself. But even the nosiest scandalmonger smiled at the little girl's sweet face and assumed it was her mother's city sensibilities that made the child a bit wild.

Mama rewarded the children each and every Sunday with a grand mid-day dinner, a Southern tradition unaffected by both time and the Second Vatican Council. After Mass and Sunday school, the dining table was set with a platter of fried chicken, fruit pies, and other delicacies: garden vegetables cooked in salty pork juices, peppered gravy poured over white rice so fluffy it could almost fly. Mama's biscuits were unconsciously presumptuous, even when unbuttered, and she brewed sweet sun tea like it was the eighth sacrament. It was a proud legacy from her own mother.

Early this Sunday morning, Peaches wandered into the kitchen, looking for Mama to zip up her dress. Brother sat at the round wooden kitchen table, stumbling as he read loudly for Mama to hear from the laundry room. His teacher had sent a note home saying he was falling behind.

Brother's tie was tugged loose, and it hung halfway down his shirt. When he saw Peaches coming near, he read louder, stumbling over words like a shoelace had come untied in his head. He stuttered on, posturing and leering in princely fashion, because although he was barely literate, he knew his little sister couldn't read at all.

Peaches glared as she walked past him into the living room and toward the bookshelves. She chose a book thick with fairy tales of witches and wise warrior queens, climbed into her daddy's old chair, and propped open the big book on her lap. She picked a page at random and began to recite a story from memory as her eyes obediently followed her finger's lead.

The printed words hung shadowed and untapped in the background, until a revolution occurred in Peaches' brain. A smooth piano played softly somewhere in her mind as a feather-like wand softly caressed a cymbal. Her eyes reported the letters to her brain, which carried them quickly as sounds to her mouth. The words greeted her as a friend, and her voice trembled as she bade good morning to the families that each letter was born to. Peaches dared not stop what she had started, fearing the power might go away as easily as it came.

Trudging through the room with a full laundry basket, Mama paused as she heard Peaches. She propped the basket on her hip and listened carefully. She waited until the girl took a quick breath, then said, "Peaches, are you reading?"

Mama dropped the clothesbasket on the floor and reached over Peaches' shoulder to flip the book a few pages ahead. "Start from here." Mama pointed to a sentence in the middle of the page, trying to assure herself that her wee daughter's precociousness was not just another of life's little tricks.

Peaches looked down and the words looked back. Her eyes recognized them as she read them aloud. "And Marianna alone traveled the last path to the golden city to become the princess of her new land."

For Peaches, it was a moment of vivification and other giant words of celebration she didn't yet know. Her three-year-old self felt like a new being, truly and fully alive. Her exhilaration was the stuff explorers sailed towards, whispered mysteries awaiting in strange and novel climes.

From the kitchen came a loud clatter as a furious Brother threw his book across the room. Mama squeezed Peaches' arm lovingly before sailing in to comfort Brother. He mumbled kindergarten curses at Peaches— "Stupid face" was a favorite—but she didn't hear them as she skipped ahead to read aloud an ending she already knew by heart.

That night at bedtime, Peaches went into the bathroom to brush her teeth and found her toothbrush tucked unhygenically behind the toilet in the far corner of the tile floor.

Peaches dropped to her knees to snag it, bumping her head on the white porcelain as she stood up. Pain bloomed quickly, then quietly died like a wet firecracker as she padded softly in her green and white-footed pajamas down the hall towards the kitchen.

She dragged a chair to the sink and ran hot water from the spigot, holding the bristles of the toothbrush underneath the stream until they puffed up, steam-cleaned from the heat.

Walking into the kitchen, Mama yelped when she saw Peaches standing in front of the boiling-hot cloud of water that rose from the sink. Peaches, hypnotized by the rush of the steaming water, jerked at her mother's sudden half-scream. Water bounced and spattered off the toothbrush bristles, landing hotly on her hand. A rebel drop misfired to the corner of her eye, searing the thin skin with a parching mark.

Mama ran to comfort and to scold, holding her child as she searched the refrigerator for butter to coat the burn. Peaches wrenched away in glazed panic. "No, Mama! Don't cook me!" she screamed as her mother chased her around the kitchen.

Mama finally coaxed calm from the child with a lump of brown sugar sharpened with a shot of bourbon in a brightly colored sippy cup. On the way to the hospital, Mama watched her daughter carefully in the rear-view mirror. Peaches seemed to float in a world much farther away than the backseat. Mama turned on the radio, and Peaches' eyes brooded, and then brightened beneath a gentle, gauze veil. The music didn't heal, but it brought the little liquored-up child closer to earth.

Peaches didn't cry when her puckering wounds were salved and bandaged by a nurse, though her eyes bulged bloodshot and agonized. As her hand healed, it bore an ashen scar like a birthmark. A small indentation in the shape of a tear curved from her eye, a perpetual memento of a troubled moment in a little history.

A Penance to Father Time

On warm, summer nights in the south Georgia town, the tardy twilight came dutifully. Lightning bugs twinkled gold through the trees. The girl Peaches always thought they helped make up for the lack of snow at Christmas, which happened to be another time of wonderful, sparkling lights.

Peaches skidded across the living room floor in her socks, stepping easily out of her graceful slide at the kitchen doorway. She searched the cupboards for an empty peanut butter jar with the label scrubbed off. She then poked holes in the plastic lid with a fork. Ripping off her socks and tossing them on the kitchen floor, she ran full speed through the screen door, whooping because the lightning bugs were out, and so was she!

The moon hung full and heavy in the early night sky. Peaches stalked the blinkers, plucking bugs from the air and pushing them inside the jar nestled in the front pocket of her overalls. She felt restless and unsmooth under the full moon's watch. Beneath her skin, blood undulated in waves as her heart murmured old stories whose telling was masked by blood's rhythmic beat.

Suddenly, a figure of death stood at her left swinging a tennis racket. Fat bugs rained down upon the earth like a biblical plague. Peaches tried to shield them with her body, but their hysterical blinking was like a beacon to the evil Brother. He continued his bludgeoning, leaving scattered beacons flickering in the grass.

Peaches ran, grasping her jar full of captives and mourning the fallen. . One plucky living thing squeezed from its translucent jail cell and rose to hover around her head before taking a zigzag flight back to its comrades. She tossed high a hope that martyred bugs went to heaven and wondered how Brother could kill such tiny, benign beings.

Hearing a rustling nearby, Peaches feared Brother was coming around the side of the house. She dove beneath the hydrangea bushes that bloomed purplish-blue. Sprawling on her stomach underneath its branches, dirtying her overalls with the black topsoil layered, she held close her jar of lights and listened to crickets chant evening prayers as birds sang their nightdreams. From the calmed songs, she knew Brother had gone. She unscrewed the top of the jar to release those she caged, hoping as they flew away that she was safely forgotten.

Peaches walked onto the back porch and entered the kitchen, ambling to the counter to pluck a piece of fried chicken off a platter. She tilted her head, gnawing on the cold chicken leg and philosophizing as she chewed the delicious, encoated flesh. "Mama, why do things die?"

"I don't know, Peaches. Time has different ideas for everyone." Mama answered as she rolled biscuit dough. Flour caked her hands and speckled her fists and wrists as she quickly cut out thick circles from the dough.

"What does Time think about me?" Peaches asked, reaching for a piece of sticky raw biscuit.

Mama popped at her daughter's fingers with a dusted hand as she shook her head. "I don't know that either, Peaches."

Peaches stared with puppy-dog eyes until Mama tossed high a strip of the dough. The girl caught it, and then wrapped it around her finger like a ring, admiring it before swallowing it in three quick bites. "I hope Time likes me. She has to!" Peaches nibbled again on the drumstick, wondering why she wasn't being scolded for snacking before supper.

"Why do you think Time is a she? Haven't you heard of Father Time?" Mama questioned. Gram had rung Mama a few hours earlier, on fire to know about her daughter and her grandchildren. The call was exhausting, as most things were. After hanging up, Mama had lain down in her dark bedroom with a cold washcloth over her eyes, rising only when she heard the screen door slam when Peaches ran outside.

"Mama, everything is a he," Peaches' eyebrows scrunched together in exasperation. Mama clucked her tongue "Where's your brother, Peaches?"

Peaches frowned in remembrance of the dead. "Killing stuff, Mama."

Mama's next words were too soft for Peaches to hear. "Ah, just like his daddy." She hoped there was time enough to draw her first husband's poison out before Brother was fully-grown.

Peaches noticed the biscuits on the cookie sheet were messy and imperfect, as if Mama was a bit off her cookie game. She poked with something new and different to see if it brought her mother back. "Mama, I saw the Klan go by, and I stuck my tongue out at them."

Peaches was lying. Weeks ago, a schoolmate had told her of finding a still smoking cross deep in the woods while visiting family in Michigan. Her friend spoke of stealing sips from a few of the beer cans scattered around the glade, where burnt wood smoldered wetly in the morning dew. Peaches' stomach had lurched at the thought of Klansmen, especially at the thought of drinking after one. But she herself had never seen the Ku Klux Klan.

"Honey, don't cause trouble." Mama sighed, reminded again of the lax grip she had on her daughter.

Peaches dove in. "Mama, was my grandfather in the Klan?"

Mama's bent frame snapped upright, shocked by the blaspheming of a good, fair man like her father. "Of course not, Peaches. The Klan hated Catholics."

Peaches mulled that, trying to figure out why religion mattered, why color mattered, why little things made such a big difference. "Why, Mama?"

Mama flattened the last little bit of moist dough with the rolling pin. She tossed the responsibility for an answer elsewhere. "I think you'd have to ask a Protestant, Peaches."

Peaches had another question. "Mama, how come people let all those bad things happen?"

Mama paused in her labor to try for honesty. "It just happens, I guess. Things just like that still happen all over the world." She looked ruefully at Peaches and began a confession. "Sweetie, when I was a child…"

It wasn't exactly the Southern experience as told by Hollywood. Her childhood was cool and fine, before the wrongs stood out bright white all over the world and protest righted it.

Mama remembered marching once in a protest with her own mother through Atlanta, where colors had mixed in a way they hadn't before—or since. Now she looked at her daughter contentedly nibbling on a chicken leg, and she wasn't sure she could tell any of it to Peaches.

Mama shook the past away in the flour, feeling like a thief digging up an old grave. "I never saw the Klan, Peaches. Only in photos or on television." Mama lied. She had seen the Klan at a march her mother had insisted she see. "Once they hit sunlight, most of them went home."

Peaches found another question bristling in her mind. "Who do we hate, Mama?"

"Come learn how to make biscuits, Peaches. Every good Southern lady needs to know how to make biscuits."

Peaches was immediately suspicious, thinking it was one of those things that once done must continue forever. "I don't want to be a good Southern lady if it means I have to make biscuits all the time, Mama."

Brother pushed into the kitchen through the screen door. The tennis racket hung over his shoulder like a hunter's jacket after a long day in the bush. One small bug was jammed in the netting, blinking a postmortem farewell. "Yeah, make me some biscuits, girl!"

Innocent words from her mother were liquid spite from Brother, as if his greatest gift was turning speech into fists. "Hell, no, you piss-ant!" she yelled and stuck out her tongue.

"Peaches!" Mama was aghast and chastising. "For swearing, you can now make biscuits for your brother."

Peaches watched as the sporadic flashes on Brother's racket reached a complete brownout. She refused again. "No, Mama!"

"Ha, make biscuits for me, girl." Brother sneered at Peaches, a shock of hair flipping to cover his eyes.

Peaches felt funny. Her body grew heavy, almost condensed, as her eyesight fuzzed black and white like an old television. She found it hard to think, like her head had separated from her neck and was about to float away.

"Now, Peaches!" Mama rapped on the counter with a wooden spoon. Peaches' brain waded through the muck, searching with broken eyes for the source of the faraway drumming.

Mama misinterpreted her daughter's slowness as passive disobedience. She grabbed Peaches' hands, briskly dusting them with flour until the pink turned white. Peaches dutifully kneaded the dough mechanically as her head buzzed and her eyes fogged like glass. Suddenly, her world tilted sideways and her hands stopped, gobbed up in the solid, yeasty mound. Peaches slumped to the floor, leaving a sticky lump on the counter. She lay unconscious on the cold linoleum. Her hands curled into claws, her body went fetal, and her eyes rolled back under half-closed lids.

Mama was a ghost, but Brother thought the little girl was playing possum. He prodded her lightly in the ribs to get her to move. Mama bent down to lift the dead weight into her arms. As they carried her down the hallway, Peaches woke up in bits and pieces. Brother saw her eyes open and pinched Peaches on her arm, his scruffy fingernails imbedding deep into her skin. "Aw, she's just faking it, Mama."

Peaches was still fuzzy. Brother's fingernail pain seemed distant, as if it were happening to someone else. She lay pale and weakened in her bed, sipping from a glass of water. Mama sat with her, trying to figure out what had brought the wrath of the gods down upon her child.

It was the first time Peaches passed out, another knotted loophole in her endeavor to survive. Mama called the blackouts, "visits from the fainting fairy," and the fairies came visiting once or twice a year. Sometimes Peaches got warning of their presence as different senses and body functions began to slowly shut down. When the world turned shades of gray, her ears forgot to listen, and mouths formed words she could not hear. Peaches, dizzy, would stumble to a safe place and and sway towards full collapse.

The doctor ran tests, but found nothing. A genteel liability of birthright, it was assumed. Gram said it was perhaps a genetic abnormality rooting from female ancestry wearing corsets so tight that their inner organs shifted. The old lady figured that was an inherited penance for womankind's proud membership in the cult of thinness.

Peaches later read about a species of Kentucky fish living in the dark pools of deep caves that were not only blind, but had in time grown scales over where their eyes had been. . Peaches took comfort in the fact that the women who came before her had not deigned to live their life in utter darkness. As for the affliction, she felt blessed that she could forget about it until the next time it happened. Mama's own reading was that Peaches must sit and act like a lady, or be punished by keeling over from time to time.

Family Reunion

School was only in its first year, brand new for Peaches. Already she was horribly unimpressed. Her class wasn't writing yet, just barely reading, discerning what sank and what floated, and naming the colors of the rainbow. It was pseudo-learning and Peaches felt trapped.

She stood with her classmates waiting for the bell to ring as rain dripped from trees onto the roof, gently spattering the jacketed students huddling beneath the eaves. Brother stood at the school's front doors, taking bets on college football and local Little League games. He scratched numbers in a notebook with a pencil, while dollar bills plucked and faded out of the air as older boys registered with the grade school bookie.

Brother didn't bully kids out of their lunch money; he merely waited for human nature to guide it to him. Peaches sometimes wondered if there was an empty hole where his goodness should be. She did her best to avoid making bets with Brother, because he hated losing to her and would cheat her mightily. When they played blackjack for gumballs, he always dealt. It was exasperating not to be able to jump as far or run as fast as him, but one thing she could do. Peaches refused to lose a perfectly dealt hand to a slippery House.

She leaned against the wall and watched her kindergarten friends play hand-slapping rhyme games as they waited for the bell to ring. Staring around her small world, she wondered how the rain made green grass glow and dandelions stand out as bright spots of buttery yellow fluff.

The school bell tolled, and she walked towards the door, tracing her fingers along the rough bricks making up the wall. Each solid chunk of clay was part of the whole, though Peaches noticed each was slightly different from its neighbor, like snowflakes or fingerprints.

For the first few hours of the morning, her class was sleepy and subdued. Rain fell and the sky stayed as dark as on the day Noah set sail. She grew bored with the stories of Dick, Jane, and Spot and stared around at the circle of readers in the colorful classroom. Suddenly she leaned down and bit the little redhead beside her. A half-moon puffed and rose like a misshapen, doughy biscuit on the little girl's arm.

The wounded girl screamed and the classroom erupted in laughter and babble, stirred by Peaches' anarchy. Before her teacher could even sort it out, Peaches slid from her chair and walked down the hallway to the principal's office, taking Brother's seat on the red bench outside.

"Peaches, why did you bite her?" her mother asked over the phone.

"I dunno, Mama." Peaches thought her head had decided, then told her mouth, and she was the last to know. She didn't know her brain could go around her like that.

"Do you not like that little girl?" Mama tried again. "Did she do something to you?"

Peaches was surprised, and then grew stricken. "No ma'am, she was just sitting there. I like her fine, but I bet she doesn't like me so much anymore."

"Peaches, if you ever do anything like this again, you'll wish you hadn't."

"Yes ma'am, Mama." She apologized to the victim at lunchtime and gave her the cookies from her lunchbox. By the dismissal bell, they were friends again. Rain clouds gave away to a bright blue sky.

Peaches walked home reading a book held chest high. Brother ran past and knocked it from her hand. It flopped open on the roadside in a spine-crippling way, bouncing to land among weeds and scattered green shards of a Coca-Cola bottle.

"You'll get yours, Brother." Peaches stole the line from an old movie and delivered it like a gang moll, but with no cigarette. Her yellow braids swung like double pendulums. Brother tossed the book back at her in mock fear.

Trailing slowly towards home, arriving a few minutes after him, Peaches wondered why Mama wasn't waiting for her on the front porch. A partial answer came crashing through the window as a dish landed broken at her feet. Peaches stared at the porcelain pieces as if they were a message from God she wasn't born to understand.

In the doorway she stifled a little-girl scream. A burly stranger teetered in the middle of the living room, ponging the air with a blue cloud of animal stink and liquor fumes. Propped near the door was a lean silver shotgun, another sure stranger in their house. Peaches hated it on sight, thinking it made the house look trailer trashy. She saw Brother clutching Mama's side and was aghast to see the boy of stone in tears.

"Look at him." The man growled at Mama. "You gone and raised him a damn gurl."

The brute reached out to slap Mama with one of his big paws, clasping her face tightly before flinging it back. Mama's head whipped to one side. Blood trickled from her left nostril and her face radiated scarlet.

Brother began to hiccup and almost hyperventilate like the skinny, asthmatic boy he wasn't. Something in Peaches, notified by the angry popping of bubbles, buzzed loudly and demanded that this was not the way it was supposed to be.

Her legs geared up like a cartoon character readying for takeoff and her brain boiled as she ran tripping and stumbling towards her enemy. She embedded her teeth in his ankle, biting deep into his meaty leg. She pushed her teeth through khaki skin, layer after layer, heading for bone. He smacked her and whirled her up against furniture, trying to get her to loosen her hold. As he crashed his full weight upon her,

Peaches' eyes closed sleepily as the breath in her lungs grew stale. Something pounded on the thing that trapped her, and pounded again and again. Finally, the big body rolled off of her. Peaches slumped over, weak and puppet-like; her collapsed skin puckered, her veins refilling after being squeezed dry.

Mama stumbled backwards, dropping the bloody encyclopedia she had used to beat him when he was crushing Peaches. His skin had broken under the repeated slamming of the book and red poured thickly upon its pages. The black-haired angel called Mama reached out to dust his jaw with a final swipe. Her tiny, clenched fist made something crunch inside his mouth.

Mama shoved Brother towards Peaches, and he dragged his sister into the nearby linen closet. Peaches whimpered and tried to fold inside herself. Brother told Peaches to hush and be still. But her whimpering grew louder—and angry.

Brother told her again to be quiet, because it would all be over soon. Peaches called him names, angered because he didn't pull Mama into the closet with them. Brother tried to hold her back, but Peaches burst out of the closet, yowling like a cat in heat as she slunk surefooted to the man's back.

Mama now lay mannequin-still on the floor. Doors slammed shut in her mind and locked. Peaches jumped back into the brawl like a movie sailor. Mama's mouth opened slightly as she recited old prayers to patron saints, slurring through lips swelled from an earlier hit.

Peaches seized a piece of firewood and hoisted it slowly over her head, and behind the intruder, her legs apart, balanced like a gymnast ready to jump the beam. It dropped like a cop's baton, bashing the man's skull with a spray of blood and popping bone. Goliath fell to earth as the girl glowered above him.

Mama stepped over the slumped remains and seized her daughter close. Peaches spat on the man, then began to shake. She had never spat in her life.

Mama was embarrassed to have police cars in front of the house, more embarrassed at the gathering of neighbors. Peaches wondered where they were when they were needed.

One cop bent close to Peaches, chucking her chin kindly. "You are one strong lil' gal." He looked over towards the slumped form. "That big boy ain't been knocked down too often."

Brother kicked at the unconscious pile, his little boy sneaker mussing the man's dirty, checkered shirt. The police officer waved him away. "Boy, don't kick your daddy."

The truth cleaved Peaches' soul. Peaches stared at Mama, but her mother's eyes were glazed over and unseeing. She hoped no one thought the man was *her* daddy. Peaches held her side where it hurt, and the policeman turned to Mama. "Your gal's rib might be broke, ma'am." Mama gingerly probed Peaches' left side. Her daughter yelped like a pup with its tail shut in the door.

A deputy approached to take a statement. Mama was polite to guests. Concluding, she said: "Thank you, sir," and pointed at the shotgun leaning sedately in the doorway. "When you take him away from here, please leave the gun." On his way out, the deputy looked at Brother, arms crossed over his chest. The boy stared at his father's face in shock. He recognized a bit of himself.

As her greatest mistake was handcuffed and dragged out the door, the brute began to stir and tried to lean close to kiss his former wife. She recoiled and Brother snapped a hostile slap inches from his father's face. The door shut, and the intruder disappeared as quickly as he had come.

Alone with the children, Mama gathered her brood and waited for the world to tilt back onto its familiar axis. It was just the weird, wonderful little family again, cracked and bruised, but still breathing. Brother approached the shotgun, but Mama told him coldly: "Never ever, Brother."

After washing her face, Mama poured two glasses of creamy, white milk, and set a plate of cookies on the kitchen table before beckoning Brother and Peaches to sit down. Brother took his place at the table. Peaches waited for her mother to say something, then realized Mama had tucked it silently away.

Peaches left the kitchen, returning with an orange plastic record player. She propped it on the counter and plugged it in. She chose a record from one of Mama's yesterdays, and as the music began to play, Mama seemed to float away. Peaches thought there was something bold about this manner of escape. Taking her seat at the table next to Brother, she ate her cookies and drank her milk. Her rib still ached.

It was just three of them again, mother, son, and rebellious spirit, as the old music played. A sweet smile broke across her face like morning sunshine. It was a moment when her two little monsters looked like beautiful, dirty angels, as if she had somehow managed to do things right. She adored the son of her heart and the daughter of her soul and gave thanks for the momentary blessing of easy and slow.

She thought of death and the obituaries she read every morning Every day, she threw prayers skyward in the hope she would never see her own offspring's little bodies in small coffins.

Peaches thought it felt like a good life for a moment. Turning up the volume on the record player, Brother stood to grab hold of his little sister's hand. He swung her around, and they danced like Lilliputians for the giant.

Mama smiled, watching them with her chin resting on one hand. Then she stood tall, throwing her arms in the air and roaring like a grizzly bear. Brother and Peaches squealed as they scrambled towards the living room. Mama chased them, catching Brother first and flipping him over her shoulder. She tickled him as Peaches clambered over the back of the sofa in a hasty getaway.

Mama caught Peaches with ease, careful to avoid her bruised left side. She hooked her arm around the little girl's waist and swung her high. Mama held both her bundles of joy close, one laughing so hard she couldn't breathe, while the other was as silly and gleeful as the giggling little girls he despised.

The song glowed as if something holy and strange acted upon it. Its transubstantiation grew wings and blew what was stagnant and past far out of sight, birthing new life in each fresh echo of strings.

Mama forgot the child coffins, Peaches forgot that she was a biter and a fighter, and Brother forgot that he was the son of a beast. The family slept peacefully that night, dispersing dreams in communion with each other and with all the souls beyond.

Amazon Mama

One good thing about the town of Peaches' birth: it was landlocked. That allowed it to avoid the fury of hurricanes that blew apart other towns on the nearby Atlantic coast. Here, nature's wrath merely slackened into tropical storms. Rain gutted the landscape, streets flooded and sewer drains ached to swallow the rivers of water pelting down. But nobody stayed up all night to watch it all, and nobody died.

Peaches awoke during one such storm, listening as the sky crashed down outside her room. She found sleep again once the storm turned into murmurs and rumblings, and rainwater dripped from the roof onto the pine straw below.

When Peaches rose for school the world was still dark and wet. Mama had that look on her face that said no hot water was running through the pipes. She had gone underneath the house where nature's own cold water sometimes ran high and doused the pilot light.

Brother and Peaches sat at the kitchen table, sleepily munching bowls of cereal speckled with banana slices. Mama came in, outfitted with heavy, green galoshes and a giant flashlight, her sole weapon against the crawlspace darkness. "Y'all get your raincoats and stand outside in the backyard. I have to light the water heater."

Mama reached in the kitchen drawer of sundries that held everything from toothpicks to a bright buffet of colored pens. She took out an oversized box of wooden matches that were nearly as long as Peaches' arm.

37

"Mama, why do we have to go outside?" Brother asked, his mouth full of sugary color. Mama's smile was as humorless as a killer clown's. "Because if I do it wrong, the house will blow up."

Peaches grew wide-eyed, but Brother thought there might be a trick and dawdled another moment or two. He scooped another spoonful of breakfast, and then finished his juice. He popped his vitamins as if it might make a difference that he was both sated and healthy when blown to bits.

As Peaches and Brother stood hooded in the pouring wetness, sheltered beneath the branches of a full, young dogwood, they saw their mother bless herself before ducking through the small door to the space underneath. The children stood waiting for the end of the world or for nothing at all. Peaches had faith in Mama, but Brother wasn't so sure. "Peaches, do you think she'll take out just our house or the whole neighborhood?"

Peaches thought she had an Amazon Mama. She always figured Mama's height was an advantage because she could see so much more from way up there. "Brother, Mama can fix most everything in the house when it breaks. She's just lighting something now. Plus, she's really tall."

Under the house, Mama bumped her head on a beam and swore as she trudged through the moist crawlspace. Her anxiety bubbled to near bursting as she held the flashlight in a clenched fist and squeezed one eye shut to strike the long wooden match. Carefully tucking the flame inside the water heater's belly, she saw flame poof and spark. Fire, do your best, Mama thought, smiling in relief. She moved quickly towards the door, finding that the world on her shoulders had lightened its load a bit.

Emerging from under the house like a kid pulled from a well, she took the children inside and shooed them off to school. Her morning and early afternoon turned out peaceful, but when the clock hit three, a whirlwind roared its way home. The porch door slammed open as if it were kicked. Two small feet pounded into the kitchen like Bonnie in search of her Clyde.

"The South had slaves!?!" Peaches shrieked, spitting out the words like dirt. "Why didn't anyone ever say anything!?!" Peaches demanded. Dominos fell and heroes died as myths shattered and baby belief systems came tumbling down.

Mama turned from the stove where fresh tomatoes and ripe peaches were ready for canning. She wasn't sure how to tell her child that not quite all the ugliness was gone. Some of it had just changed shape.

"I thought you knew, sweetie. I'm sorry." She walked to the freezer and took out a Klondike Bar. "Unfortunately, the South is known for other wicked things long after slavery ended. A lot of people think we're just as evil today."

Peaches, dumbstruck and lost in thought, ignored the ice cream. She had known there had been a war when the country's sons fought each other over slavery and cotton, or something of the sort. Now, she was floored with the realization her people were the Cains in that battle.

"You're a Southern girl--a Southern white girl--and with that label comes baggage. But, Peaches, it's not the only label you wear." Mama paused to sip her coffee, dark and sweet like raw sugar cane. She was cryptic and roundabout, circling like a sick vulture over flattened roadkill. "Being a Southerner will always be an annoyance, no matter how you behave. Being female is another roadblock."

Peaches nodded slowly because she had been a girl her whole life. "Like in sports." She was hopping mad the local churches wouldn't let her play t-ball, as if she would take to the field in a dress or weep girlishly if she struck out.

Mama's smile grew wistful, remembering her youth when she took being an athlete as far as she could. "I could have been a great basketball player, Peaches." It was a secret for her daughter, a treasure from her before-life, and Mama let it loose like a beautiful butterfly.

Peaches was shocked by the tall tale that couldn't be true. "You can't play basketball, Mama!"

Mother and daughter went outside to where the cotton net hung still in spite of the afternoon breeze. She took position at the foul line, bouncing the ball and listening to it bullet against the pavement. She held it close, pressing her fingers into its rubbery thickness and tossed the ball high in a clean arc that ended in a cool swish.

Peaches rubbernecked her stupendous Mama. Her fingers loosened their grip on the ice cream bar, its inner whiteness landing in large drops on the ground. Mama's hand stayed hooked above her head as a crowd in another time and place sang and cheered. She remembered a thousand such swishes, and her grin grew into a young, foolish smirk.

To Mama, basketball had made sense of her height. She had inherited her longitude from her daddy, along with her surname, and then given up both shortly after adolescence. She was once a girl good enough to play with the boys, learning brute things in their games she wasn't allowed to use with her own kind. She would tie her hair back, lace her high tops, and play rough, throwing elbows in kidneys so hard they forgot what she was.

Mama lost herself in thoughts of her father. He had been proud of her court skills and often remarked that it was too bad the world wouldn't let her play after high school. She never heard him wish for a son with her talent; he merely voiced disdain for a system that couldn't see her as a player.

As she dreamed of days gone, the feel of the pebbly, orange leather against her palms triggered off a bomb inside, the same way a certain subtle shade of blue china gripped her mind with claws. Then Mama left the basketball behind and put away the little girl dreams, the lost years she had chosen to exchange for the blessed privilege of being a mother and a wife.

Peaches watched as her Mama fled inside. She was furious there was no one around to document the firecracker moment. Peaches caught sight of Brother coming down the drive, his face like a blue tick hound. She prayed he was a witness to the strangeness as she called out to him. "Brother, did you see Mama sink it?"

Brother looked at Peaches like a stranger, Mama's eyes embedded like blue diamonds in his pale face.

Later, from inside the house, Peaches watched him through the window as he tried to match his mother's feats. From her place at the counter, Mama grew edgier with every bounce of the ball. Finally, she burst out the door to see Brother fail again, sweating enough that his dark hair glistened black. "Play, Mama," he cajoled. He swaggered around her. Peaches emerged from the house to smell a heated battle underway as the son huddled down in shining defense against his mother.

After Mama sunk her first shot, she saw the look on Brother's face. She realized only then what she had gotten into. If war was violent, then a game of basketball was pure politics. Mama let Brother duck past and score each time she made a basket. The winning point drew close, and Mama couldn't decide if it was better to lose for her son or win for her daughter. The grand game ended in a deliberate draw.

Brother was doleful at first. A tie meant he couldn't boast to his friends about beating his mother, but he decided it wouldn't have impressed them anyway. It never crossed his mind that Mama could have handily shut him out from the first dribble.

But Peaches knew it, and Mama knew she knew. The mother tried to catch her daughter's eye, as if they shared a valuable secret. Peaches, wanting no part of the pitiful compromise, looked away. Brother's tied-game was his sister's loss, and Peaches couldn't understand why Mama chose so wrong.

The Violent Catch It

Peaches had graduated to learning cursive script and fractions, but she found she was tired of desksitting. She had been tired of it from the day when school was baby-chick new. The little girl doodled at her desk, waiting patiently for recess, that godsend of fresh, unfettered outside time. She had woken this morning with a desire. She was going to play baseball. With the boys. The girls at her school shunned the game, which was off-limits not by law, but by general custom. Peaches decided she had spent far too much time in the backyard fielding Brother's hits to waste her skill at school.

As teachers marshaled the students through the doors to the outside, Peaches contemplated a strategy. She knew if Brother was in a good mood, there was a possibility he'd let her join his team. She approached him with her head hung low in embellished reverence. "Hey, Brother, can I please...?"

Brother knew her wants before they became words. "No, you can't, Peaches. You know girls can't play ball around here."

Peaches bunted back even though she wasn't yet in the game. "Says who, Brother?"

He elbowed one of the other boys, so that someone might hear his clever comeback served with a sloppy side of sarcasm. "Well, Peaches, Little League, high school varsity, and, oh yeah, the Major Leagues."

Peaches was sweet, but careful. "Brother, I really don't think this is the Major Leagues."

Another boy ducked his head into the conversation, nudging Brother and snickering. "Let her play, B. Even a girl could play better than you."

Brother's eyes darkened, and Peaches knew she herself would pay for the boy's words. Brother had already flubbed an easy fly ball in the opening inning. And he had slipped on the grass because Mama had made him wear different shoes that morning.

Brother shoved her to the ground. Blood seeped from bare legs, and Peaches hoped that since Brother made her pay he would now let her play. She was wrong.

Brother grabbed a thin stick and raised it high to whip her across the shins. The other boys ran off and returned with their own thin branches, circled around her, and thwacked her in rhythm.

Looking at the ring of shiny belt buckles circling her, Peaches gripped one boy's hair and grabbed another, buckling him to his knees. She tightened her hold on her two hostages, her fists pulling hair on the whimpering boys' heads. Their hot tears dripped down on her face as she cracked the two skulls together. Their bodies dropped upon her like dead weights.

A teacher finally swooped inside the circle, raised a hand, and scattered the pack. Bending to lift the beaten, bloodied girl, she bore Peaches to the infirmary, chattering uselessly: "Well, I just don't know why they would attack you like that."

Peaches was mute in her knowing, as the nurse bandaged raw wounds. "Peaches, what did you do to stir them up?" pressed the teacher.

Peaches stared at her now striped legs, remembering how they once looked. Her hands were balled up and hidden beneath the folds of her skirt. The women couldn't see how they were shaking.

"Honey, are you scared to tell what you did?" the nurse inquired.

Peaches ignored her. The teacher finally departed and Peaches saw the nurse hiding a grin. "You tried to play ball, didn't you, girl?"

Peaches stared at the lady who knew her secret. "Maybe I did, ma'am."

The woman laughed deeply as if they were sitting at a lakeside barbecue. Peaches angrily demanded an answer. "Ma'am, why can't I play? Aren't we all supposed be allowed to play?"

The nurse drawled like a low country preacher. "Honey, I think everyone should be allowed to play."

"Isn't it against the law not to let me?" Peaches was desperate to be right. "Why did they do this?"

The woman spoke in a way that suggested a shared experience. "Tell me when you find out. That question is older than you and me."

Peaches' brow dropped, holding back her tears. "I hate them. I hate them all."

The nurse looked at her, her face still and thoughtful. "Do you know any of them?"

Peaches paused for a beat, and then answered honestly. "One of them was my brother."

The woman's eyes crinkled in surprise, then smiled. "Honey, he sounds like the kind who'll take himself down long before he manages to do it to you."

"What about the rest of them?" Peaches was humiliated. She swung a fist in the air, as if to strike one of "them".

The woman took Peaches' hand. "It's likely most of them are going to be too ashamed of themselves to give you any grief."

The nurse sealed the final bandage snugly and helped Peaches stand up. At the doorway, she braced her by the shoulders. Sometimes the world felt like a bus that Peaches was about to meet head on.

She went back to class and before the day was done, a good half of the boys approached her, cowering like struck pups, mortified by what they had done. One boy's heart bled tears as he apologized. She touched his cheek where wetness dangled and hung. The clear drops glistened from the whorls of her fingertips, and Peaches wondered whether they would taste bitter or sweet.

Brother glowered with a sick man's pride at her wounds. Peaches gritted her teeth and ignored him. She didn't tell Mama the truth. Peaches didn't want to enlighten her mother to the damage her son had done.

Mama concluded Peaches got scratched up running through a briar patch. She salved them with hydrogen peroxide and new bandages. "Looks like they were after you, Peaches." Mama chided her child. "If you start behaving like a lady and stop running wild through the briars, you wouldn't get hurt."

Soon after, Mama noticed Brother and Peaches rarely spoke to each other. She wondered why her two children couldn't get along. Both Peaches and Brother wondered why she thought they should.

A Pageantry Played Out

On her way home from school, Peaches sometimes stopped at a little corner grocery, a banjo-looking building of wood and nails. Its walls were covered with hand painted signs that proclaimed and priced fresh vegetables. Homemade jams nestled near plump red and green tomatoes that burst forth from woven baskets like multiplying rabbits. Melons and citrus fruits were stacked like cannonballs. Homegrown Georgia peanuts boiled and steamed in a black cauldron atop a wood fire.

Peaches breathed in the smell of hot salt, finding it nearly as pleasing as the juicy little buds that were tucked inside each peanut. She was still stretching to reach her first decade, but she had long known how to break through a boiled peanut's wet shell with only her teeth. On this day she pushed through the store's door, and a bell rang a welcome above her head. The old gentleman behind the counter teased his little customer. "Are you playin' hooky, Miss Peaches?"

Peaches tilted her head in mock defiance of the elephantine man. "It's after three, Mister Beauchamp. I'm free."

Peaches browsed the candy shelves as Mister Beauchamp popped a pan-sized chocolate chip cookie into a brown bag for her. The store's homemade cookies attracted a stream of regulars, as did the takeaway sausage biscuits earlier in the day that nudged the morning's grease through their wax-paper wrappings before the buyer was out the door.

Peaches dropped a quarter on the counter for the cookie. Then she searched her pockets and found two dimes for a couple of Cow Tails, wiggling strings of sugar-dusted dough coating a creamy middle. She bid adieu to Mr. B and recoiled—as always—at the pickled pigs feet floating in jars on the shelves behind the old man's benevolent smile.

Peaches tucked the cookie in her book bag for later. The candy she bit open, sucking the sweetness from the wrapper, trodding the familiar path home on a sun-soaked sidewalk. A honeysuckle vine rose above her. Peaches plucked the darkest yellow blossoms, the sweetest of the bunch, and drained the dewy drops from one end. She stayed there tasting from the vine, until the ground was scattered with hollow buds that she had emptied and tossed aside.

Ambling along the quiet country road, she was startled by an oversized truck that screeched and smoked to a stop beside her. A man dropped to the ground from the passenger side, closed on her fast, snagged her shirt collar and yanked her towards the truck. She wriggled and fought, her legs whipping in the air as he pulled her up into the truck's cab. Peaches tried to claw him, but he held her close, muffling her against his chest. Her fingernails grated uselessly against his stubbly face, and the truck door slammed shut like a prison gate.

Shoved backwards between him and his buddy, Peaches stared past him at the door lock, the door handle, at anything but him. "I know your Mama, baby girl," he grunted. His lean arms were blackened and blurred with homemade designs, and a caterpillar moustache drooped over his thin lips. His skin, gleaming like old butter, was cracker white.

It was Brother's father, and he pulled her to his lap in the shotgun seat. She slapped at him until he yanked her hands behind her. He twisted her right arm and slapped her across the face, searing her cheek like a lick of fire. She quieted and stared out the window, looking desperately towards home.

Reaching into the glove compartment, he pulled out a brass flask, took a deep swig, then turned her around to face him, tilting the flask towards her mouth. He twisted her arms more, and tipped the blistering liquid to make a burning path down her throat.

Peaches' belly rose up to repulse the fire and spewed forth a spraying arc. The giant truck jerked and lurched. "You're a tiger, aren't you, kitten?"

"No sir, I'm a dragon."

He tugged her braided pigtails playfully, and Peaches conned a sweet, saccharine smile. He countered with a drunken grin of his own.

Their driver ripped a quick u-turn as he tossed a suspicious look towards Peaches. The big truck flew down side streets to her house, the driver bumping it over the sidewalk out front, splashing dirt high into mud flaps as the giant tires squealed to a stop inches from the picket fence. Both men laughed gleefully at the churned grass shredded beneath them. Peaches bolted from the truck, stumbling to her knees.

Brother popped through the screen door with a weapon in hand. Flattening himself on the grass like a trained sharp-shooter looking for a sweet spot, he lay a few yards away with his shotgun raised and centered on his father. One stubby finger clicked back the safety, while another readied the trigger. His boyish fear was dead and gone. He was a man with a gun.

"Boy, you best put down my damn gun!"

Brother imagined himself a soldier and kept a steady bead on his father's skull. He smiled toothily like a Jolly Roger as he watched brown eyes blink from above the barrel. He inched his trigger finger and motioned Peaches to step away from the man.

Mama came through the porch door, wiping her hands clean of kitchen duty. It was her son looking through the sight that froze her cold.

The big man stared at Mama with a gunshot look. "Honey, you better beat your son before I do." He spat meanly, glaring at Brother and his silver-black gun. "I might just kill him."

Brother chuckled viciously, the grand marshal of his own parade. He lowered the gun, and then raised it, blowing a hole through the truck's wind-shield. Shock waves boomed within the taut silence of the street. Phones began to ring as neighbors made sure everyone saw the pageantry being acted out down the street.

The truck's driver screamed as glass crackled down the hood of his Tonka. "Sweet Jesus! What kind of boy shoots a man's truck?"

Mama was stiffly polite, "I'd leave if I were you. I can't stop my son from shooting you next." She stood behind her little mutineer, smiling as if she were offering a slice of hot apple pie with ice cream on top. "Goodbye." The smile dropped from her face like a brick from a skyscraper. "Don't come back now, y'hear?"

Brother's father blotched purple from his forehead to his fists. He grew furious as it dawned on him that Brother by birthright was himself. His eyes clicked on Peaches as his target. She stood with one hand on her hip and the other across her midsection to deflect the blow. Peaches didn't realize she needed to cover her ears. "Lil' girl, did your mama tell you that I was driving the engine that flattened your daddy?"

Suddenly, Peaches was leveled, splintered, altogether undone.

"There was a big ol' popping pow when we slammed him, and then his pieces went everywhere. Lost my job 'cause of it." Brother's father looked up, almost thoughtfully. "That was a damn shame."

He whirled towards Brother to throw a handful of poison at him. "Did you know I'm your daddy, boy?"

Brother's face closed. He clicked the trigger with the ease of flicking a rubber band and blew a hole in his father's leg. The knee detonated like a fat cat feeding on a firecracker, leaving the man howling in pain and surprise. "Boy, you ain't shot your daddy!"

The big gun recoiled and smacked Brother in the face. His nose bled like a mountain spring as he called out: "I shot him, Mama! I shot the bastard."

Inside Peaches' head, a long note played deep and loud and her heart beat like an ancient, drum. She watched blood flow from her Brother's nose and from his father's knee, her brother gleeful in the shining afternoon like it was his birthday.

Mama felt as if she was walking sideways through life. She remembered she wasn't walking alone and that was the kinetic force that kept her standing. She envisioned ancient warrior women facing the world with spears, arrows, and babies strapped to their backs.

Danger had arrived unannounced at her front door and now had been dispatched.

She took a breath and lifted the gun from her son's hands. Then she walked her children into the house as the driver of the big-wheeled truck helped his meaty-legged partner toward the broken truck. Mama watched for a moment through the window, before clicking the single lock on the front door. They drove off slow.

In the kitchen, Mama pulled up the cast iron skillet and set out a jar of bacon grease from the refrigerator. She warmed up the black skillet and neatly divided two chickens, baptizing each piece in flour, pepper, and salt. She juggled the innards into a separate pot, the gizzards, the heart, and livers, to form the base of a rich giblet gravy. She cooked solemnly like a priest at the altar, following rubrics that transformed the physical into something nearly spiritual.

Brother sat at the table holding a Mama-wrapped towel full of ice against his nose. He fidgeted proudly, as if he had hit a homerun with the shotgun. Mama spoke to him in the voice of a troubled ghost. "Brother, that's not the way to change things."

Brother couldn't believe her words. "It did change things, though, Mama," he protested.

Mama stayed silent over the crackling, popping pan, watching bacon fat meet chicken skin, searing its flesh down to the bone. She felt like a fragile piece of glass, transparent and reflective of her surroundings, still unshattered, but very still.

Outside on the sidewalk in front of the house, a small crowd had gathered, pointing at the blood on the grass and whispering stories about the characters in this neighborhood horror story. When the stove went cold and the grease stilled, their chatter seeped inside, leaching the peaceful air out of the warm kitchen. It jarred Mama into discomfort, and she doffed her apron, smacking it down on the counter. She strode to the door with confrontation in her eye, but stopped with her hand on the doorknob, suddenly too scared and ashamed to proceed.

Her daughter, brazen, pained, and peeved, swung open the front door and marched down the porch steps towards a showdown. Brother slid up to stand beside Mama in the doorway. "What is she doing, Mama? Who does she think she is?"

"Brother, watch your sister. She's got a better weapon than a gun."

Peaches stood at the fence gate in front of people she knew by name, children she had played with, and grownups her Mama had cooked for when their kin took ill or passed away. They looked at her hard, and for a moment, she was scared, too. She took a deep breath and disappeared around the side of the house.

The group craned and shifted as Peaches unwrapped a long garden hose. Her fingers touched a small strip of yellowed tape on the hose, and Peaches realized her own father had put it there long ago. His shade of green eyes stung on her face as she looked at the duct tape that survived him. Peaches stroked it like a teddy bear's ear or the corner of a blanky, trying to override her feeling of want. She wanted to hop over the back fence and find a lonely place somewhere else.

Instead, she twisted the flower-shaped handle, turned on the water, grabbed the mucky hose and headed towards the blood puddling in the Bermuda grass. Peaches' disdain of the crowd's uselessness rose inside her, but she smiled through it. She twisted the hose and sprayed the blood that had soaked through the grass.

When the blood was gone, she clamped the nozzle shut, wearing a smile like a Bible salesman. "Mama told me to clean the fence the other day. I really should do it right now, don't you think?"

Peaches arced the spray smoothly across the fence as if she were a little floppy-hatted lady tending to her roses in the evening cool. The hose's splash speckled the clothes and faces of the neighbors, misting them with gray fence-grime. They grumbled and muttered as they began to disperse. Then Peaches put up the hose and headed back inside, tired from the dogfight that had just ended on her front lawn.

Mama's hand was at her mouth when Peaches walked through the door. Peaches shrugged it off. "I just thought you wanted it to be normal again, Mama. The neighborhood standing out front wasn't normal."

"Peaches, you shouldn't have lied. I never asked you to clean the fence." Mama waited for a heartbeat, then looked at both her children. "Now, look here, we're not going to talk about what happened outside of this family."

Brother was angry. "Mama, if the neighbors know, the whole town's soon going to know. If anyone else cared, they'd know too."

Peaches had something else on her mind. It was less of a question and more of a direct punch. "How did you end up with him, Mama?"

Mama's face slammed shut. She would rather explain the birds and the bees in street slang. "None of that matters anymore." Mama sighed the breath of the prey, trying her hardest to put the day away. "Let's take you to the hospital, Peaches. Your arm isn't going to fix itself."

On yet another ride to the emergency room, Peaches rode in the backseat of the car, away from her mother. Brother stayed home. Mama thought it was just as well, since nurses were about as keen on him as a barefoot walk-in. Mother and child rode in silence until Peaches burst out: "Do you want me to lie to the doctor, Mama? Say that I fell off my bike or something?"

Mama thickened her accent and glued her daughter to her history with her words. "You can tell them that a sorry bastard did it, Peaches."

Peaches smiled into the seatbelt strap. She waited to ask a final question once they had parked in the hospital lot. "Mama, why don't we just leave this damn town?"

Mama silently prayed for a new answer. Her late husband's life insurance and the settlement from the railroad was enough to feed the family and pay down the house. It allowed Mama to embrace her role as a mother full-time. Despite their stability, Mama felt stuck.

"Peaches, I've thought about taking you all to Atlanta, because I think it would be good for you. But your brother….well, I think we'd lose him there."

They approached the hospital's main doors, and Mama held Peaches close to her side. She knew she couldn't bring herself to sacrifice her son, even for her daughter's sake. She wanted to tell Peaches she loved her more than anything else in the world, except for Brother, whom she loved almost as much.

Deep Diving

Peaches' world steamed up hot by mid-April. Her fellow students sweltered, refreshed only by mirages in the classroom windows. Once school finally let out in early June, the days seemed as endless and plentiful as boiled peanuts and pole beans.

Brother and Peaches temporarily put aside their enmity and soaked up the sun's glow, slicked down with sunscreen at the local pool. The water was blue, cool, and clear amid the shimmering greenscape, a taste of heaven for the town's youth and grown-ups alike. Mama's two children often hung at the pool from open to close, quietly soliciting each morning dollar bills from their mother's purse to buy crinkled-wrapped goodies from the snack bar. Sometimes, she packed them a cooler, but both children thought carting forth turkey sandwiches and juice boxes in their towels was like introducing the school year into paradise.

The pool snack bar was a Pinocchio's funhouse, and Peaches and Brother loved it like blue skies. A storage room at the base of the clubhouse contained a lone teenager who stayed partly hidden in the shade behind the window. Money slid in. Food slid out. The sun-soaked children with their bills and coins thought the boy a demigod. Brother, uncowed by deity, inevitably sneaked goods, sometimes sharing with Peaches if he made a substantial haul.

In the hierarchy of all things poolside, if the snack bar teen was a god, he had apparently sprung from the head of a lifeguard. The lifeguards were the Titans of the cosmic struggle to mix and socialize and just be cool.

They shared pizzas with their favorites and gave others bars of candy to scrub gutters. They braided or spiked the hair of their child pets into wet Mohawks while scanning the pool for death, gossiping about pool romances and their own riotous nights. Their thrones were on the lifeguard stand, which held two chairs and a radio, enough room for a scattering of underage groupies to sit with their legs dangling. The radio sung a soft soundtrack of summer. Baby teens flirted and little children with oversized tummies imped about.

Once a week, whistles blew and guns fired as children dove off starting blocks to race under brightly colored flags until dusk fell and underwater lights bloomed. A utopia of ribbons and free pizza slices straight from the delivery box were the climax of the evening for every kid in a bathing suit.

During summer, the art and act of moving through water was Peaches' everything. The clear water muffled all sound, and quiet filled her mind as if she were swallowed alive and contained gently by a leviathan. Without goggles, it was a blurry and soft world. With goggles, it was blue crystal within white walls, an underwater kingdom too large to have been made by human hands.

The children loved playing Sharks and Minnows, Bull, Fish, and Marco Polo. But Peaches loved sinking slowly to the bottom of the twelve-foot diving well, hanging in the depth to watch sunlight slip through the ripples and play onto the walls and across the pool floor. Everything was shrouded except for the bubbles that rose from her mouth and nose, perfect transparent spheres outlined by the peculiar world above.

Sometimes she lay on the pool floor and pretended it was the bottom of the ocean, and she was a legged mermaid, daughter of an absent father, the King of the Sea. Juveniles of different shapes and skills hurtled off the one-meter low board into the deep diving well. Peaches watched their feet implode in soundless bursts upon the smooth surface as their shining bodies dropped into her silent, spaceless place. It was a procession of cannon-balls, eggrolls, simple jumps, and avian dives. Sometimes a freefaller plunged knifelike without a ripple. Those guys, Peaches thought, know I'm here. But she was actually visible to all of the divers, except in her sub-aqua mind.

One day, a boy broke through the blue-water ceiling in an awkward bellyflop. Peaches nearly laughed out loud underwater at his pain. His bubbles rose in a wrong-way waterfall as he sunk. Peaches held her breath, waiting for him to recover and ascend. The boy's arms flapped stiffly as he kicked to reverse himself and rise. He was almost near bottom when Peaches realized he was failing.

Quickly, she pushed off the gritted bottom and split through the water like a stingray. Her heart beat fast and goosebumps formed as the cold water slid across her skin. She heard the muted echo of children screaming and playing and knew other kids were waiting at the diving board, murmuring impatiently and assuming the sunken boy was merely taking his sweet time getting to the ladder.

The drowning boy's arms and legs were spread like a limp parachute. Boy muscles had started to grow from his arms and legs. Ribs still poked here and there in a rack down his sides. His large brown eyes watched as

Peaches swam up, hooked her arms under his and began to kick upwards slowly. He began to kick with her, and she couldn't figure out how to signal him he was only getting in her way. Her lungs screamed murder for air, and Peaches thought he might kill them both as their legs tangled together. She finally gave him her arm to hold onto. He gripped it tightly as they rose.

The ladder at the pool's side ended the shared nightmare, and the boy coughed and threw up water into the gutter as Peaches perched on the corner of the ladder gulping sweet air. A ricochet of spray drenched them as the next diver in line left the board in a one-and-a-half can opener.

Peaches nudged the boy gently up the ladder, but he turned and shoved her arms with a scowl. She fell back, banging her knee against the molded plastic of the ladder. Climbing from the water, she saw an attentive, sunburned audience surveying them like the audience of a puppet show. The boy hurried half-bent towards the bathrooms, waterlogged and humiliated, but not dead yet.

A pool parent beckoned Peaches towards the lifeguard stand, where he stood next to the pool manager, a young sorority girl with dreams of teaching in Appalachia. The old man spoke in a voice that echoed across the water. "What happened down there, honey?" he asked.

"Nothing really, sir." Peaches thought it was transparent and obvious, and not her story to tell.

He sucked on an unlit cigar. "Kids like him can't always swim. We welcome 'em here though, 'cause you know, it's not like before."

"What do you mean, sir?" Peaches asked him, becoming irritated by his easy affability.

He spoke softly, though the whole pool heard. "Cause their parents can't usually swim. They couldn't go to pools back in my day."

Peaches again felt the past creep up to bite her. She'd heard of the signs that warned a particular people to stay away from the pool gates and cool off elsewhere. Anywhere but here.

The pool manager stared at the man. Peaches remembered a play she read about a teen-aged girl with the skills of a champion, whose ancient religion prohibited her from her club's swim league.

An eavesdropping lifeguard sitting on the stand poked his head into the now silent conversation. "I read somewhere that those boys drown more than any other group."

Peaches turned to him, her eyes cut into slits. "Shouldn't we be teaching them, then?"

The lifeguard's face trickled with reddening guilt before he shrugged off her boldness. Peaches turned away and walked to the edge of the shallow end. Before she dove in, she heard the pool manager speak sharply to the lifeguard. "Why *aren't* we teaching them?"

Peaches coasted underwater towards the steps on the far side, where the toddlers pranced and played as their mothers tanned. Brother's head popped up suddenly in front of her. "Was that kid really going to drown, Peaches?"

Peaches looked down and studied her wrinkled wet hands: "I don't know, Brother. Maybe so."

Brother punched her on the arm, familial and friendly. Peaches was surprised, forgetting Brother was a golden boy in the summertime. "That was cool of you, Peaches." He floated in place and grinned as he pushed his slick, wet hair out of his eyes. "I'm gonna get us some candy." He ducked beneath the water and pushed off the side, jettisoning across the length of the pool easily.

Brother's quirky amiability confused Peaches as much as anything in the past few minutes. She knew he had to see himself in something to have any feelings about it at all. Peaches wondered perhaps if he identified with the boy she had saved.

She looked around and saw that very boy on the edge of the pool across from her. His legs dangled in the water and a towel was slung over his head, hiding his face.

Peaches swam slowly up to him, but didn't meet his eyes, knowing full well he could see her. "If you meet me here tonight, I can maybe teach you to swim." Then swam away. The boy tossed a whispering nod in her direction and flashed two spread palms and a finger, before he disappeared through the pool's front gate. Eleven o' clock.

Night Swimming

That night, Peaches waited until the house hushed completely, then rose from her bed. Already wearing a bathing suit, she swapped her pajamas for a dark t-shirt and shorts. Then she crept from her room, down the steps, and out the porch door. A pre-teen loose on the streets after dark.

Even though she was barefoot, her quick tread consumed the blocks and she arrived early for her swim date. She waited in the dark shadows of an old oak whose roots broke boldly through the black asphalt of the pool parking lot. Crickets chorused and an owl hooted, but the low din of nature was the only sound as the town slept through the night.

Peaches settled amid the tree roots to wait. The giant branches cooled the tepid night air. She jerked in surprise as the boy sidled up beside her, tapping her on the shoulder. They moved to the pool quietly, scanning the landscape for an illegal entry through the barbed wire fence. He spotted the hole where a ditch created a crawl space and slipped underneath, then held the fence to let Peaches through.

The pool was calm and quiet in the moonlight, its ripples smoothed and the surface stilled. It was chaos in the sunshine, but at night the water pulled into itself and erased the memory of the invaders who had kicked and pummeled it throughout the day.

They approached the sacred water. Peaches sniffed the air, fearing the lifeguards might have added chemicals at closing time. Peaches told him what she was doing and he sniffed too. She smiled at him and he smiled back, and the pool reflected the pair of them.

"What's your name?" They were his first words to her. Though Peaches had held him close that day, he wasn't real to her until she heard his voice.

Peaches hesitated, expecting the usual commentary or ridicule that came with the telling of her name. "Peaches."

He held his hand out to her, and they shook like they were sealing a business deal. "I'm Kahlil, Peaches."

They stepped towards the edge of the pool. Peaches undressed down to her suit; Kahlil took off his shirt. They stood half-naked, gazing across the length of the pool. The crickets were quiet and the only sound was the water kissing the sides. Peaches waded down the steps into the shallow end of the pool and beckoned Kahlil to join her.

Tentative and slow, he walked down the steps. In the occasional streaks of moonlight, Peaches saw goosebumps rise on his arms and legs. When they both had reached the pool, he made ready to follow her in a silent game of underwater copycat. Peaches plunged beneath the surface and emerged dripping, her yellow hair slicked back and framing the unspoken dare. Kahlil inhaled a deep breath, then submerged, a shadowy underwater silhouette. He rose gleaming and drenched, shaking the wet from his hair and ears languorously as if he had done it a million times before. Peaches grinned gleefully at her almost-twin as they stood shining in the white moonlight, bound by their shared delinquency.

Every night for a week, they met for lessons. By the end, Kahlil could race full lengths and leap off the diving board with a grace his instructor had never possessed. On the seventh night, he whooped loudly as he tried a curving flip off the board. His sound echoed across the water, and wary of discovery, they ran away with their clothes in their arms.

The next afternoon, Kahlil brought his younger brother and sister to the pool to teach them what he had learned. They were nervous and excited and Peaches tried to help, but they screeched and splashed fearfully. Around them, pale mothers with litters of pale, wet offspring murmured, exchanging looks.

Kahlil grew angry at his flesh and blood, finally herding them out of the water. Peaches shared ice pops from the snack bar while they wrapped up in towels, readying to leave. Kahlil told Peaches he was bringing them back at night because a different fear would keep them quiet then. She smiled when he asked her to come, too. Peaches loved nightswimming, when the pool was theirs alone.

The siblings learned quickly and so did their friends, and for sundry nights, more and more boys and girls swam undetected, aided by the parking lot and thick groves that isolated the pool from its neighbors. The water of the pool and the dew of the night were co-conspirators that held the noise close. Under the cloak of moonlight, they spent joyful hours in the water racing, playing games, and listening to a radio that bumped and buzzed softly at the pool's edge.

Peaches thought the nights weren't terribly different from the days, but when both intertwined, it made a fantasy summer she couldn't have created in her own mind. Eventually it had to end, she knew, and it finally did when the felonious group gave themselves away with irreversible imprints of their after-hours existence. There were too many mornings when the staff noticed scraps, souvenirs, and, occasionally, chairs out of place. The world had found out about their night play.

Cops came, unwisely warning the swimmers of their approach with red and blue lights that flashed across the water. The gang of miscreants ran through the fence gap and across the parking lot. Only Peaches flashed bright dangerously white in the dark.

From a shadowy branch high up above in the oak tree, Kahlil watched as his water sprote was tucked into the back of the police cruiser. Then he jumped down from his perch to find his brethren, saying a quick prayer to Jesus that Peaches' mama would go easy on her.

Match Point

The cops switched on the blue lights upon reaching her driveway, a sociable service to forewarn the neighborhood of Mama's approaching humiliation. Behind the mesh wire in the backseat of the police car, Peaches had found it didn't smell so good.

Blinking sleepily in the doorway, Mama was polite to the police officers, but Peaches realized her mother's serene visage had nothing to do with how she felt about her daughter, who was soon yanked through the door.

Inside, the troubled child floated in purgatory as Mama spoke with the police outside. Her Mama wrapped a long lock of black hair around her finger like a ribbon, and the boys in blue said things Peaches knew were close relatives of not good. As the police car backed down the driveway to go flood some other neighborhood with blue light and grief, Mama stopped tugging her hair and Peaches heart sank. Brother hid in the shadows of the stairs, amused that Peaches was the troublemaker. That role was usually his.

Mama paced about the house, through the living room, into the kitchen, and back again. Her eyes shot blue ice into Peaches. "Sweet Mother Mary, Peaches. What do you think you were you doing?"

Peaches thought to lead off with a glory story, since the truth was actually breaking, entering, and trespassing. "See, Mama, I was teaching this kid to swim."

Brother tossed a life raft to Peaches from the dark staircase. "Is that the kid you saved from drowning?"

Mama covered her face with her hands, wishing things were sometimes ordinary with this child. "What? You saved someone from drowning?"

"I'm really tired, Mama. Can we maybe talk about this in the morning?"

Mama's face shaded a deep red, and her hard, angry mask slid into a blur of sorrow and sadness. Tears sprang from the gray fountainhead as she froze, staring at something playing out behind her mind. Brother saw the unhinging and ran up the stairs to his room, leaving his sister alone with their mother, who now wore a peculiarly remote smile as her mind drifted away. Peaches took a seat on the sofa to patiently await its return.

Behind her eyes, Mama dreamed in movies. She was sitting by herself in a dark movie theatre watching grainy film spool across the wide screen while she ate buttery popcorn through a bright smile. Mama was the star of her own memory, playing on a movie tennis court.

In this recollection, it was winter and the surrounding trees were barren, except for the old pines that nature never stripped. Off in the distance, the swimming pool was tarped over and floodlights began to flicker as late afternoon started its slow bleed into evening. Brother was a toddler and scampered after balls like a chipmunk. Mama, meanwhile, pounded overhead serves to a wooden practice wall.

It was a moment in Mama's biography when days were nights and nights were sleepless pacing. A confusing time. Mama's racket was old, and she wore sweatpants and a hooded shirt, but she had bundled up Brother like a stubby sausage against the chill of the season.

For nearly an hour, Mama smacked the ball like it was her life until she heard the metal fence rattle and realized someone was watching. She didn't recognize the man leaning against it, but she wasn't worried because at that moment, there was no way she looked like easy prey.

The man's voice broke into her concentration. "Want a game, ma'am?"

She looked at him and replied honestly. "I don't think you want to play me. It wouldn't be you that I was really playing."

He winked at her. "Then maybe you'll win." She noticed his eyes were green like springtime. The same bottle green irises she saw every day in the eyes of her little girl.

The game started. Mama beat Peaches' father soundly. She didn't feel bad about her game with the stranger. Her dark-haired, light-eyed son was there, and her ring finger was bare. She was sweaty and dressed about like a housewife on strike. It had been the beginning of love and wonder in her life, and now it was only a movie in her mind.

Mama was enthralled by the memory of that day until the dark dream became too much. She stood and the film began to skip and blur as the lights flickered on and off. The theater shut down as she fought the memory, before light zapped through her skull like a shock of electricity. She returned to the real world and saw Peaches in front of her, watching her mother with worried eyes.

Mama remembered her nowadays, and her face softened. Peaches thought her mother looked younger than she had ever known. "Go to bed, sweetie."

Peaches hesitated, but Mama remembered why they were up this late. She stared pointedly at her daughter. "You know that I can punish you until forever, Peaches. Your brother wasn't even brought home by the police until this year, and he's older than you." Mama momentarily recalled her horror at learning her son was sneaking onto trains, then jumping off when the tracks crossed the river, dropping through the air to bullet down into the water below.

Peaches had forgotten her own misbehavior during the slow minutes in which Mama's mind went on holiday. She gazed at her Mama's face and suddenly felt accountable for everything that ever went wrong in her mother's life. "I'm sorry, Mama."

Mama stood up and kissed Peaches on the crown of her head. She led her to the stairs and nudged her gently up the steps. "Go to bed, sweetie," she said again.

Peaches began a slow trudge as Mama closed her eyes. She held out her hands as if she could hold everything in place. She had miscarried a husband to inherit his daughter. For one moment, everything stood still and nothing changed. She thought it was enough. "Wait, Peaches...."

Peaches stopped and turned on the stairs. Mama thinned her eyes and made a slow, cutting gesture at her throat. "Stay in bed tonight, Peaches."

Peaches was surprised by the dark humor. She obliged quickly because she was glad to have her Mama back. "Yes, ma'am."

Peaches headed towards her bedroom and sleep. She realized that as much as she knew about her Mama, she didn't really know anything at all. But Peaches knew she loved her anyway, more than anyone else in the world.

Questioning of Belief

Each Sunday during Mass, Peaches sat with
Mama in a pew up front and stage right of the altar
where bread and wine became Flesh and Blood. Every
week, Peaches watched the consecration of the host
carefully, hoping to see the transformation, but like a
really good magician, God was too quick. Brother's place
was near the priest with the other altar boys, bowed in
prayerful black and white. Peaches desperately wished to
join them, to be a part of the service, rather than
dutifully encased in stone for an hour.

Her eyes wandered, studying the lines of the
church, a thick limestone building that oozed spirituality.
The stained glass was dull and dark, until the sun broke
through and the stretching windows glowed deep reds,
golds, greens, and a particularly vibrant blue. Each floor-
to-ceiling window was a piece of a story that began or
ended with the extravagantly crucified man hanging
above the altar.

When Peaches was young, she had imagined that
a leprechaun lived in the eaves, ready to do her bidding.
He would jump and run around the church, mussing the
priest's hair and making rabbit ears behind the cantor's
head. Peaches wished she were powerful enough to
make her imagination come to life. She wasn't jealous of
God, but she was thoroughly impressed with His
building.

For Mama's sake, Peaches pretended to possess
the dignity of a young lady, spending the time at Mass
lost in profound thought. Long before now, she had
given up the futile effort of opening herself up to divine

intervention or the sacred feeling that kept everyone else coming back each week. But she did find comfort in the beauty of something so old. She loved the scent of candles, the incense in the air as if the congregation was inhaling and exhaling God, and the thick pew missals filled with songs familiar and beautiful. Sometimes, though, it wasn't enough to keep Peaches from wishing for a wailing gospel choir and a bit of clapping to break the solemnity.

But it was the repeated kneeling and rising that took the greatest toll on her, especially her little-old-lady circulation. After the sermon, and then again during the priest's consecration of the host, Peaches' world often began to turn gray. She would struggle to remain standing as her knees buckled and her brain strained towards the light. It was not a feeling of being born again, but of dying slow.

One time, her world shifted so hard, it caught her like a solid fist to the jaw, and she toppled. Peaches missed the divine moment of consecration as her head cracked against a pew. Wilted and unconscious, she was carried by ushers through a side door, waking up a few minutes later in the sacristy. Mama sat beside her, stroking her forehead and holding a handkerchief of ice to a notched lump on her daughter's head.

Another hand patted Peaches on her arm, owned by an old priest murmuring words of consolation. His touch was unfamiliar. She thought a man of God should feel less like a stranger. His murmurs poked at her, as if he thought she could rise from his words alone.

Peaches asked a Peaches question, born of a hundred Sundays' lost thoughts. "Father, why can't women be priests?" she murmured.

He blinked in surprise. "Because they can be sisters," he replied.

Peaches found their dialogue a sudden stimulant. "Yes, sir, but sisters are only equal to brothers."

The priest shot a frustrated look at Mama, who smiled back politely, busy with her prayers of thanks at Peaches' return. She was trying to remember all the patron saints she could, already successful in plucking Ursus of Ravenna from her personal treasury.

The priest tried again. "All Jesus' disciples were men, little girl."

"What about Mary Magdalene? And Mary, the Mother of God? And all the other women Jesus knew? Don't they count for anything? We can be saints. Why not priests?" Peaches was recovering.

The priest leaned close as though offering last rites, in a whisper so Mama wouldn't hear. "Jesus was a man. All priests must be like Jesus."

Mama patted Peaches' head, still not listening. She was proud her daughter was talking religion with a man of the cloth.

She leaned forward into the priest's ear and her defiance peaked. "God lets Mary sit beside him in Heaven. I can't even be a damn altar boy."

The priest stared in silence at his little blasphemer. Behind him a painting of the Virgin Mother backlit his balding head, making hornlets of his stray wisps of gray. Peaches borrowed a little of the Blessed Mother's smile for herself.

Mama thought her daughter had never looked so sweet. She was pleased Peaches had recovered so quickly from her spell and she turned towards the priest gratefully. She was shocked by his face: an exorcist at the moment his rite had failed. He scrambled to leave, "I've got to say the next Mass."

Peaches climbed off the sofa and crossed another invisible line. "Maybe I'll just have a life of making biscuits, Mama."

Confused, Mama shook herself out of her reverie and went to find her other child. Brother was in the sacristy, taking off his cassock and surplice.

Mama watched Brother push through the cluster of bobbing little boys in front of the vestment closet and thought of how nice it would be if Peaches could serve Mass, too. She turned to the old priest as he slipped a long white alb over his head and asked what she thought was a fresh and original question. "Father, can little girls be altar servers?"

He muttered and stomped off. Mama looked on bemused.

City on the Edge of the World

Spring flung itself across the South's landscape, and Mama thought it felt different from the resurrections of nature past. Her children were yearlings, moving and thinking without her. That was a blessing because Mama found she herself wasn't thinking very well at all. Sometimes her brain crackled like an embered log and she lost time and place, until a smooth wave soothed her back into the present.

Peaches noticed the change in Mama. It scared her, but she didn't say anything. When Mama disassociated and went somewhere else, Peaches snapped on music to bring her back. Concern for her mother became baggage that she carried along with her own. When it tugged too hard, Peaches invariably decided to think about it tomorrow. As his sister drifted into hideaways of silence, Brother tread upon the world like a colt unharnessed. He was stilted and stuck in his same old self, but now too big for even Mama to handle.

Peaches' two best friends were Kahlil and an old camera she had bought at a garage sale. The three were always out and about: Kahlil, the camera, and Peaches. Every hand-carved cornice, old building, brilliant sunset, and town citizen had been etched into film. Peaches was running out of things to focus on, her cameras emptying the town of its visual treasures.

Her young life was a cage and her birthplace an Attica. The constraint was as tangible as if razor wire had been set around the town. She could walk the perimeter blind for how well she knew it.

Sometimes she pulled Kahlil along to stand on the overpass above the interstate to watch the cars below. She was jealous when she saw the license plates from other states. At other times, she skimmed the small print on boxed and canned foods to see where it had been, places that she hadn't seen, faraway-seeming places that were sometimes just a state away, sometimes an ocean. It woke something in Peaches that burned red hot, and she was angrily certain that she'd never go so far.

Kahlil was a ready companion, not as desperate as Peaches, but still willing to breathe different air. He nudged her with easy words, telling her she could leave home if she just wanted to. Soon her thoughts joined his, and together they felt an audience of angels cheering them on as they fantasized an escape.

One Friday morning, they both skipped school, grasping their wheel of fortune and spinning it recklessly. They were going to Savannah, taking the train east like newlyweds on honeymoon, headless of consequences.

Kahlil's escape strategy was simple. He faked sick, then waited for his parents to leave for work. Peaches thought she wouldn't be missed at all and forged an excuse note from home, signing Mama's name without a second thought of her deceit. (Later, Mama focused her upset on the forgeries. "Maybe if you had just left, Peaches, I wouldn't be so angry.")

For the first three hours on the train, it was cows, crops, and small towns, each looking just like the one they had left behind. Paint peeled and old barns slumped, seemingly determined to remain unchanged. Peaches took photos, because she had a bagful of film.

Kahlil slept, because he had both the time and inclination to dream.

Peaches skimmed railroad pamphlets that listed train tables and routes, recognizing the names of only a few of the towns. Most were brief stops or pass-throughs, never destinations, and they all lacked the bold print awarded to the cities. Peaches thought of the universal curse of the small town, its inability to attract attention unless there was a tabloid occurrence like the birthing a two-headed calf or an onslaught of teenage license and disease.

She thought it was unfortunate that they remained unnoticed. It seemed to her that small towns played the world's game, diligently spending their little bit of cash on self-promotion as they allowed an occasional swath of concrete to cut across their land. Their inhabitants were loyal and good people; flag-waving and God-fearing, living and dying and producing more like themselves. Peaches didn't think small-towners were so different from anyone else. It was just they were not very different from each other.

The vegetation changed as the train drew closer to the sea, near the shores of the Atlantic where adventurers had landed long ago to chase away the mosquitoes and the inhabitants. Chubby palm trees replaced tall, lean pines. Damp green grass replaced pallid fescue. It was an ever-blooming, ever fertile world, and Peaches poked Kahlil awake to share the finding of it.

They kept to their patience carefully as the train slowed through Bloomingdale and Garden City, waiting painful minutes for the advent of cosmopolitan Savannah. Soon, clusters of noble buildings and exquisite homes huddling thick as oysters signified its coming into their lives.

The two travelers stepped off the train to stand under cerulean skies. Savannah. Their first time in any city, and the city was Savannah! Peaches thought photos had been poor replicas, two-dimensional sketches of three-dimensional wonders. The authentic hurt her eyes and evoked her amazement.

They absorbed Savannah in the endless forms in which she presented herself. Kahlil suddenly pondered aloud what Atlanta must be like, if it was indeed the sovereign of the South. Peaches said that Atlanta was newer and had a skyline crested by buildings built so high they were topped with blinking lights that warned planes away. Savannah sopped with the old, and Kahlil said that was money, too, that old was good for tourists, and book writers, and moviemakers.

Peaches came back with a history lesson. Back before cotton had a tagline, she said, Savannah was governed by planters and their factors-- the technical term of the day for commodity brokers. In this case, the commodity being living humans:, blood brokers, as busy and as efficient as the gas chambers of a century later. During the Civil War, when soldiers set fires that ended the slavery and burned throughout the rebellious region, Savannah was saved by its own charm, forwarded in a famous telegram as a Christmas present to a friend of the conquering general, said friend happening to be President of the United States. Now, art and culture thrived even while the city mortgaged its antebellum soul to enchanted newcomers.

Kahlil and Peaches took a lumbering bus to the ocean 17 miles away, and Peaches walked straight into the water. Kahlil hesitated at the cusp where the reach of the waves dribbled into foaming sand. Peaches pushed him further in.

Under a beast of a springtime sun, the boy and the girl waded and watched. Kahlil said he thought a beach had enough sky for anybody. They stared at silhouettes of steamships and sailboats traveling easily on the horizon, moving platforms of humans who walked on water in the only way they knew how. Peaches took pictures of the dark sea as it returned from touching continents far away. She captured Kahlil staring off into the distance at the ghosts of his capsized ancestors struggling to reach some new shore.

They took one final taste of the salt air, mocked the crying seagulls— "rear! rear!" – and caught the bus back to the city and the riverfront, two starving kids in a candy factory. They ambled through cracked, stained neighborhoods where once-beautiful houses sagged, scalded by sun, salt air, and neglect. A hundred shades of people walked the sidewalks and sat on stoops under the old trees, while children played and shouted across the gritty pavements. Peaches observed through her camera lens, while Kahlil took it in through his bold brown eyes.

A few blocks later, the city center washed over them in vibrant watercolors. There the lives of well-fed inhabitants were as lived out, serene as the river coursing close by. Bracing art galleries and somnolent cafes held space in buildings encrusted with century-old molding. Sidewalks ended in dappled green squares, shading courtesy of moss-covered oaks. Tree roots rose in knotted knuckles from the ground, splitting street from sidewalk and wrenching the pavement out of shape. Peaches found the trees' effect nearly as charming as all the museums and cafes. Nature, life, earth intersecting with man, craft, art—that was Savannah.

Peaches and Kahlil stood looking over the busy river that stretched through marsh and tidals to where they had waded in the great, gray sea. A few miles upstream an arcing bridge rose gracefully to reach into the flatlands of South Carolina. Spunky tugboats and vast cargo ships sailed by. Train tracks no longer used for riverfront cargo led to an Italian bronze: an islands woman frozen in place as she hailed passing ships and sailors, holding with both hands above her head a great cloth aloft in the wind, her ave atque vale from Savannah to the world. Under her gaze, the two children counted their money and bought a fried scallop and bacon sandwich that they shared bite for bite.

In a nearby candy store, Peaches purchased a giant speckled jawbreaker for Brother, but gave it to Kahlil instead. Brother didn't need to know about their journey. A Moonpie clock behind the candy man told them it was time to consider their train. As they walked back towards the station, Kahlil sucked on the golf ball-sized ball of sugar, his tongue etching through color after color of the marvelous candy.

They stopped in front of a record store and stared through the window, having previously only seen such ecstasy in films. Peaches photographed their reflection on the glass, and Kahlil made a face at the camera before pulling her through the door.

Inside, they both fell over their heels drowning in a dream, as if popular music was their newly reformed native tongue. Kahlil flipped through a messy stack of posters, while Peaches searched through albums. She chose one release from Los Angeles and another for its cover art, which was a kind of dreamscape. Kahlil slipped on a t-shirt bearing a particular genre's messiah, and then froze as he tapped Peaches and looked at his wrist. She blanched, realizing that only an act of God would prevent their train from leaving them behind. They spoke of calling a taxi, despondent at their exodus from paradise and fearing retribution if they didn't make it home on time.

The sales boy was watching them with cool appraisal. Peaches watched him back, feeling something like fascination for the boy whose black hair was split and spiked in gelled chunks and a tattoo that spread like green moss from his elbow to hide under his shirtsleeve. Peaches smiled sweetly, just like a girl. "Y'all are a little young for a cab, kids," the sales boy said.

Peaches questioned, "Is there an age limit for cabs?"

He laughed, and it rolled across the counter like an ocean wave. "No, but, aren't you supposed to be in school?"

Peaches looked at Kahlil, both remembering their little sin. Peaches turned it back around. "Aren't you?"

He laughed again, impressed. "Actually, yeah, I'm supposed to be in a class right now, but I had to work." He studied her and thought of his little sister, still in pigtails. "Save your cash, lil' girl. Hang on, and I'll get y'all a ride."

He leaned over the counter and called down an aisle to a young couple perusing the shelves. "Hey, can y'all drive these kids to the train?"

"No, man. Sorry." The male waved in apology. "We don't have a car."

Peaches' newest crush threw keys from his pocket towards the couple. "No worries, take mine." He turned back towards Peaches, who was drowning in puppy love. "Kids, don't take rides from people that you don't know." He looked at Peaches, delivering his next line like it was a reason not to do things in life. "You're a girl, y'know."

Kahlil blockaded that, declaring in a voice down a register, "She's with me, man. She'll be fine."

Peaches rolled her eyes. "No, he's with me. We'll both be fine."

The black-headed boy laughed so hard he nearly lost his breath. "Y'all are funny." He was still chuckling as Kahlil and Peaches followed their new hosts towards the door. "Have a good trip, kids. See you next time."

The old, green hatchback covered with stickers of unknown bands. The girl cranked on the stereo and rustic music drummed through the car pure and loud. She turned it down suddenly to swear at her forgetfulness. "Aw shoot, I'm thirsty. I meant to buy a Coke."

Kahlil spoke like the polite Southern gentleman he was. "I'll run in and get you one." He ducked his head, slipped out of the car and back into the store.

The driver grinned over his shoulder at Peaches. He pulled on one of the knotted twists of hair that hung from his scalp like a rainshower. "You know what these are?"

Peaches was small town, but she was aware it was a big world. "Dreadlocks?"

"Ya, I Rasta. What 'bout you?" His words were a humor song, and she thought his voice sounded like a deep bass drum.

Peaches contemplated the question, unsure whether her answer should be related to race, culture, or religion. "Catholic?"

The girl beside him grinned as she turned around towards Peaches. She had thickly twisted ginger knots hanging from her head like octopus legs. Peaches secretly wanted to touch one to see if it felt like muppet skin. "Me, too. Or at least I was."

"You can change?" Peaches was astonished, as if trading religions was traitorous. She wasn't sure she was ready for that kind of personal revolution.

"Yeah, but it's weird. Some stuff always sticks with you." The girl was frank, mulling over her reply as she fingered wood and clay beads wrapped around her neck. "Or to you."

"Every life experience molds you," the driver declared. Peaches sensed hot sun and something British in his accent.

Kahlil returned and slid in the backseat, handing out chilled bottles of Coca-Cola as the driver prodded him with a new question. "Hey, little man, is that your girl?"

Peaches stared at Kahlil with one eyebrow raised high. She knew most girls would demand an affirmative, as if it was a shiny coin they could tuck away for later.

Kahlil steered away from a likely fuss. "No, man. We both stand alone. But we're next to each other, y'know." The girl in the front seat smiled sunshines on him.

Peaches looked out her window, hiding her grin as something syrupy and warm flowed under her skin. She turned and kissed her champion on the cheek quickly, and it was Kahlil's turn to stare out the window.

Peaches saw his face flush and his throat move as he tried to swallow. He turned back to grab her hand, the one between them on the seat. Kahlil smiled as Peaches smiled, then they laughed at each other. It was the sound of caramel and soda water combining together in a delightful roar.

The girl riding shotgun had seen it all and raised her bottle to Peaches in a toast, as if they were in the same secret club. The Coca-Colas clinked and both took a slug while the two bemused males looked on. Like a competent Jeeves, the driver flipped the rearview mirror to regard Kahlil and Peaches. "What time does your train leave, kids?"

Kahlil was hesitant, because the clock was unfriendly in its honesty. "Um, in about three and a half minutes."

The passengers were thrown backwards as the little car leapt through a yellow light, its tires squealing and exfoliating across the pavement. The girl up front directed the driver through side streets shaded by leafy canopies and tangled with moss, which hung like witches' wigs from the trees.

Peaches pulled her camera from her bag, and the pair in the front seat turned to pose as the car stopped for a traffic light. Peaches' finger paused on the shutter, and instead caught them a moment later when the light turned green. Their movement and gestures matched, and it was the picture Peaches wanted, a perfectly balanced contradiction.

Kahlil saw it, and he muttered aloud. "The problem is that everyone has something in common. But they insist they don't."

The little car turned into the train station lot, and Kahlil and Peaches readied for the run of their life. They slammed doors and yelled their thanks as their mamas had taught them. Peaches heard their charmed chauffeurs laughing as the car putt-putted off. Quickly they sprinted into the shadowed cool of the depot.

Seconds before the train caught the tail of the westward ocean breeze they were seated and began their homeward glide out of the station. Peaches and Kahlil looked at each other with fortunate eyes before breaking open the casing that enfolded the stories of their day.

When the train finally stopped in their small-print town, the arrival was unsettling, leaving the pair feeling both revived and blue. Peaches and Kahlil expected the day to disappear like a dream, as if all their new thoughts would crash and burn upon the reappearance of their old way of being. It didn't, and they split up to head towards home.

Kahlil walked slowly, lost in thought. Peaches scurried mentally to match up her day with that of school dismissal. She thought about how good it had been, but the buzz died when she came upon Mama in the kitchen, her arms crossed as if she were holding down a hurricane. Even Brother had been shocked by the news of Peaches' brazen truancy. For the first time, Peaches realized it might seem a little strange she had wandered so far.

Mama's composure collapsed into jabbering that climaxed with: "Peaches, you could have been sold into white slavery!"

Peaches' young face looked surprised. She had never before realized that was a danger for her kind. "Really, Mama?"

85

Mama paced a line around the kitchen table. Her exasperation was her anxiety transformed, and she finally paused in front of Peaches. "Are you ever going to do something like this again, Peaches?"

Mama's eyebrows arched at an impossible angle, distracting Peaches as she tried to shroud her desire to leave again. It was a long, telling moment, then she delivered the right answer. "No, ma'am. Never again."

Mama understood the pause well enough. She made one last desperate attempt to tame her girl, telling Brother to take his sister outside and teach her the basics of how to defend herself.

Lessons Learned

Peaches didn't hear him come up as she sat on the porch after the boxing lesson. Brother had grown man-size in the past year, his face and body thickening. He had also stopped looking in the mirror. He didn't like to see himself anymore. He looked too much like someone else.

When Brother sat down beside her, a sweet-sour tang trailed him. His voice was morose and frank, and Peaches found it strange. "Peaches, shoot me if I become like him."

Peaches couldn't help but think it was too late, not because her brother looked more like his daddy each day, but because he always had the man's imprint on his soul. She kept quiet and let him talk, as if porch therapy might help.

"At least I don't carry his name, thank God."

He continued to reflect, and it was almost a foreign language for him. "Your daddy gave me his name. Maybe I never had the other one. Maybe Mama gave me granddaddy's at first. I don't remember." His smile was hard and bitter, as if he remembered something he wasn't telling.

Peaches wanted to grab and hug him, but she knew better. Brother drew back from affection like it was shattering glass. He stood up, looking straight ahead, his cheeks dry, but his throat moving fast. He left the porch and walked back into the yard.

Brother turned back once before reaching the fence. His voice broke from somewhere inside his throat. "Sometimes I think I'm like him because it's what everyone expects. Maybe if your daddy hadn't died, I'd have been different."

Brother wandered off, his head bowed, leaving Peaches alone under a hundred thousand stars. She took a mental picture, wanting a memory of this particular Brother forever stored in her mind.

Later, Mama came into her bedroom and Peaches paused with her hand on the lamp's switch. She looked at the woman in the doorway, seeing parts of her own face in there. Peaches knew the color of her eyes was from her father, but it was their shape that made Peaches her mother's child.

Mama sat at the edge of Peaches' bed, fingering a long rosary looped through one hand. She reached to gently trace the sore spots near Peaches' eyes. Her fingertips were warm, but felt like needles, and Peaches quivered at her touch.

"Your Gram once said you would go places." She clicked off the light and walked to the window. She stared at the peach tree that watched over her daughter as she slept. When Mama spoke again, it was the echo of another voice. "I think we may have peaches soon."

"Oh, make a pie please, Mama." Peaches' voice was muffled in the pillow in a way that made her face hurt.

Mama heard her from the doorway and replied with a threat and a smile that matched the one pressed into the pillow. "I'll make you into a pie."

Peaches fell asleep. She wished in her dream she had seen a Savannah nighttime, so she could determine if it was the same as here. Mama washed dishes in the kitchen until tiredness rubbed her mind clear of thought. She was in bed nearly asleep when she heard Brother finally come home. His footsteps on the stairs were heavy and old.

Extinguishing a Phoenix

It was a ding-dong day of celebration, and Peaches beamed with the white-hot energy that surged within her teen-aged self. She circled around the roller rink on orange-wheeled skates, watching Mama wave to her from a table piled with tributes to the child's birth. Peaches skated at top speed towards her mother and hit the slick rink's curb, her young frame sprawling, light rug burns appearing on her knees and elbows. She dusted herself off, and the scrapes were quickly forgotten. It was her day, and Mama was the picture of normality, the lady Peaches knew and loved most of all. It was the best present, having a day without any worry that the cracked flagon might shatter.

Peaches reached to hug Mama tightly. "Thanks for the party, Mama." Peaches was thirteen, an ancient age. She thought she was too old for a party, but Mama was always bully for an event to cook up for.

Mama hugged her back, looking hard at the girl who always made her wonder. Mama fingered her silver plait of hair, while Peaches tugged on a chiseled metal necklace, a birthday present from Kahlil. Both felt disturbed by something they couldn't discern, a flickering that tilted their world slightly, a wispy nudge from a very large ghost.

The daughter was dressed in loose old-man pants, a ripped v-neck, and jewelry that seemed more urban than small town. Mama's tone switched like a record with jazz on one side and blues on the other. "Peaches, couldn't you have dressed like a lady just for today?"

"Mama, I dressed like a person today. That's all I want to be." Peaches held down her teenage irritation as she tried to shake off the dread that still bussed her nerves.

As the partygoers gathered around, Mama pulled matches from her purse to light the candles in unlucky numbers. The yellow cake with vanilla ice cream brought a stifled sigh to Peaches' throat, and she wished for color or chocolate or both. She blew out the baker's dozen, suddenly aching to leave. As thin lines of smoke rose from the cake, a woman burst in from outside. Her hushed words hit Mama like a thrown knife. She told of a bullet that was now lodged deep in Brother's neck.

Mama fell to her knees, her arms cradling nothing. She held onto herself, a silent scream wailing in her head. Peaches was blank, thinking first how strange it was. Then she flinched, realizing how real it was. Her horoscope in the newspaper that morning flashed to mind. It had said nothing about her brother getting shot in the head by a friend.

The partygoers scattered, while the skaters rolled unaware around the rink. For the next few hours, Peaches and her mother sat mutely in the hospital waiting room as nurses passed back and forth and doctors stayed out of reach. Friends and neighbors came, but Mama's face was stone. She spoke only three thoughts aloud. "The world is getting meaner. Boys will be boys. Thank you for coming."

Brother didn't die that day. Death was mocked by a strong heart that continued to beat, but his arms and legs couldn't move at all. Weeks later, he came home in a wheelchair, and his lanky appendages hung from it. The sight of Peaches infuriated him. She had emerged the chosen one, the child determined by fate to be fit and survive. The eldest male lost his place on this fateful day.

Already a birthday and a deathday, this day became the boy's own crippling moment. On the day Brother returned, Peaches walked in on her mother and found her scrubbing the floor, dressed in a man's seersucker suit.

Brother sat stiffly in his chair, his eyes demanding that Peaches do something. Mama looked up. A dodgy grin curved across her face. "Help me before your daddy gets home, Peaches."

The breaking point. City walls fell, the good leader was slain, and Peaches had only a quaint colloquialism at hand. "My Mama's lost her mind," she whispered.

Brother's chair shook as if he nodded vigorously in concurrence. Peaches gritted her teeth and plucked the cloth from Mama's curled fist. She helped Mama stand, and then walked her to her bedroom. Peaches lay her mother down on the bed, unsure whether to rouse her or keep her still.

Then she dialed Gram's number in Atlanta. It rang and rang, and Peaches wasn't sure what she would do if her grandmother didn't answer. She knew she couldn't allow the small-town neighbors to watch live color footage of men in white coats taking Mama away.

After a double-digit number of rings, Gram answered and Peaches found it hurt to speak. "Gram, it's Peaches."

"Peaches, honey. How are you?" Gram was outside when the phone rang, and warm sunshine still sat sweetly upon her. She waited for Peaches to answer, and suddenly smelled rain.

Peaches whispered, so that Mama wouldn't hear from where she lay still and quiet like a china doll. "Gram, I think that Mama's mind broke. She's talking about my daddy and saying he's coming home. She's wearing his suit."

Gram's heart ached for her daughter and grandchildren. "Peaches, I'm getting in the car now. I'll be there before nightfall."

Peaches handled her mother as if she were a child, helping her out of the seersucker suit and into one of her housedresses. Pushing away, Mama took over and tied her hair back. Brother's eyes burned in fear at the sight of his mother returning in conventional garb.

In the kitchen, Mama got lost in a frenzy of food preparation as if there were a party planned. By the time Gram pulled into the drive, two chickens had been roasted, two more fried, and an eight-pound ham gleamed with honey near a triplet of cooling peach pies. Mama was stirring pudding and Peaches pitted olives, then cleaned the silver, obedient to Mama's strange demands.

Mama looked up, excited by the apparition before her. Then her blue eyes narrowed, as if she were expecting someone else. She bit down hard on her bottom lip and slung the rolling pin across the room. Gram tried to look stern as she ducked it. "Honey, how are you doing?"

Mama wiped her mouth, smearing the blood from her lip across her face. Gram grimaced. She had not realized it would be this bad.

Mama replied, "Peaches' daddy is on his way home. I'm not sure we have enough food."

Her arm knocked over a glass of milk, full and forgotten on the counter. Gram cringed again, but Peaches quickly set the glass upright in its puddle.

Her mother started crying, reaching to hold onto her own mother. "Mama, I don't know how to do this anymore," she wailed.

Peaches sat still in her chair. She had never before seen this Mama. Her mother had never been a widow like in the movies or on television. She had never worn black or stared forlornly out a window. Peaches had never heard her mother weeping in the night. For Peaches, her father's absence was as familiar as his presence.

Gram tried to rebuild a little. "You did your best, sweetie. It's what happens afterwards that matters."

Mama lay against Gram, and Peaches watched her mother sob like a child. Gram gestured to Peaches for the phone and dialed a number from a slip of a paper. With one arm around her weeping daughter, she booked Mama into a hospital in Charleston.

"Peaches, we're leaving now, your Mama and me," she said. "We'll be there by morning." It had to be now. If they waited till next time, there might not be anything left of Mama to take away.

Gram sedated Mama with a handful of old lady pills and tucked her in her car. The full moon shone through the windows where Peaches stood near her father's piano, a silent gravestone in the tomb of a room. Gram lifted the piano lid, plunking the keys slowly and gently at first, then a little harder like a newsman on a sticky typewriter. Gram birthed an old hymn with the dusty keys, certain that Peaches would recognize the tune if not the line: "Time like an ever-rolling stream/Bears all her sons away," she sang gently.

The music shone nobly. Peaches tilted her head and listened, remembering only a feeling of something warm and snug, like a body blanket. Gram stopped playing once a smile broke across Peaches' face. It disappeared when the music stopped. Gram gently pushed the child's mouth back into a smile. Peaches hugged her grandmother tight fingers pressed into thin old frame. "Thanks for coming, Gram."

Gram kissed Peaches on the forehead and loosed her from her hold. "Bring your Mama's things out to the car. I'll get your Brother."

Peaches staggered out the door with the bags and moved slowly towards the car, in no hurry to send Mama so far away. Only her two children saw the neighborhood's most talked-about resident depart in Gram's classic Cadillac. Mama was a silent angel as the car pulled away, waving slowly as if she were on a ship headed out to sea. She thrust a small, white handkerchief through her window, letting it kite in the breeze before her numbed fingers dropped it. Peaches watched it float towards them, then land in the gutter. She thought of picking it up, but she wanted nothing at all kept from this damnable day.

Peaches brought Brother in the house and parked him in front of the television, then went back outside. She stretched her head back towards her spine and stared up at the milky black sky. She dared God to shoot a star, certain that on this night of ruin only a mother could fall so far and so fast.

A Ghost in Sunlight

Few stopped to look up at the passing train. It was no different to them than the wind or the rain. At one house, in one little town, a young boy hung high in a tree at dusk until the branch broke and he fell to the ground. Mama saw him from the train and gasped. The boy dusted himself off, then ran to his little sister, who sat brooding and staring at the train. Mama remembered her two children and went blank again.

At the hospital, Gram watched the attendants tug her tall, fractured daughter through the double doors to a new life, panicky, wriggling, staring back at Gram over her shoulder.

Back home, Peaches had slipped from her perch outside, spending the night asleep on the hard ground. When the sun rose, Kahlil was there and helped her up. Things stuck to her, but she didn't shake or brush them off. She felt dewy, messy, and different. She sat down on the porch steps and rubbed her eyes, trying to tackle awakeness, if not for herself, then at least as a favor to her friend.

Kahlil had run to her house as soon as he had heard the news at his breakfast table. "They say you're going to live with your grandmother. They say you're moving to Atlanta." He whispered the last part, ghosts of another man's words spoken long before his birth. "South of the North, and North of the South, the city of a hundred hills."

Peaches wondered if the neighborhood gossip was right. "I've never had a new life before, Kahlil."

Kahlil murmured, his voice flattened by fear. "Don't forget me, Peaches. Don't you ever pretend I never existed."

Peaches couldn't remember a time when she didn't know him. A lump parked in her throat. She stood up and heard something crunch under her foot. A shattered snail lay dead, from its own shell fragments.

Kahlil caught her as she stumbled. "Peaches, just because you're gone doesn't mean you aren't here. It doesn't mean I won't see you when I walk down the street."

They stood together in the early morning shadows. He kissed her under the peach tree, first on her right eyelid, and then her left. Kahlil hugged her and in their embrace, the two fit together like a skeleton key in a stuck lock. In the middle of the nothing, Peaches felt love for something.

The world was blue and green from sky to ground. High and low were colored prettily on a hard day's canvas. Peaches broke away from Kahlil when she heard Brother inside, his chair shaking violently in the only voice he had. She wheeled him to the porch, a first since Brother usually refused to allow the neighbors a chance to see him. He blinked like a ghost in sunlight as he looked around the yard, reserving his special insolence for the sight of Kahlil.

It was actually on the return trip from Charleston that Gram had determined Peaches would come live with her in Atlanta, not knowing the little town had already decided for her. Gram was ready to take Brother too, but he refused her offer. As Gram laid out the choices around the kitchen table, his response consisted of stubborn, angry eye-movements. The next day, Gram left for Atlanta in her Cadillac. Peaches had negotiated that she would follow a day later, wanting to breathe a last lungful of small town air.

Brother's lot was to remain hidden inside a house closed off from the world as the ward of an elderly nurse. Gram had arranged care through the parish. The nurse would feed and clean him in exchange for the use of the house and a modest monthly sum. Both his care and his mother's was financed by dead men, one a husband and father, the other an Irish-born bachelor from another century who had left his earnings from horse-swapping and land-dealing entirely to the church. Brother was moved into one downstairs room, while his nurse lived in another. The rest of the house stayed dark, waiting for the day of Mama's return.

Cemetery Stop

It was child-killing hot on the day Peaches arrived in Atlanta. The air in her new city was thick with a taste she wasn't used to. But the heat felt good. She liked the sticky humidity that beaded on her skin like wet plastic wrap.

The day began with sweet dread. Peaches had only a few hours of sleep tucked away—it had been hard to sleep since her mother left. It was a journey she had always wished for, but not for this reason.

Her last breakfast home was entirely forgettable. Brother seemed happy to see her go. Or was he? He wore a silent grin as Peaches headed out the door. She planted a sterile kiss on his forehead where black shocks of hair grew, and then she departed.

She and Kahlil gave themselves time to amble down the main street of town and past the massive stone gates of the cemetery. It was the sole burial ground for the entire county, broken up in sections by religion, race and social status. Some of the older plots were sunken after years of wind and wet had spent great effort to rub the names of the dead away. Newer gravesites were decked with bouquets of flowers, some plucked, some plastic. Oaks shaded the dead from hot sun and dripping rain.

Peaches suddenly entertained the wild hope that maybe her father was buried there. She tugged Kahlil inside the gates, skimming every headstone that looked about her age.

Kahlil realized what she was doing. His doe face softened, then stretched back into its stiff, loyal profile, the look that reminded Peaches of a nickel. He tried to speak gently, but his voice was rolling thunder when he told her the truth. "Your daddy's not here, Peaches."

"How do you know?"

Kahlil answered her bluntly, though his face spoke sympathy. "Peaches, I think the whole town knows more about your family than you do."

"What are you talking about? Where is he then?"

Kahlil wished he could just write down what he knew and hand it to her. He felt like he was reading gossip to a celebrity. "I heard that your grandmother took him back to Alabama."

It dawned on Peaches then that she had had another grandmother somewhere. She buckled, and Kahlil nudged her gently towards an oak. "Peaches, let's go sit over there."

Peaches sat beside him on the broad tree root that poked through the ground. She looked out on the field of tombstones that marked platoons of bodies, people old and young, resting within the soil. Hers was a half-told history. She turned to Kahlil. "Tell me everything you know, Kahlil. About me and my family."

Kahlil tried to convince her she was going to miss her train, but Peaches wouldn't budge. Finally, he started the story that had begun before Peaches herself. She listened as he spoke, staring at the tree looming above, trying to hear its ancient heart. She tugged at blades of new grass, tearing pieces from them and twisting the sticky strands until they bled wet and green on her fingertips. She studied Kahlil's features, from his patrician nose to his carved, copper cheekbones, to the firm jaw supporting a mouth that was often a pleasure beam, but now moved humorlessly across his face.

His telling was general, without detail. Kahlil said Mama entered the small world of the townspeople as the sudden new wife of a homegrown boy who had played college basketball in Atlanta. Mama was laden and heavy with a growing Brother, when her husband came home from school with her and his blown-out knee. The town's thinking was that his injury was only a sign of deeper breaks; he began to show it by taking it out on Mama.

Soon after Brother was born, Mama divorced both her child and herself from him. She soon remarried, this time to an Alabama boy of genteel aspirations who had swooped into town to work for the newspaper. He worked hard until he was killed in a train accident on the day Peaches was born. Kahlil reported that his rough Alabama mother had never approved of her divorced, Papist daughter-in-law. She returned with her son's body to the small Alabama town from whence she came, angered by the lack of a male heir as if a monarchy was at stake.

Kahlil's story ended there, at the point when Peaches' life began. "That's all I really can tell you, Peaches. Except that nobody really knows how you got your name."

Peaches was glad something of her life was untouched by the masses. She shared the secret with Kahlil, a simple gesture of thanks for his storytelling. "My daddy planted a peach tree, and loved it and cared for it. Mama wanted him to watch me like he watched his tree."

Kahlil smiled, because her pleasing little tale smoothed his rougher one. As they left the cemetery for the train station, Peaches thought Kahlil was the complete, perfect boy. Something that was him ran deep through her, clear and cool like a creek. She hated to leave him and the town he lived in.

In front of the station, Peaches took a final photograph. She stretched out the camera in her hand, and they both faced it, trying to smile. Peaches put the camera back into her bag once the shutter clicked. She would not capture any more beauty here.

Kahlil chose to leave her at the train station's entrance. They hugged goodbye like strangers, discomfited by the loss their touching signified. Peaches was hushed as she focused on her friend's face. "I'll write you, Kahlil."

Kahlil sighed like an old man parked at a bar. He nudged her towards the door, towards the train, towards her new life. "Don't, Peaches. Just go."

After she bought her one-way ticket, Peaches turned to wave. Kahlil had already gone. She was on the train instantly and sat unmoving like a cemetery angel cut from stone. When the doors closed and the train started on its way, something small and bright awoke inside her. She chivalrously pushed it down, knowing full well it would rise again.

Peaches didn't watch out the window as the train rolled out. She knew it was just another day in the eternal cycle, and no matter what she did, it would happen with or without her.

She wondered if her train was the one that killed her father. It was the same railroad. Her life crossed paths where his life had ended. There was reason to go to Atlanta. To walk in her Mama's footsteps. To start walking in her own. To end up somewhere different. To become.

Her Mama wasn't dead, but she was gone, and Peaches doubted there would be a quick return, considering how long it took for her to get there.

Resurging, More or Less

Peaches' passage through the state would take mere minutes on an airliner, but required hours by train. Each second clicked by slowly as a classroom clock while the train chugged towards the South's gaudy crown. She was too harried to read, and she tried to draw, but grew scared of what she sketched. She settled for tracing the train's path on a map, crossing through names of towns they passed with a fat black pen.

With a blessed sense of relief, Peaches finally found the next stop was hers. She pulled out her camera to snap pictures as the train moved inward towards Atlanta's center. She marveled at the massive spread of the Southern capital, a hundred cities making up a grand metropolis.

The proud place of her mother's birth was announced in a mumble over the speaker system. Peaches grabbed her bags, ready to jump off even before the train slowed to a stop. She walked through the compact red brick station slowly, taking pictures of its stately interior, old but new to her.

Peaches had kept her arrival time secret from Gram, because she wanted to make acquaintance with her new home by herself. She had a map and Gram's address, and she figured she'd eventually find her way. She wandered out on Peachtree Street, past strolling suits and students, along a smooth avenue brimming with bikes, cars, and buses. Even her trip to Savannah didn't prepare her for the crowd of people that was Atlanta. A block later, Peaches thought she had seen her first million already, and wore a poker face so they wouldn't know she was a stranger.

Peaches found an underground station and paid a dollar and some change to ride. She rode past only two stops: Gram's house was mere blocks away. Peaches had never ridden in a subway before and could have stayed on forever. She emerged from the cool dark into the bright heat and walked west until she found a most extraordinary thing.

Gram's house was born old in a city that was still new, a quaint piece that seemed to chuckle at its own irony. Tucked between giant skyscrapers, the residence was a beacon of yesterday, the sole remnant of a once sleepy hill town. Peaches walked a front gate to the side yard where a huge oak tree stood, thick with the decades. She traced her fingers over its rough bark, thinking today was an entirely different animal than yesterday. For the first time in her life, Peaches was unknown and undefined. She nearly choked on her own musings and sat down outside the house, winded emotionally by the change of the past few days and physically from muling her bags around the state.

From the ample yard, she scanned the city as if it were a stage. Cars and trucks rolled past as birds swayed on telephone wires, their song silenced by the late afternoon's heavy heat. A vehicle slowed in front of Gram's house, then separated from the masses to park at the curb. A man in a flash suit stepped from the car to walk towards Gram's front gate.

He didn't see Peaches, his invisible audience of one under the shade tree. His voice hit a high note as he clumsily tried to garner the attention of the lady inside. "Ma'am?"

In the kitchen, Gram heard a voice calling from beyond the picket fence, but she was expecting her granddaughter, not a stranger. She continued to wash beefy tomatoes in the sink as pots of peanuts boiled on the stove.

"Ma'am, are you home?" The man wiped sweat from his forehead as he walked along the picket fence to confirm that the big white Cadillac was indeed parked in the drive. Gram rinsed crumbs of soil and from the tomatoes, then dropped them in a basket as the man spoke again. "Ma'am, I know you're busy in the kitchen."

One of Gram's many philosophies was to ignore the rude people of the world, especially those lacking the gumption to brave her front door. She dumped another batch of tomatoes in the sink. "I'm up to my arms in chicken giblets. Come back later," she yelled out the window.

The visitor made the mistake that sealed his fate. "This is a prime piece of real estate you've got here, ma'am. I'm prepared to make you a generous offer."

Gram couldn't see him through the curtains, but she heard the gate creak open and knew he was trying to slip inside the fence. The bravery that came with bollocks of money got her temper up. She ran through the house to the front door, ripping it open as heat hit her like a church set afire.

"Sir, don't even think about crossing the property line." The old woman was staidly polite, standing at the door with a long, thick cane at her side. This man was spoiling her skyline view.

"Ma'am, you really should talk to me about this." He felt a fragment of self-importance, until he saw the mean staff she lifted high in warning. With it, the old lady could make his temples pour blood, along with his ears, nose, and whatever else she hit. He crept his foot back to the safety of the sidewalk as the gate creaked shut in front of him.

Gram whistled sharply. Growling and barking boiled from within the house as a toothy black and white Boston bull terrier heaved himself down the hallway, rumbling like a canine hurricane. The man heard it and leapt back from the gate, stuttering from the safe side of the fence. "Ma'am, I don't think you understand what this land is worth."

Gram ignored him and headed back inside, letting the pup take her place as spokesperson. She knew exactly what it was worth, since every real estate developer in town had bothered to tell her at some time or another. She had decided that it was worth even more never to let them have it.

The dog pawed excitedly on the screen door that strained and shook like a summer cyclone was bursting through. The man dashed back to the safety of his oversized sedan, taking one last wistful look at the house, as if Gram might suddenly reappear, lobotomized and willing to sell.

He stood with his car door ajar, as cars honked and swerved into the next lane to avoid him. One black pickup screeched to a stop, and a woman with a mane of curling hair spit a curse out her open window. "This ain't New York City!" The woman flicked her cigarette butt at him, and it exploded like a little fireworks show across the hood of his car. He slammed the door and started the slick sedan, pulling into a flow of traffic that greeted him with a cacophony of outraged horns.

On the grass out front, Peaches hurt from laughing at the one-act street play. She heard Gram's melodic bass chortling from inside. The old lady was back at work, stirring her peanuts before draining the pot into the sink. She dumped the peanuts still steaming from their salty boil into a colander, and then brought them and the tomatoes to the front porch. She took a seat in her chair and rocked as she arranged her foodstuffs. Gram paused, feeling the presence of someone else within the boundaries of her yard. "Hey, there, who's here?"

Peaches emerged from beneath the old oak, drawling in a Hollywood hick accent that no true Southerner would ever claim. "Hey, Gram, it's me. Just watchin' you scare them damn Yankees."

Gram matched her granddaughter's inflection, raising it to a slow, suffering twang, as if they were playing a game of enunciation poker. "Aw, Peaches, I hate to say it, but that was probably a homegrown boy. This damn city is eating itself now."

Gram stuffed a few plump tomatoes into paper bags, plucking them quickly from the large straw basket at her right. She slipped back into her own light, sleepy accent. "Come here, honey, and give your Gram a hug. I've missed you fiercely, and it's only been a couple days since I saw you last."

Melancholy splayed sadly across Peaches' features as the memory of those days rose inside her. She slapped a smile in place, choosing to keep close the sadness. Gram thought Peaches was too much her Mama's child, and tried to nudge her granddaughter into conversation about the hard things. But Peaches spoke only about her train ride until Gram's fingers reached straw at the bottom of an empty basket. Gram tossed a bag of boiled peanuts in Peaches' direction. "Take these and go on inside and wash up, Peaches."

Peaches entered the kitchen and looked around. It had been built before modern conveniences were designed to save space and waste time. An oversized gas stove stood in one corner, near two ovens implanted in an adjacent wall. Most of the room was taken up by counter space, including the giant island set in the middle. There, a jug of whole milk sat alongside a butter dish, both warming to room temperature. Peaches put the dairy products in the refrigerator and smiled when she turned and saw that Gram used her microwave as a breadbox. A large dishwasher stood half-open and filled to the brim, a seemingly welcome newcomer in the old kitchen.

She passed a dog resting near the doorway, who wiggled excitedly at her approach. Peaches leaned down to scratch his ears in greeting. "Hey there, you must be Beauregard. Nice to meet you, boy."

Peaches left the kitchen to move through the rest of the downstairs. She had heard only a little about the house, and now it was her new home. Down the shotgun hallway past dark bedrooms was a high-ceilinged dining room that connected to a well-furnished living room. Peaches thought some of the items might be as old as the boats that first came to the convict colony. On the other side of the hall was a comfortable den, where an old television and stereo sat in front of recliners dating back a couple of decades. Back down the hall and towards the kitchen, Peaches found a door to a long enclosed stairwell leading to the second floor. She opened it and climbed polished wooden steps that creaked as if in welcome.

There were several large rooms upstairs, including the old house's eccentrically placed original kitchen, dating to a time when air-conditioning didn't exist. One bedroom at the top of the stairs was especially intriguing. Peaches knew it had been her mother's room, though the décor was now guest-room generic, and the remnants of previous residency were few.

Peaches dumped the clothes from her bag, tossing them in closets and drawers. She tucked three shoeboxes of photographs under the queen-sized bed as far back as they would go. The final item out of her bag was a leather scrapbook, neatly slim and empty, still wrapped in a thin plastic cocoon. Peaches had found it in Mama's closet at home, enclosed in pink paper with a dusty pacifier adornment around the ribbon. The card attached was from a well-meaning, but out-of-touch friend of her father's, congratulating him on the birth of his child. Peaches figured the gift rightly fell to her now.

She pulled back the plastic and opened to the first page to place her train ticket to Atlanta there. Flipping to the back page, Peaches inserted something else she had found in her Mama's closet. It was a black-and-white photograph of her father poised on beach rocks, holding a long two-pronged spear above an incoming sea. His face was blurred, but he held himself like the sea god his daughter had once pretended he was.

She put one final picture on the next-to-last page, a clear message to her that life was rarely like photographs. It showed Peaches and Brother carved in black and white shadows years before. She was in a little girl dress, crocheted at the collar and probably pastel in color, since Mama loved when she was dressed like spring. Brother wore a sweatshirt and blue jeans, thin and lean, a slick, smart kid. Each had an arm hooked around the other in a half-hug. Peaches couldn't remember the photo being taken, or even a memory of ever being so close to him.

She shut the book and lay back on the big bed. Snapshots of her life played through her mind in quick Kodak color, until Peaches fell asleep in the cool, dark room. The ceiling fan swished as the real world outside her window whined soothing tunes, a passive soundtrack for her peaceful imaginings. Peaches slept deeply in the shaded room. Her slumber was comfortable and needed. It was forgetful but it was good.

Evensong

While her new boarder unpacked upstairs, Gram sat outside on the porch, scooping peanuts and filling paper bags to the brim with their sweet, salty goodness. She kept one sharp old eye on the road in front of her, waiting for the traffic to signal the beginning of the evening stampede. Peaches was out cold, in a deep sleep after the day, and the week, and the life she had led. Gram estimated Peaches' shift from the old to the new was now underway, and it was time for the next phase.

Finishing the peanut sacks and lining them on a pushcart, the old lady placed them and the bags of tomatoes on a red wagon. She whistled, and a paw immediately scratched open the door on the screened porch. "Beauregard, honey, let's put your wheels on."

Gram grabbed her sunhat from atop the icebox, then leaned over to wrestle a harness onto the tiny dog. She hooked the tiny latches of the harness onto a wheeled contraption her late husband had constructed for the little two-legged fellow. Beauregard then clattered down the porch steps, wheeling around the front yard to check the grounds for new smells, wheels trailing behind him. Gram followed, cramming her hat further down on her head and smoothing her dress.

At the curb, Beau stretched out on the pavement and Gram placed her folding chair on the sidewalk. She propped a sign in front of the pushcart that listed her wares and their prices: P'nuts - $2, Tomatoes- $2, Two for $5. She always chuckled at her marketing math and at the motorists' lack of change.

Hers was a business model that worked, allowing her to tuck away a tidy amount for a rainy day. Gram hid pickle jars of cash around the house and brought the proceeds twice a month to her bank. She had lived in the same house since her marriage. Not so long ago the city had crawled right up to her front yard. Where once there had been a neighborhood, now towers and twelve-lane interstates stood. Shortly before his death, her husband had said it was like waking up one morning to find that the neighbors had been swallowed up by the city while everyone slept.

Back when they were a pair, Gram and Marcus rocked together on the front porch every night, watching the world pass by. During weekdays, they gazed on office-building drones. Late nights were for college kids searching for soothing, and pretty club boys holding hands. Weekend days belonged to families and skateboarding teens. Around the clock the homeless claimed their ownership. At some point, after the air smogged up and the tap water colored, the value of their land inflated absurdly. It was then that Gram's husband waited in fear for the urban city to trespass across his property line. He often woke in the middle of the night from dreams that his land had been stolen and seared in front of his eyes.

One hot day, with a fried chicken leg in his hand and a napkin tucked at his chin, he slumped suddenly in his rocker. As he struggled to breathe, he clutched his heart and pointed at the house, and then towards Gram. It was his last gesture before his eyes rolled back, his face grew slack, and he began to sleep his longest night. Gram rocked beside him until sunrise, praying through

Mary to Jesus that even a mere man would rise again with the sun.

When Marcus didn't get up from the rocker the next morning for breakfast, Gram sat a little while drinking coffee before laying plates of eggs, bacon, hash browns, and biscuits around his body. It wasn't until the mailman came by at midmorning that Gram accepted the torch she had been passed and rang up the funeral home. It was her strangest day and her saddest. Marcus had been a good, good man.

These days Gram missed her husband, but she was a self-sufficient, clever woman. Besides catering farm goods to the rush-hour crowd, she sold pies when her mini-orchard dropped fruit. It all kept her busy. Besides, her husband had left more than a few dollars behind from his pursuit of a vocation no one was too clear about, but which seemed to have gotten seed-money from distilling spirits in Tennessee.

This day, as her granddaughter continued to sleep, the setting sun snuffed itself, and darkness began to take control of the skies, Gram continued dealing with the line of cars waiting at the traffic light. She was affirmed again in her belief that if anyone sat in traffic that resembled a parking lot, they'd want—indeed, require—a sack of tomatoes to bring home or salty peanuts to snack on.

During red lights, she flitted expertly among cars, chatting with each driver as they transacted business. When the light changed to green, she sat in a chair on the sidewalk, tucking dollar bills into her pockets. Each day, she marveled on the cosmic experience that brought to her stand hundreds of vehicles with different people of varying shapes, worths, and backgrounds.

If one of these cars missed its chance for a buy, it would often pull in the nearby liquor store to park and then the driver would walk over and purchase from her on foot. She would remind her customers that nothing tasted better with hot peanuts than a cold drink, which satisfied her merchant neighbor, who was pleasant enough if a few of her customers dropped change in the Coca-Cola machines outside his door or picked up beers inside.

Traffic slacked, and Gram packed. By the time she picked up her chair, the painfully potent sun was just a memory. She belted Beau to his wagon and brought everything into the house. Then she assembled a light dinner of cold roasted chicken, saffron rice, and pole beans, while warming up a broth of chicken giblets to pour as tasty stock over Beau's kibble. Before they ate, she and her dog, Gram gave thanks for the child sleeping upstairs, and prayed for the souls of all those gone before and those left behind, her own daughter and grandson among them.

After clearing the kitchen, Gram climbed the stairs to check on Peaches, who still lay fully clothed and asleep on her mother's childhood bed. Next to her was the scrapbook. Gram opened it to the front page, fingering the train ticket that had brought Peaches her way. She flipped through the other pages, and came to the photo of the little girl and boy holding each other. Then, Gram saw the picture of the girl's father. The drama of change weighed the book heavily in her hands. She closed it and held it for a moment, the record of yesterday and a new slate for tomorrow. Gram laid the album on the bedside table and covered Peaches with a blanket from the closet. She crept down the creaking steps, smiling in the glow of the nightlight in the hallway.

Reaching her downstairs bedroom, Gram knelt beside the bed and said her rosary, lips moving silently as she recited the great prayer comprised of many little prayers. Finished, she drew a bath. Before the moon had peaked, she lay clean under the covers, next to the shadowed imprint left on the mattress by her late husband. The house's human heartbeat this day had doubled. In the dark night shared by half the earth, as someone somewhere laughed and someone somewhere else cried.

Breaking Fast

When Peaches awoke on her first Sunday in Atlanta, the world outside was dew-soaked and still dim. She crawled from bed and padded down the steps to find Beauregard waiting in the hallway. The house was shadowed and quiet. Peaches followed Beau to the kitchen door where light peeked out and smells of cooking food slipped through. She opened it and found Gram standing at the stove, frying up viands for what seemed like far more than just the two of them.

"G'morning, Gram. Am I supposed to eat all this?" Peaches teased as she dropped down in a chair. Beau, meanwhile, dragged his legless hindquarters across the slick linoleum.

Gram tilted backwards from her position at the stove to pat Peaches on the head. "Good morning Peaches. We've got guests."

Peaches shuffled to the screen door and heard a murmuring in the backyard. A small crowd sat beneath the fruit trees around picnic tables, drinking coffee and juice from Gram's good china and crystal. It was the most people Peaches had ever seen on a Sunday morning outside of church, especially at first light. They looked to her like extras on a movie set, or figures in a Jungian dream. "Who are they, Gram?"

"They're people wanting breakfast, Peaches." Gram played the stove like a violin, cracking a dozen eggs two at a time as she stirred a king's ransom of grits.

Peaches munched on a piece of slick, salty bacon that she snagged from a draining board. "When do we eat, Gram?"

"We eat last, my dear." Gram piled scrambled eggs, biscuits and gravy, bacon, sausage, and buttery grits onto large heated platters that bulged to overflowing.

At Gram's direction, Peaches carried the food two platters at a time out to the long buffet table on the back porch. Gram followed with plates, napkins, and utensils, then stuck her head back through the screen door to grab a nearby tray of salt and pepper shakers. She stood on the porch and shook a small, delicate crystal bell, sounding the call to grub with a silvery tinkle.

Gram said grace, according to the ancient formula. "Bless us O Lord, and these thy gifts, which we are about to receive from Thy bounty, through Christ Our Lord. Amen." The lines of people piled their plates high from the steaming buffet. Conversation glowed in the dewy air, as the morning sun broke open and bled its brightness into the yard.

Peaches saw Atlanta differently in the fresh light. The city's buildings stood stock still, watching like lords over the serfs' feast. It was the ageless time of morning when ancient juices seeped from underground and touched bits of yesterday to today.

When breakfast ended, Gram's guests, as always, offered their assistance, but she politely shooed them away. Peaches was put to work scrubbing dishes as Gram stacked trash bags. When Gram walked back into the house, she announced her firm desire to take her granddaughter to church.

"Gram…" Peaches whined like a homesick pup from the sink, where china plates and silver were piled high, soaking beneath bubbles.

"You need morality." Gram was adamant as she shoved pots and pans caked with Sunday breakfast residue into the dishwasher. "And religion gives you an idea of it. You need to know that the world is bigger than you. Regardless."

As they drove out, Gram took a moment to request protection on the trip from her guardian angel. Peaches conceded it was an idea with benefits, since Gram regularly scraped the car's passenger side against the bushes on the way down the drive, thumping over the curb and hurtling the tailfins into the street. Peaches hoped Beau knew to keep his head inside whenever he was in the car. She figured he did, since he still had it.

Gram turned left at the first intersection and barreled north down a one-way street that had more lanes than many great motorways. She pressed the gas pedal to the floor, shooting through a lucky string of green traffic lights, then cranked up the radio to sing loud and proud like a teen queen. As the road split towards the interstate and the city's show street, Peaches crossed her fingers and hoped that Gram would stay off the highway. She did, and they crossed the hidden border from the glossy midtown business district into the Upmarket famous for its noble homes, smug restaurants and endless stores.

The road curved as it approached the apex of the area's center, where three stately churches held faith. Gram pointed towards an imposing golden structure high upon a hill. "See that, Peaches? That's the Episcopal cathedral. The Catholic cathedral made the choice to build right down the road instead of there."

"Why, Gram?" Peaches was curious. The hill was obviously a prime vantage point over one of the loveliest stretches in town a block down the way. The Catholic cathedral sat politely to one side.

Gram shared one of her stories of days past. "Decades ago, the Klan was flat broke, since their membership was at a blessed all-time low." Gram chuckled as she wheeled the car into a parking space. "The bishop of Savannah looked at both spots, bought the Klan headquarters, tore down the mansion, and built a new church on top of it. Ha! Of course, the Episcopalians when they built their cathedral ran out of money so it came up about 22 feet lower than the plan. They kept that pretty quiet. Episcopalians aren't known for running out of money! "

"Now that's spiritual cleansing," Peaches thought about the Klan story. She tried to detect the presence of white-hooded ghosts in the plaza as they walked up the limestone steps of the petite neo-Gothic cathedral.

Peaches followed Gram in genuflection and thought again of her inequality in this sacred place. It was a thought that always returned: Girls can be sisters.

The organ intoned the processional hymn. The congregation stood. The crucifer, acolytes, and priest began their procession up the center aisle. Peaches seized Gram's arm tightly and pointed at the cross-bearer leading the little army of God. "Oh, my gosh," she said. "It's a little girl altar boy."

Peaches was completely floored and extravagantly jealous. She wondered why word of the city's emancipation had not yet spread to the towns. Gram smiled and whispered: "Halfway there." Peaches wondered why it took God so long to do a little for the faithful, if the faithful were girls.

Shops

Atlanta grew into a comfortable second skin for Peaches. She pretended to forget everything that had come before. She didn't want to write to Kahlil, the hurt seemed easier that way. Brother refused to speak to her on the phone, but, then, he didn't talk to anyone. Mama was voiceless in Charleston. So Peaches' past soon went silent, though it endured in every breath she took. Gram let her do all this, knowing that taking the girl out of the past didn't ensure that it would leave the girl alone. And that is how, one day, in celebration of novel ways to be and to live, Gram and Peaches went shoe shopping.

They first drove to the elite shopping district, where sculpted drecht and designer constrictions left Peaches uninterested. Their next stop was a rough and tumble excuse for architectural expression whose coming laid waste to a segment of city blocks. There they entered a deliberately graffitied store hung with phallic replications and Far Eastern artistry. At the top of a staircase shaped like a long, black tongue, Peaches found exactly what she was looking for. Calf-high, blue-black British boots capped with steel.

Gram dangled them from their laces as if they might bite. "Sweetie, are you sure you want a pair of shitkickers?" asked Gram.

"Yes ma'am, every Southern belle needs a pair," Peaches teased. They were better weapons than cheese straws in any case.

Gram looked thoughtful as she raised the boots to eye level, deep in thought about days gone by. "Yes, these would've been nice."

Peaches carried the bag of boots out of the store. She laced them on as they stopped to eat wide slices of pizza under a stunted dogwood in the middle of a concrete sea. All around them, the cracked blacktop of the high street was dotted with in-your-face bars and cheap restaurants. All available wall space was veneered with ripped, scrawled signs announcing bands, shows, and release parties for a long list of unknowns. Gram pulled up the average age of the populace by a few decades. Peaches laughed when Gram said it aloud, because she felt she had more in common with her grandmother than with her peers. Besides the wandering collective of miscreants loitering, selling, or begging, there were also grumpy punks, fat Goths, and deadened junkies. They walked the same streets as tempered Rastas, crazed eccentrics, and rich-kid runaways. Dated hippies and scatterings of girly boys and boy-like girls made up the rest. There was even the occasional ordinary youth who was simply out of place. Peaches studied the segments, conformists of their own, all in desperate denial of mainstream's pull. "They all look like the people who look like them," she said.

Gram heard the solid thunk of a target well hit. "As much as they think they can be whoever they want, they can't help being whatever everyone else thinks they are. But, what about you, Small Town Sally?"

Peaches smiled as the sun shone down on her. "I'm a city girl now, Gram, and it doesn't matter too much to me what anyone else says about it."

Gram leaned to pat Peaches on her golden head. "Ah, that's my colleen bawn."

They found their way back to the Cadillac, parked on a sidewalk halfway down a one-way street.

Gram pulled out a trash bag and collected debris from sidewalks and gutters. She shot a glance at her granddaughter, who immediately bent to lend a hand. When Gram tossed the bulging bag in a nearby dumpster, Peaches was the only one surprised to hear a disturbed shout from the man living inside.

Gram floated the car on the long route home, sneaking around downtown neighborhoods that were both decrepit and charming. Peaches scanned the radio before finding something tilted and strange on a fuzzy university station. She remembered how when she first arrived in town, the generous number and genres of local radio stations had impressed her. That lasted until she realized that almost all of them played the same things.

Gram steered across an avenue once famous for music that flowed sweetly from dark until dawn, pulling in an audience that traveled miles to hear the locals play. The pair paused at a red light where the name of a white Southern editor intersected at the corner of a street named after a black Southern shepherd. It was one of Atlanta's invisible monuments, a symbolic handshake between two long-gone giants. Gram pointed it out to Peaches, thinking someone should put a marker there before the people who remembered the monumental pair were dead, too.

They drove deep into downtown, and the radio played a blend of pretty guitar and indignant bass thumps. Peaches' mind drifted as the melody ran over her. Her life ahead seemed like a gift, a promise to rebuild for a house that had been burnt to the ground. She felt a twinge for something old, but she wanted it to fit with all that was new. "Gram, can we please have fried chicken for dinner?"

Gram was vehemently pro-fried chicken, even though it had been her husband's last supper. It reminded her of her mother and grandmother, of family gatherings and warm kitchens. It was also one of the rare vestiges of the Southern people that wasn't controversial or trashed elsewhere. "Yes, ma'am, we can."

Once home, Gram put Peaches to work on the porch swing snapping pole beans. She pinched the stems and halved the long, bumpy, green bodies, tossing the trim pieces into a large, metal colander. When it was full, she dumped them in the pressure cooker, where a mingling of butter and bacon awaited the sacrifice.

Gram attended to the bubbling black skillet for the chicken, where dollops of lard and rounded tablespoons of salty bacon fat melted down to clean liquid grease. She dusted the pieces of fowl in paper bags holding flour, spices, and a few family secrets. When a pinch of flour sizzled brown in the skillet, she politely introduced the chicken to the fat. Even a chicken's death should have meaning, and Gram was kind enough to send the deceased pullet off in glory worthy of a queen.

Gram then sent Peaches out of her kitchen. The girl snapped on the stereo in the living room and stepped out to the porch, first sneaking one of the long, thin cigarettes Gram occasionally smoked. Peaches wasn't quite sure she was doing it right, until she gulped a solid stream of smoke that hit her lungs like a forest fire. She wheezed and hacked to keep from coughing. Once the storm passed, she breathed in again foolishly like a pup weaned early. When the butt was half-burned, she stubbed it out and tossed it in the bushes before walking back inside.

After one of the best fried chicken dinners she had ever tasted, Peaches sat on the porch staring as Gram smoked a cigarette. Peaches found herself wishing for her own smoke and wondering in the name of God why.

Bloody Mad

The school year came around, and Gram enrolled Peaches at Peerless, an elite old Catholic school downtown, overriding the protests of her belligerent granddaughter. Gram staunchly refused to send any child under her care to public schools: across the country and especially down South, she thought, there was something sadly, abhorrently off in the education offered at such places, even if it was for free.

On the first day, Peaches learned her mother had been one of the first skirts to graduate from this former military school, which had lost its crusader instincts only two decades before. Peaches tried to disregard all the older black-and-white photos on the office walls, in case her Mama was there. Her mother had certainly left her mark. Her afternoon play one practice day with some of the members of the boys' basketball team had launched a stampede, and the first girls' team of any kind at Peerless was formed as a result. Peaches let a smile trickle across her face, slouching a little less on the bench as she and Gram waited for entry into the headmaster's sanctum.

A girl came and sprawled on the couch next to her as though she were Peaches' lifelong friend. Her hair was jet black, and her eyes were dark almonds rimmed with circles of pecan brown. She wore a navy hooded sweater over her uniform shirt with the sleeves pulled down, hiding her wrists and fingertips.

The headmaster's secretary sighed tiredly, as if she were chained to her desk for eternity. "Oh, Bloody, what did you do now?"

The girl pulled up the sweater cuff and showed a design, large and black, scrawled meaninglessly on her shirtsleeve. "My teacher says I need another shirt."

The secretary stood up, shaking her head. A teacher passing stopped to speak with the girl. "Hi, Bloody. Listen, can you think about being on the Jeopardy team? We could really use that brain of yours."

Bloody thought for a heavy moment, as if contemplating whether to be queen. "Well, I can't make practice, sir, but I can probably be there for the competitions."

The teacher broke into a smile and said, "Good, good, that's great. Thanks, Bloody."

The secretary came back with a clean blouse and another request. "Bloody, can you be in a picture for the annual report this afternoon? We need one more student."

The girl smiled civilly and agreed. "Yes, ma'am." She glanced in Gram and Peaches' direction as she whispered in a stage voice: "Ah, diversity."

Gram burst out laughing as she nudged Peaches with a whisper. "There's a girl you should know. She's going places, despite her name."

Peaches watched in astonishment as the girl changed clothes in the middle of a busy office. She held back from rolling her eyes. "If you say so, Gram."

Peaches learned quickly about the hierarchy of attitudes and behaviors that dominated the school. The boys seemed smaller to Peaches than those back home. They were groomed like lap dogs, and absorbed with new toys instead of after-school jobs: cars, electronics, watches. The girls saw each day as a fashion show, regardless of the limitations of a plaid schoolgirl skirt.

Their hair was done and dyed as if they were thirtysomethings fearing forty. Peaches found them nice enough, but soon decided if she tried to become one of them, it would render useless everything she had done before. A lot of the boys and most of the girls suffered from the primeval fear of standing alone.

One day Peaches sat contentedly on the porch swing, bagging, but mostly eating Gram's boiled peanuts and sipping a bottle of Mr. Pibb, her personal ambrosia and most probably one of God's, she thought. Gram sat near her, painting a picture. Her old hands manhandled the brush into quiet submission. The painting was of the city, how Atlanta once looked, combined with its present vision. It wasn't a symmetrical split or segregated scene, but a blend of an old black-and-white photograph merged with a recent color Kodak.

The traffic outside the house pulled and flowed like a river, but it wasn't yet thick enough for it to surge and dam in front of the house for tomatoes and goobers. A shiny black car suddenly screeched to a halt at the curb, and a young girl jumped out. She angrily kicked the door shut, cutting off the shrill epithet of the woman in the driver's seat. "Naughty girl…!"

It was Bloody. She stomped towards the sidewalk as a ring of house keys flew behind her, clattering as they landed in the gutter. She waited until the car pulled away to retrieve them, dropping them in her bag. Bloody turned towards the people on the porch and thought for a moment she had fallen into yesterday. A beautiful old house with a wraparound porch trellised with roses, ivy, and flowering vines stared back at her, as did an old woman and a girl about her age. A full vegetable garden burst forth beside a giant oak in a side yard, where lariope grass framed islands swelling with color. The dwelling was an enigma in the concrete city, but Bloody found the discrepancy as refreshing as it was surprising.

Gram called down politely, recognizing her as the only other girl besides Peaches who wore school uniforms but looked like a junkman's daughter. "You looking for something, honey?"

"You have a beautiful house, ma'am, and this is a great location, too. Say, have you got a match?"

Peaches rolled her eyes at the girl's boldness. Bloody leaned close to Gram's outstretched light.

Gram thought she should say something about the girl's unfortunate habit. "Honey, you're kind of young to be smoking, though that's probably your mother's business, not mine." "Gram, it's that girl, Bloody," Peaches whispered.

Bloody returned Gram's serve deftly. "Freud would say my mother weaned me too quickly, and I developed an oral fixation." Bloody looked around, trying to get her bearings. She unconsciously picked up on Gram's soft slur of an accent. "Scuse' me, but where exactly is public transport 'round here?"

"Freud…" Gram snorted, then studied the girl in front of her. "I'll drive you home, if you can wait until after the rush hour."

"Why, yes ma'am, I'd appreciate it. Very much in fact." Bloody, it turned out, usually knew where she was and where she lived, but never how to get from one to the other.

"All right then, it's time for me to get to work." Gram pursed her lips to whistle, and Beau popped his head out of the screen door, initiating their weekday ritual. "Beauregard, honey, let's put your wheels on."

As Gram settled in to make her street trades, the girls set out to kill time, leaving the house to walk east towards the main drag. Bloody yanked Peaches to a stop in front of a large subway map. "So, how does this train thing work anyway?"

Peaches shook her head as she studied the map. Some areas had a gluttonous number of stations within walking distance, but the majority of the population was forced to go a distance to reach their closest stop. "Depends on where you live, "Peaches replied.

Bloody named her personal environs. Fingers scanned over the map until they found her street in the east end, on the fingertip of the city center. Peaches provided a critique. "This system is horrible. It's made like all four and a half million people in this city live across these two lines. But you're one of the lucky ones. You've got a station you can walk to from your house."

"Really?" Bloody was euphoric at the news that an escape from her house cost only a few quarters and a short stroll. "Where's school? And where are we right now?"

Peaches showed her, and the girl nearly danced a jig. It was a landslide moment of sweet liberation.

The girls kept walking; it would be a couple of hours before Gram finished her sales. They decided to visit a century-old expanse of green and trees birthed after the Civil War. Like Gram's house, it was rare for the city, a place unspoiled.

The girls entered the park through its back gates, walking past the lake where the tops of distant office buildings peeked through the trees. The ground was hallowed, soaked with soldiers' blood and echoing with a freeman's speech. Few of the park's visitors knew they stood where the first motion picture ever played.

The sun was close to disappearing behind the water reservoir hidden west of the city. Peaches squinted into the setting sun, and her eyes stung, wetting her eyelashes. She thought guiltily about how much she loved where she was. Something was always moving or new. Something on the landscape was always shifting slightly from the moment before.

Dusk fell like a feather. Peaches and Bloody stood on a bridge overlooking the expressway. Thousands of brake lights winked from surrounding streets as commuters crawled nowhere fast. The skyscrapers were silent observers, illumined and awake against the dimming sky. In her camera, Peaches framed the remaining streaks of the sunset that hung in between the buildings.

The girls stood quietly on the border where the two halves of the city, the Elder and the Younger, kissed like kin. Older Downtown was like a miniature Manhattan of buildings packed tightly together, cutting out the sun. Youthful Midtown was a concept of smart urban design, still stretching its adolescent legs. Between the two and always apart lay a single plinth memorializing the modern city's corporate creator. The classic red script was etched against the background of cobalt sky. Peaches rather liked the company's blatant brand on her city. God watched over the earth from heaven, and Coca-Cola had its eyes set in Atlanta's skies

Bloody and Peaches waited until the traffic eased, then left the bridge for the sidewalks. They walked under orange streetlights with their footsteps echoing, as if they and their shadows were the only mortals for miles. Bloody moseyed along, seemingly content, but a feeling of loneliness chilled Peaches, crawling across her skin like a spider web. Even Gram's house, lit in the distance, seemed for a moment foreign and new to her. The groove of melancholy lasted until her new friend grabbed hold of her arm, and they raced like foolish children back towards the house.

Gram was in the kitchen when they returned. It was against her Southern religion to let a guest go unfed. She apologized to Bloody for the simple spread of chicken salad hiding slivers of apples and pecans, and the sides of sweet homemade biscuits and cherry-red tomato slices dolloped with mayonnaise and sprinkled liberally with black pepper. For their dessert, a layered gelatin crowned with whipped cream chilled in the icebox. Around the table, dishes and plates were passed in slapdash rhythm, like a smooth jazz band. Bloody sang the praises of both the cook and the kitchen until the last bite was gone.

Afterwards, Gram, with Peaches and Beau, drove her home. Hers was an old neighborhood dripping with something unshakable and dark, like a homicide in high society. Sweeping magnolias veiled huge manors and their carriage houses. Peaches almost expected to see men tipping hats and women hiding their ankles as they strolled along sidewalks glowing in the dim light of gas lamps.

As the Cadillac cruised into this land of yesterday, Bloody pointed left to a house that was no larger or smaller than the others on the street, though similarly exceptional. "Mi casa, senora."

Gram pulled into the cobbled drive and up to the house and let the girl out. As Gram turned the car around, Peaches watched astonished as Bloody climbed a trellis to a small portico. She opened the glass doors with a key hung from a thin chain around her neck. With that, she slipped into her house unnoticed, as if her parents didn't expect her to be anywhere else but there.

Gram muttered from the front seat, patting Beau's head as she sheared bushes near the mailbox. "She ain't a pore' chile. Unless she gets to feeling poorly in that house."

"Most kids at my school have money, Gram." Peaches enlightened Gram with the obvious. "Or their parents do. I think the kids think it's theirs, though."

Gram turned up the radio where a local threesome sang supremely, a dying breed of true songbirthers. "Not you, Peaches."

Peaches shrugged as she stared out the window. They soon found themselves on back streets where time got stuck and never got loose. Tucked in between swathes of prosperity, poverty pockets stood out starkly. Housing projects nestled in the shadows of the state capitol's golden dome. "Money is opportunity, but most people just use it to buy more stuff." Peaches leaned towards the front seat and playfully poked her grandmother. "And I'm flush in my Gram. I think that's enough."

Gram laughed, pleased with the poetic response. Peaches bounded over the front seat to sit in between her and Beau. Gram spoke a thought shared by Peaches. It was a moment of color in the black and white night. "I think you found a good one in Bloody, Peaches. I hope you meet more like her."

La Madeleine

Soon enough, among the school's sameness, Peaches found another girl who bravely stood out, though in muted fashion, rather like a clouded-over sun.

Peaches originally assumed Madeleine Bennett was as dead-eyed as her group of friends, ensnared in life-long comas of narcissism. On the contrary, Madeleine contained a hundred or more souls, which only made her social group love her more. She was their special one—born unto them, looking like them and for them that was enough. She just didn't think like them. Peaches met her through a random pairing by a religion teacher, a Nazi of theology.

The two girls were required to meet over the weekend to do the homework assignment. Gram dropped Peaches at a house off a suburban motorway. Deep within the sweeping tracts of super-sized, all too similar houses, Gram abandoned Peaches and happily headed back to blessed urbanity as fast as her Cadillac could carry her.

Peaches circled down a bricked path around the back of the house to a lower back porch where a stereo blasted a thrumming resound of guitars, in notes smart and wonderful.

Outside, Madeleine sat scribbling on scraps of paper. She looked up to greet Peaches like a long lost friend. They entered a furnished basement apartment, a panorama of teenage freedom with a galley kitchen, a bedroom, and a lounge. Every wall was dominated by posters of bands and artists that had a thread of commonality Peaches couldn't place at first, until it hit her that they were all quite dead.

Peaches asked Madeleine why the posters. She was told simply that they might be gone, but their music remained. Madeleine thought that made them immortal. "Peaches, what I really want is a jukebox of only dead musicians. I think that's as close to rock and roll heaven as I'll get."

Madeleine switched off the stereo with a click, and the silence was deafening. Outside, the birds chirped and squirrels dropped nuts through the leaves of trees. Through the half-open sliding glass door Peaches saw a swimming pool and a backyard lake. She found a seat on the plush, oversized sofa. Madeleine collapsed in a beanbag on the floor. She looked up at Peaches earnestly. "Peaches, don't be offended, but I already finished our project. Religion class is the same every year."

Peaches pardoned the peccadillo, since she had no personal attachment to homework. "No worries." She spotted a bleached brown guitar on a stand in the corner. "Hey, can you play?"

Her skill was shocking. The guitar dripped wet with music and Madeleine's voice sounded as though from another time. The girls moved out to the patio, and the endless panoply of people within Madeleine sang the afternoon away.

When Peaches later reported on her overbred new friend's singularity, Bloody didn't hide her doubt. She was born suspicious of anyone suggesting perfection. "You just can't be cool from that part of town." Bloody said. "It's scientifically impossible."

Peaches looked pointedly at her friend, not saying a word about pots and kettles. Bloody was defiant. "Hey, my neighborhood is old school cool, Peaches. Her area is nothing but a stage set."

When Peaches told her about the posters of the dearly departed, Bloody showed a flicker of interest.

It wasn't until Madeleine later escaped in their direction that Bloody was finally won over. It was then Bloody affected her own change on the girl. She decided to call Madeleine "Mad Bean."

In The Palace of Art

Peaches felt less like a hobo now. Sometimes she wondered if her baptism as a city girl meant the end of her old life in its entirety.

Somewhat in the manner of her mother, Peaches found her sleeping mind often played night movies of the times that she was trying so hard to forget. Many mornings ached as a result, and many daylight hours were spent pushing the past back to where it couldn't trouble her. The effort failed.

Peaches' first nightmare in the series was of a homegrown holocaust--corn on fire and rain pouring red across the fields. Brother and Mama were trapped as Peaches ran freely through hot flames, liberated from whatever held her kin. Horrible.

Her strangest dream, however, was a full-length tale that plunged her back into the old days of childhood, into events that never happened. The dream began when Peaches awoke in her bed at her old house on a soft summer morning. She went downstairs looking for breakfast. Instead, she found bags packed and waiting by the front door. Gram had arrived before dawn to say her husband, Mama's father, was close to heaven. Mama had spent the last worried hours of early morning readying her mind for the trip back home.

The dream cut to the family waiting in the town train depot. Peaches and Brother were dressed in their best, though it wasn't Sunday. Brother yanked his tie loose, then walked to the tracks to spit across them as far as he could. Peaches stepped forward to join the game, but Mama frowned and pulled her back. Peaches watched Mama thumb a rosary of polished, sand-colored stones laced with woven silver, praying as if the day was already hitting her like a brick to the head.

Their train came, and dream Brother bowed low, his arm stretched towards the door. "After you, ladies."

Mama made Peaches take the seat beside her, then sat back and closed her eyes as if to nap, but Peaches could see slips of blue between her cracked lids. They instantly arrived in Atlanta. Mama was excited, leaning close to muss Brother's hair, then pulling Peaches into a hug. Peaches rolled her eyes, and Mama rolled hers back. The dream skipped to Peaches and Brother following Mama like two yellow ducklings across a busy city street.

In Peaches' dream, family and friends clogged Gram's giant porch and out into the yard. Gram saw them first and greeted her daughter and her two grandchildren with a benign papal wave. Mama shook her head in disbelief. "Mother?"

A solid tear ran from one old blue eye, crossing every wrinkle and crevice on Gram's face. Mama's face matched her mother's, breaking apart into liquid grief that ran like rivers down her cheeks. Then Mama fainted on the sidewalk, down as quickly as a rabid dog shot clean through. Everyone disappeared, and Peaches found herself on the porch swing with her grandfather, Marcus, separating bug-eyed heads from shrimp.

"You're not going to leave here, are you?" Peaches asked.

He shook his head and looked towards the city. His smile shone vividly from his sunflower eyes, irises glowing green. "Beautiful," he said, addressing her, "I was born in a small sea town. I'm going to grow old in a big city, and I promise you, I will die in this house."

The dream ended, and Peaches awoke, intensely missing a man she had never met. Her wet face was silhouetted in the moonlight, and her tears leaked upon her pillow. She plunked a thumb in her mouth and slowly drifted into tumbled sleep, until her alarm sounded and she rose for school.

At breakfast in real life, Peaches lost her temper. She had missed her mouth and orange juice dribbled down her chin. A loose jumble of profanities trickled out with the juice. Peaches was secretly thrilled by this unexpected command she had over bad language, until Gram admonished her with a superior tongue-lashing.

Peaches retreated, changed her wet shirt upstairs, and took off for school on a silver and black bike she had bought with some of the money she received in return for having a dead father.

When Peaches had first biked to school, she found a uniform skirt and a bicycle made a horrid combination. She either flashed her underpants at someone every other pedal, or she got the skirt caught on the chain or in the spokes. Her solution was getting Gram to pull in the hem, so she simply flashed bystanders like a beguiling cheerleader. Peaches avoided indecency by wearing gym shorts over her skivvies, ignoring the occasionally bawdy commentary from the various peanut galleries as she whizzed past.

She often lost herself in a lovely, cosmopolitan pageant of whizzing down streets and jumping curbs. She didn't realize she had become a regular morning fixture to many of the onlookers in their cars, along with their cup of coffee or a favorite morning deejay. She pedaled on the wide sidewalk past the morning traffic clogs, never grasping that the ease with which she moved in and out of the clumps of cars was due to the kindness of motoring strangers.

Peaches often met up with the strangely named friend Bloody outside the underground train station located a couple of blocks from school. Bloody would wait in a street space filled with folk art sculpture, smoking cigarettes until Peaches arrived. Sometimes, Peaches brought her a stolen smoke from Gram to keep Bloody from picking up dog-end butts left by strangers in the gutters.

"Oi, Peaches! Wait up, girl!" Bloody cried as Peaches rolled teasingly by.

Up ahead, their contemporaries gleamed around the ancient school doors, the boys combed and trim, the girls over-accessorized. Some of the girls had a way of making adolescence seem like a job. Peaches paused, wanting terribly to go any other direction than the one her school was in.

Bloody caught Peaches' hesitancy. Her id kicked in, as if impatience and boredom were its scriptwriters. "C'mon, Peaches, let's take a breather today."

"Bloody, we can't go anywhere dressed like this." Peaches gestured at their schoolgirl uniforms. "We look like a dirty old man's dream."

Bloody found the sweet spot on their Achilles heel. "Nah, we're dressed like studious students, so we just have to act studious. C'mon, we can go to the art museum." The bell rang, she ditched her bike, and the two girls sneaked away.

The museum sat north on Midtown's edge. Peaches had the flickering thought that maybe they should go further the next time they decided to escape. There were eyes here.

The museum was a curved, cylindrical building, encased in glass and slicked up bright white. If the city was young, the museum was a baby. Peaches and Bloody made it to the locked front doors before realizing it wasn't open yet. Field trip buses were still sitting back at their schools.

The girls headed back down the long arcing sidewalk, through side streets and into a dim restaurant adjacent to an all-night club. The denizens slept in shadowed rooms during the day, then lived at night beneath epileptic flashes of replicated sunlight.

In the cafe, the two girls drank Cokes and ate curly fries. The owner regarded them curiously as he handled a stream of old men's sports bets. Peaches watched his murmurs, the handshakes and his scribbling in a notebook, and remembered her Brother, the grade school bookie. She stared too long, and one man nudged the owner, pointing at his watch, and then at the girls to signal what time it was and where they shouldn't be.

The owner came over, and Bloody winked at Peaches as she asked for a refill. He shooed them out the door, following them like he was Gabriel with a divine message, the latest in a series. "Get to school, girls!" They wondered why he was so intense.

Bloody replied with a sweet curtsey, while Peaches offered a genteel smile. They moved towards the museum, now crowding up with visiting tourists and students.

Peaches dug deep into the crevices of her bag in search of cash for a day pass. Bloody grabbed her hand and swept it over their matching dark plaid outfits. She pulled Peaches in line with a similarly attired group. "Free pass, Peaches, dear."

She guided Peaches up a spiraling ramp, where a merely adequate collection of exhalations from the world's creative spirits awaited. Peaches' mouth dropped and her eyes widened at the paintings and sculptures, creations surely never wrought by human hands. Peaches eventually left a massive canvas covered with sticky ropes of paint and lifelike washings of color to enter the next room.

It was empty, except for a slight woman dressed in brown and black, a little more than a sad smudge against the white walls and squares of color. Peaches thought at first she was carved from marble. Her posture was straight, and her legs crossed as hair hung down to conceal her face. She seemed in deep scrutiny of a particular oil canvas, a Frenchman's interpretation of a flower before death, the final climax before the illusion of life disappeared. When Peaches and Bloody left, the woman still had not budged from her dead-tree position.

They completed their tour and walked outside to the square where the arts center, symphony hall, and the art school were arranged. Along the cobblestone walkway were manifold statues, including a spiraling sculpture suggesting the planet.

Both girls were startled when the still-life woman appeared beside them. She spoke in a creaking voice that sounded as if it hadn't been oiled for days. "Do you girls know why all this is here?"

After a moment's thought, they replied in unison. "No, ma'am."

"It was placed here to recall the aircraft that went down at Orly, France. Many of art's guardians died in that crash. One man had stayed on the ground; he saw it descend with his wife onboard. It was he who informed the mayor in a telephone call home. We've had so many phoenixes. And, oh God, the funerals after that one! Never-ending."

Peaches wondered what deity could take a city's spirit with a single stroke. . "That's horrible. I'm sorry, ma'am."

The woman turned and strode away.

"What was that, Peaches? Who was she?"

Peaches guessed the plane crash was personal and potent to the woman. "I'm not exactly sure, Bloody."

Bloody thought hard as she tapped a finger against her lower lip. "Do you think maybe she's a ghost?"

"I don't know if this city is old enough for ghosts, Bloody. Maybe she just lives every day thinking of one."

"Let's go get some pie, Peaches."

The fruit pie was shamelessly fried in butter, then topped with ice cream that melted down through cracks in the sweet crust. Sitting in a parking lot on a bench, Bloody and Peaches scraped their plastic forks over pie-coated paper plates.

The midtown district was behind them, the steeples of the skyscrapers nearly touching the sky. Downtown stood in front of them, stacked like a theatre audience, eying the highway below. Two great roads joined to pour eighteen lanes of cars and trucks through the middle of the city.

It was a timeline. Buildings born during an ugly decade. Older beauties. Disco architecture here and there. Plastic facades. Classic monoliths.

Peaches spoke in a stream. "I remember that when I first saw this city, it made me think I probably didn't know anything about the world."

"So, do you like living here now, Peaches?"

Peaches stared at the blended mush of apples, crumbs, and ice cream on her plate. "Yup, I do, Bloody."

"Is it better than where you came from?"

Peaches stared at the cityscape. She had a Mama before, but a Gram now. Then, she had a Brother and no father. Now, neither. She had lost Kahlil, but she had found his girl twins. She concluded that Atlanta was an inexplicable blessing that couldn't really be compared to what she left behind. She answered Bloody as best she could. "In some ways, Bloody."

Eager to change the subject, Peaches held her new friend's wrist and tilted it gently towards her. She peered at the multiple timepieces loosely strapped along the arm, early evidence of eccentricity. None of them showed the same time. Bloody interpreted them for her: "Hey, school's out, Peaches. Want to walk me to the station?"

Peaches collected her bike on campus, feeling a little guilty. Bloody seemed unconcerned, talking about everything else as they headed towards the rail line. Peaches bade her adieu, and Bloody saluted back from the escalator as it sunk down towards the cool shadows of the tracks.

A passing group of elementary school children and a handful of their chaperones came near. One little girl with tangled hair stared at Peaches, and then popped her arms over her head. She joined them together to make a pretend cone hat. She glared at Peaches and spoke brusquely as she held her position. "Hey, I'm a princess!"

Peaches nearly fell off her bike with laughter. The girl turned to the little boy beside her, who sucked fearfully on his fingers in response. Peaches was smiling still as she biked through beggars and office workers.

It had been a good day. She would think about Bloody's question tomorrow.

A Day in the Life of the Dead

At this particular lunchtime, Peaches stood guard for Bloody, who was in the girls' bathroom finishing a stupid cigarette. The voiceover for the scene was an echoing cacophony of flushing toilet bowls.

The girls' retching kept teachers out of the bathrooms in the time between the lunch period and the first afternoon class, providing a handy context for both vices. "Bloody and the Bulimics," Peaches thought.

A beauty queen stepped from one stall wearing a practiced look of disdain, her trembling hands the only flaw in her presentation. Peaches felt blessed to have a dead father, crazy mother, and crippled brother; it made normal an impossible standard in her case. Peaches let go with a barb in the girl's direction: "Hey, do you suppose you'll grow up to be your mother, or like your sister who's just like your mother?"

The girl backed Peaches against the wall. "You think I should be like you? Or maybe sucking down nicotine like your little friend?"

More blondes emerged freshly mouthwashed and lipsticked from the stalls. Bloody tossed her smoke and disappeared through the swinging bathroom door. "Well, you know, smoking would speed up your metabolism," Peaches replied.

Madeleine appeared and quickly pushed in between Peaches and the clique. "Hey, what's up? I'm glad y'all met Peaches and Bloody. They're all right, huh?"

The bloodlust dissipated as their adored Madeleine used her sweetest smile. The clique tensed again when the bell rang, stirring fears of disgracing themselves with the sin of tardiness. An alpha girl waved the pack out the door, and they obediently filed past Peaches towards class. She returned their brilliantly capped, bright white vampire smiles as they passed. Bloody came up after them and burst out laughing when she caught sight of Peaches' grin on her way out the door.

Madeleine waited until the door had closed behind them. "Peaches, you know I'm no different, right?"

Peaches leaned against the wall, hating that a human face that she liked so much was attached to something so pitiful. The vice was awful to behold. It left eyes red from busted blood vessels, teeth stained from stomach acid, and neck glands swollen and bloated. "I don't know, Bean. Is the penance worth the privilege?"

The bathroom door swung open and a warship of a woman glared at the dawdling girls. Madeleine paled at trouble made flesh, while Peaches mentally slapped her head at her own misfortune. The dean of punishment aimed at Peaches with relish, while treating Madeleine as an afterthought. "You, Peaches! We need to talk! Madeleine, go to class!"

In the hallway Peaches got a dressing down for a full house of uniform violations, from questionable jewelry to improper color coordination. Before she finally let Peaches free, the woman smelled her hands and hair, certain she was responsible for turning the girl's bathroom into a smoking lounge. Peaches spent the late afternoon in detention, watching a football player sneakily move tobacco dip through his crooked grin into a shirt pocket spittoon.

By the time Peaches biked home, Gram was already out selling. Bloody and Madeleine waited for her on the porch steps.

"Hey, Gram."

Gram pulled her head from a client's front window. "Evening, Peaches. I met your new friend, Madeleine. It's a nice conspiracy of characters you have littering your life, my dear." Gram cracked a smile as she teased the girl.

Her young ward smiled back like a gracious thief. "You know it, Gram."

Peaches pulled her camera from her bag and stared at the world through its lens. She snapped pictures of Gram skipping through chaotic traffic, of the girls sitting on the porch, even a photograph of herself and the city. The threesome waited for Gram to finish selling as the sun burned from its glistening spot behind low clouds.

Soon the skies looked like the gates of heaven, and Gram packed it in. She made the guests stay for supper, a grand feast of fried Carolina oysters and warm dropped biscuits laden with butter and honey. Madeleine admired Gram's tomatoes, red as the sunset. Gram sliced some up, dressing them with vinaigrette and seasoning. The four ate well, sitting on the porch in the dimming light, feeling the breath of the city slow as it began to fall asleep.

When they finished, the moon was hanging, and the visitors headed home. The next evening, Madeleine returned while Gram was washing dishes. Peaches watched from the porch as Madeleine parked her mother's British cat at a haphazard angle, her beloved truck recently incapacitated by an accident.

That old Ford flatbed was an incongruity, a gift from her father, a country boy turned corporate counsel who saw her as the son he didn't have. Madeleine's mother was angered by her husband's betrayal and spent her free time disabling the truck. Once she backed into it with her husband's German town car.

Madeleine bounced up the porch steps, carrying her guitar on her hip like a toddler. She then burst through the door towards the stereo and twisted the dial to one of the country's largest college stations, declaring loudly: "Y'all, you need to boycott commercial radio. I just saved your life."

Gram brought bottles of Coca-Cola for the girls and something a bit stiffer for herself. As music poured from the speakers to drift out to the now-quiet streets, the old lady and the girls philosophized.

Gram's whiskey and Pibb disappeared in record time, as she toasted every point in the dialogue. "Good music is like a conversation with someone special."

Madeleine matched Gram's thoughts. "Or maybe it's just talking to a deeper part of yourself."

Peaches fumbled with Madeleine's acoustic guitar, trying to pick out notes. Its owner took the instrument from her and dribbled her hands easily across it, evoking a mumble from the strings. "I think the best songs are the ones that you learn to love. The ones that hit you immediately, those are great. But the ones that show you a little bit the first time, and then each time after give you a little bit more, those are the true ones."

Gram nodded over her glass, where ice cubes tinkled like tiny church bells. "Kind of like people."

In the song on the radio, a flat hand hit a throaty bass guitar. Madeleine's ears pricked up. "Hey, do you hear that? They're slapping the bass."

She looked down at the silver watch tagging her thin wrist. "Oh, I need to go. I've got a mother-daughter breakfast early tomorrow. Ta ta for now." She headed to her car in a waving, grinning half-run before turning back. "I left some music for y'all, by the way."

Peaches watched her leave. She wondered about her friend, the strange, normal girl. "Good lord, Gram, I don't think I could be that many people."

Gram flipped through the cases left behind, and pulled one from the pile. "I don't know, Peaches. That girl is going to shine or die trying, as soon as she figures she should. Put this one on, sweetie."

Peaches realized then that her Gram listened on a different level. She displayed a ritual for her initial chewing on any music. First, she let it play through in its entirety, listening to it as she dusted or mopped, taking a seat with a drink and a smoke to listen closely when something caught her attention. Some albums were so good they left Gram near drunk. Those she would start over, then sit in her rocker on the porch, drinking coffee as though to sober up.

Soon enough, Gram became a music fiend like none Peaches had ever seen. Songs raged loudly from the open windows of the house, as if the old woman was the undisputed deejay of the city streets. Peaches could tell the weather every morning by hearing what Gram played downstairs. Blues when it rained. Quick, rhythmic tunes in the fresh, new sunshine.

One day, Peaches noticed a violin case sitting closed in the kitchen. Gram said only that she had given it up decades ago, but now wanted it near, where she could see it. Music seemed to make Gram more transparent and intense. Peaches suspected the violin case would soon be open again.

The Atticus Track

Peaches spotted Bloody having a smoke and talking to a bum, who had sold her the cigarette for two bits.

"C'mon Peaches, jump the train with me. We're Alabammy bound."

Peaches read a handwritten excusal from class, forged with Bloody's best guess at Gram's signature. For the first time in a long while, Peaches remembered Kahlil.

Peaches held back, just to drive Bloody mad. "Why do you think I want to go to Alabama, Bloody?"

"Why would you want to stay here?" Bloody, ticking a win with one easy shot.

Madeleine approached. Peaches greeted her in a lazy drawl, in a faux Alabama belle mode. "How're you, Bean?"

Madeleine's smile always glowed like a tulip just cresting the soil. Today, she looked like a whole garden. "Still kickin', Peaches. Hey there, Bloody." And to the lingering hobo, "H'lo, sir."

The school bell rang. The morning's death knoll. Bloody stared at Peaches and waited for the word one way or another, tense as a child on Christmas Eve. Peaches paused for a beat, then acceded to the day's destiny. "Alabammy it is, Bloody."

Bloody clapped Madeleine on the back, then handed her their get-out-of-jail-free notes to drop off, an easy partner in crime because of her Teflon reputation for avoiding trouble. "Have a good day, oh studious student. I wish you would come. Even God travels in threes."

Madeleine adjusted her poker face of sweetness and light. She fit a small earplug in one ear, slithering the wire under her jacket, then hiding it in her long hair. "I've got a game to play, girls. Ta for now."

Bloody and Peaches stole away from school, blending into the morning crowd that swarmed the downtown sidewalks. They broke free at the city's sole train station.

"Bloody, where in Alabama are we going?" Peaches asked from behind her Southern literature textbook. She hoped against all blessed hope that it might be someplace cool.

Bloody unwrapped her surprise gift by picking up her novel and pointing at the cover. "Monroeville. We only have a couple hours there, though. That should be enough, because it ain't that big."

Peaches clapped in glee and nearly kissed the book that her friend held high. "Bloody, you're brilliant."

A few hours later, they arrived in small-town south Alabama and sought out lunch at a home-style cafe on the main square. The regulars barely glanced at the city girls as they inhaled home-cooking that was almost as good as Gram's.

Striding the nearly barren blocks around the Monroeville piazza, Bloody pushed Peaches through the door of an antique junk store, a repository of one town's leftovers. A woman about Gram's age stood politely transacting a bone-handled fork with the man at the register. He called her by her birthname and Bloody and Peaches snapped their heads in her direction. A few feet away, talking to the merchant, stood the birth mother of the roaringest little girl in Southern fiction.

The woman tucked the antebellum piece away in her purse, and nodded her cropped-hair head graciously at the girls on her way out. They smiled courteously, their hearts rising to their throats. Peaches reached in her bag to finger her camera with deep yearning. Any extant photos of the very private lady were older than both girls combined.

Feigning nonchalance, the pair trailed their heroine down the street, passing the courthouse that continued to make Monroeville a literary shrine. Bloody spoke from the corner of a mouth that struggled to remain slack. "Peaches, is this stalking?"

Peaches considered the question from the tree they were hiding behind. "Quite possibly, Bloody."

Bloody's stage whisper was as quiet as a kicked trash can. "C'mon, take a picture, Peaches."

Angst swept Peaches' face. "I really want to, Bloody, but I think that'd be worse than stalking."

Bloody's eyes bulged with ire, and her brow dropped in exasperation. She felt as if she had flown Peaches to a mountaintop to show her the world and Peaches kept dozing off. "Peaches!" she hissed.

"I can't, Bloody. It's enough just to trail her for a few blocks, I think." That ended it.

They crept along front yards like ninja schoolgirls, until the author disappeared into the shadows of a screened-in porch. Peaches was both wistful and proud.

Bloody alluded to tabloid rumors about the authorship of the classic in question. "Hard to believe such a little woman could write such a big book."

Peaches readied to defend one of her own. "Really, Bloody?"

"No. To tell the truth, Peaches, that was a book about a little girl, written by someone who was once a little girl."

Bloody stared up at the sun, checked her many watches, then blanched in panic. "Oh man, Peaches. We're going to miss our train."

It took a fired race towards the station, and then a chase after the train that was already slowly moving east. Bloody managed to grab hold of a piece of the train door, and leapt quickly onto the step. She reached for Peaches, who envisioned a faceful of Alabama gravel as she lunged for her friend's outstretched hand. Bloody pulled Peaches in easily, like a trout on a line.

Safe on the car platform, Bloody scrabbled through her bag and found a lukewarm bottle of Coca-Cola and a crumpled soft pack of smokes. Peaches scanned the land that had cradled her father, and the girls split a Coke and had a smoke under the hard blue Alabama sky before entering the coach.

Nearing Atlanta, Peaches and Bloody stared at the city's skyline with fresh small-town eyes, a pair of prodigal daughters returning home. Walking towards the underground, their slow Alabama gait was light-years faster than the deadlocked traffic. Peaches dropped Bloody off, then jockeyed through packed intersections until she came upon Gram selling her wares.

Peaches wondered if Gram had an almanac on traffic flow, because today was the mother beast of congestion. The old lady's hand trolleys were fortuitously filled with bags of tomatoes and peanuts, and today she offered sun tea as a special treat. Early that morning, she had mixed up vats of Tetley tea, cold water, sugar and sliced and peeled yellow lemons, then let the assembly brew in glass pitchers placed on sunny window sills all day long. Peaches grabbed ice-filled cups and filled them to the brim with the brew, doggedly helping Gram with her crush of customers. It was amber booze to the motorists. Barely a half hour had passed before Gram had to declare there was nothing left. The empty vats held sopping circles of lemon pulp, and that was all. The trays were cleaned of produce, and Gram's bosom and pockets were bursting with sheaves of folded crisp bills.

Gram cleaned up in the kitchen, as she sipped a glass of her own iced tea that she had saved, tweaked with a slice of a sugar-soaked lemon. She counted her take before she started dinner, chewing the last bit of sweet tea from a sugary peel.

Upstairs, Peaches sat on her bed, arranging her train ticket and her day's own receipts inside her daddy's scrapbook. She wrote about the woman who had committed a serious story to paper and published it using her androgynous middle name. Then she sketched a drawing in lieu of the photo that she had wanted to take. For a few minutes, she glanced guiltily through her schoolbooks until Gram called her down for dinner.

The kitchen counter was set up buffet-style with a slow roasted chicken, white rice and gravy, fresh spinach topped with melted cheddar cheese, and a green salad chunked up with half the garden and Gram's homemade butter croutons. Gram and Peaches sat together on the porch swing with plates on their laps, saying little as the skyscrapers blushed to a rose hue and the sun made its own end-of-day way down the sky.

When they finished, Peaches took in their plates and cleaned the kitchen. She returned to the porch with her schoolbooks, and Gram moved to her rocker as Peaches spread out on the gray-painted floor. Music played through the open windows. A few birds chirped, and a million crickets rubbed a melody from their legs. Gram hummed along.

"I really love you, Peaches. I'm glad you live with me."

Peaches smiled at Gram from over a book of unintelligible math. "Same here, Gram. I think you're the one of coolest ladies in the world."

Peaches bent back down to her book, and smiles lingered on both faces.

A Trade in Metals

Since Peaches had arrived in Atlanta, Gram had said nothing about the extracurricular activities she had noted in perusals of her granddaughter's scrapbook. She simply watched as Peaches stretched the boundaries, sloughing off her childhood and leaving it behind.

Gram, however, did worry that Peaches was getting too good at singing the freedom-song, seeking pleasure as if it were all there was. Her hope was that Peaches might find out about the rest of life along the way. Her own daughter had bent the rules at that age. Now, her granddaughter broke them outright. Gram wondered if the rebellion might not be permanent.

One night as Gram still waited for Peaches to come home from school, she found herself unsure as to whether the child would live at all. A storm rumbled somewhere in the vast north of the city, and the sky was a bruised blue. A pearl moon slept behind shifting tanks of cloud, and knotted worry betook Gram, filling her with her own little thunderstorm.

The knot loosened a bit when an ice cream truck stopped in front of the house, and Peaches jumped from the sliding door. "Hey, Azri, thanks for the ride. See you later, Bloody."

The truck pulled away with a toodle from its horn as Peaches bounced up the sidewalk. She suddenly stopped short, realizing she should have dropped a quarter on a courtesy call home. "I brought you some Krispy Kremes and Coca-Cola, Gram."

Gram ignored the gifts, taking a gander at the book Peaches was holding that was nearly as thick as a Bible. "What's that you're reading, Peaches?"

Peaches held up a bound novel about a time long gone, penned by a local daughter. Gram spoke thickly with a whiskey-tinged drawl. "Oh, that one. I liked her more than her book, and a lot more than that Scarlett." Damp curls rose from her head like angel wings as the storm approached and the two stood on the porch awaiting it.

"You know, Peaches, it doesn't matter what color or shape the person is who wrote it, but there hasn't been a real book written about the South that isn't boycotted or banned somewhere. It doesn't seem to matter whether it's about a river rat white boy or a black girl trying to grow up. It's automatically a damn dirty book if you write about the South."

Gram suddenly remembered her young colt's tardiness, and looked at the girl with a scary sweet smile. "Get me a cold Co'-Cola, will you, Peaches? Coca-Cola is the oldest thing in this town, besides this house and my own personal plumbing."

With the Coke, Gram got to musing as the storm still loomed. "You know, I remember when there was a general store on that street corner--and when little girls did not ride after dark in cars with strange men."

Peaches tried to wave off the woman's concern. "Gram, Azri's harmless. He's got his own problems. His arm is shriveled, and he has a fake shoe instead of a foot." Peaches pulled three frosty boxes out of her bag. "Besides, I got some ice cream out of the deal."

"Peaches, I never wanted to make you a certain way, but I really want to ask: Do you know who you are?"

Peaches bit a chunk from an ice cream bar, answering shortly with a teenager's brand of dismissive smile. "I'm a girl. An Atlanta girl. An Atlanta white girl, to be specific. And…that's about it."

Gram brought a hammer down. "You're more than that. Just keep reflecting on it, my colleen bawn. You'll have plenty of time to think while you're grounded for two weeks."

On the second night of Peaches' house arrest, the moon was whole and Gram drank whiskey with ice on the porch. Peaches nursed a cold bottle of Pibb. The stereo played rowdily, but there were no neighbors around to complain. The towers' eyes were closed in sleep, and passing cars blinked by without noticing the two women watching from the wide porch of the old house.

Gram took a long swallow of her drink, then looked hard at Peaches. She added to the answer her granddaughter had given about herself a couple of days before. "You said you're a white girl, Peaches. Peaches, you're not a white girl. We're not white. We can only be gray."

Peaches refuted her. "That's black street talk, Gram—look at my skin. I'm actually kind of peachy."

Gram spoke sharply, trying to slap the girl with the truth. "Listen to me now, Peaches. Everything that happened before now is yours, your legacy, this whole big family's past. We brought it down to you, with the family pictures and the plate. All of it that made it through the fires anyway and some that didn't."

Gram tilted her glass and drained it dry. The ice was melting and the whiskey was taking hold. "Illiterate, slow, and bigoted. That's the South, or how the world sees us. Even Atlanta, the big civilized city, might as well be a trailer park."

Peaches stuck to her guns. "Gram, I can be whatever I want to be, not just what somebody thinks of me."

Gram dealt the cards straight to the little gambler. "The best you can do is both. It's enough if you know about yourself, and what they think of you. But most of all you need to know, deep inside, what really went on before you. When you do, you don't forget it, and you don't let it be forgotten. And that's not just the sins of the South. That's the sins of the human race."

Gram stood up, went inside, and emerged with an ancient postcard, yellowed, with bent corners like tiny triangles. A crowd of faces, some smiling as if in celebration, others standing sternly firm surrounded by a tree, a rope, and a half-mutilated dead man. It was the worse picture Peaches had ever seen. She drank her Pibb more slowly, feeling like she needed a bath, with acid, to take her gray skin off.

"That's a little white girl." Gram poked at a small figure with a shy grin, hiding behind a woman's skirt. Gram then stabbed at the woman with her finger. "That's her mother. How lovely of a woman to bring a child to such an affair. This was most often a men's game, but not always. Our shame, Peaches, is their lack of it."

Gram spoke as if her larynx was gutted and then walked inside to refill her drink, returning to the porch with a scrapbook, one large enough to fill a drawer. It was a gallery of human cruelty that covered continents. Peaches didn't breathe as Gram flipped each page angrily. Pictures of riots in segregated cities up north, stormtroopers in the '30s in Nuremberg and sons of stormtroopers decades later in Milwaukee. Gang signs slapped screaming onto the walls of big cities and small towns. Remains of bombed children littering various world grounds.

The world at war and still at war, as if civilization was only a backdrop for war.

Gram was now slurring as she wobbled in her rocker. She leaned close to her granddaughter. "Back then, women were there and we just submitted. We complied with keeping people down and miserable. That's how we stayed gray. Just keeping people down."

She plugged a hit from her drink. "A hundred years ago, a woman ran for president, and now nobody remembers her name. Nothing much is different now from then, except young girls can dress like whores, and their mothers can be indignant when they're called that. It's a strange world, Peaches."

Gram sighed, sat back and went silent. Then she handed the glass with two inches of sparking coppery liquid to Peaches. "Pour this out for me, sweetie, and help your poor old Gram to bed."

Peaches helped her off the porch and down the hall to her bedroom. The moon shone full through thick, white curtains. Gram took a blanket from inside a chest and lay it down for Beau. The dog turned three times, and curled into a doughnut at the foot of her bed.

Gram lay back on her pillow with her eyes closed, fingering a rosary she had pulled from the bedside table. She paused from her prayers to the Virgin Mary to offer one last chunk of wisdom to her granddaughter. "Peaches, remember this. You can be Southern, and not be a bigot. You can be Southern, without being stupid. You can be black, white, Irish, Lebanese, Asian, or Hispanic, and still be a Southerner."

Gram reached forward to grasp Peaches' face in between her hands. The cool smooth rosary beads tickled the girl's ear and neck. "Peaches, my dear, you can be a girl and rule the world. And don't ever think you can't tell the world what you know."

Gram dropped her hands to pray again. Peaches knelt beside the bed, head low and listening as her grandmother jockeyed through Hail Marys like a professional auctioneer. When she finished, Gram's eyelids were hoods, and Peaches took the rosary from her to put it carefully back on the table. The woman smiled as her eyes closed and found the world on the other side.

Peaches collected the glass of liquor from the porch, drained it, took a pen and scrap of paper and wrote: "Under the paint on our skin, all girls are silver, not black, white, or gray."

The next day, Gram found it and posted it on the refrigerator. There was something extraordinary about her granddaughter, she thought. She was determined to find out what might happen when she let her loose upon the world.

Broken In

As two weeks passed, Peaches remained grounded and close to home. She bagged vegetables for Gram, painted the picket fence, and picked fruit off the trees. She often rose before her grandmother, making coffee and setting up for Sunday breakfast, working the tables like a combination politician and waitress, being charming and nourishing to the hungry congregants.

Gram was happy that Peaches had mellowed to good behavior. A twinge of guilt shivered through the old lady for the sanctions she had imposed upon the girl, and she decided she would discuss an offer of probation with Peaches in the morning. Outside her closed and curtained window, a handful of leaves fell from the gutter as the front gate squeaked open in the dark, and a car motor rumbled quietly at the curb.

Gram awoke suddenly a couple of hours later, rose from bed and glided down the hallway and up the long staircase. She knew Peaches was gone, even before she saw the vacant bed and open window. Gram was fully awake when the single profanity erupted from her lips in the dark bedroom, where her own daughter had once played the Rapunzel of the neighborhood, leaving through the same window. Gram noticed an ad from a local show weekly on the floor.

Minutes later, Gram screeched the fat white Cadillac down the driveway, clipping the mailbox. Country music streamed from her open window. Gram slowed to avoid a passing man on the sidewalk, sure he was a junkie who wouldn't know there was a street in front of him until the Caddy had run him down.

She yanked the car into a parking lot adjacent to the concert hall, making a mental note to hold Peaches accountable for the five dollars it cost her. Gram scouted outside for Peaches or one of her likely partners in crime. There, behold, was her granddaughter sitting in the bed of a truck with two boys of questionable age. Gram hid behind a car, and watched as one of the boys slipped his hand onto her granddaughter's leg. Peaches immediately countered with an elbow to his ribcage. He rubbed his side, and Gram saw him thinking about trying again. She hoped Peaches knew how to aim lower. By then Peaches had decided to move on. She climbed over the boy and jumped out of the truck.

Peaches was on her way back inside, when her grandmother stepped into her path. "Hey there, Gram," Peaches said innocently.

Gram grabbed her by the shoulders. "You know you'll never be answerable for many things you do. But they will leave scars, Peaches. Everything costs something."

Peaches' mouth went crooked and she nodded slowly. "Yes ma'am. I'm sorry, Gram."

Gram shook her head and looked away, choked by the sudden imprint of her daughter's face on the child in front of her. "You owe me money for parking, Peaches."

Peaches grabbed Gram's hand, pulling her towards the entrance. "Come into the show, Gram. I'll get you a ticket."

Gram paused, stuck. "Oh hell, why not?"

First Bloody, then Madeleine kissed Gram in greeting, then Madeleine guided the group through the crowd, pushing through with her sweet smile. A path grew for the rough old gentlewoman and her trio.

As the band came onstage, the dark shadows of the hall erupted with fiery comets and shooting stars. The sound was giant, a monster swelling from tsunami tides. Gram listened, her eyes shining like gypsy's rings as she stared at the lead singer, a descendant of long dead queens of soul. "Bloody, how old is she?"

"Near fifty." Bloody whispered as she studied the singer. The woman's hair was bobbed and colored black with slashes of deep blue and white. Bloody made a mental note for herself when she reached middle age.

As the music climbed inside her head, Gram saw a blank tablet where thoughts of color became concrete and real. The guitar sound bounced off the wall, and the bass spoke low as the drummer played timekeeper, flipping and twirling as he showed off for the crowd. The singer's words were dark and layered, delivered with a tone that was somehow louder than everything else. The music leapt around the necks of their listeners in a hungry chokehold, forcing them into a whole.

Peaches stood near a speaker yards away, watching the guitars strive for the point where something shackled and unworldly was freed. She was drawn into the whirlpool of sound, the place the musicians created, one that rose above the smoky clouds hanging beneath the streaming beams of stage lights.

Peaches didn't notice the first signs of her body's shutdown. The singer's hair slipped down like a mask across her face. Peaches' vision turned to black and white fuzz, and the screeching violins in her skull clashed with the band's outpouring.

For a long moment, Peaches stood steady and straight before full disencumberment hit, then passed out in a long, slow slip down the dark concrete stairs at the side of the stage. Blood flowed on the smooth stone ground where she lay blackjacked and unseen, out cold.

When the final encore ended and the crowd dispersed, Gram and Bloody searched for Peaches in the bathrooms and mod lounges. Madeleine prayed to "little Jesus lost and found, show me where to look around," and found herself steered down the strange staircase, where her friend lay curled and bleeding.

Madeleine dropped to her knees and clasped her hands together as she stared into the poached white of Peaches' rolled-back eyes. At a loss for what to do, Madeleine softly sang an old lullaby as Peaches blurred in and out.

Soon, Peaches' eyes opened, shining a dull, curved moon reflecting a sliver of the single light bulb above them. The girl's face matched her eyes, pale white and green. Her lips were cloned by a gulping gash across her left cheekbone. She tried for vertical and slowly pulled herself to almost standing. Peaches used Madeleine as her crutch to stagger up the stairs like a three-gallon drunk.

"What's it like to pass out that way, Peaches?" Madeleine questioned her sodden friend as they stumbled past the stage, now as quiet as an empty church.

Peaches swallowed drily, and the words dragged slowly from her mouth. "Like you're so sick, you're throwing up your soul."

Madeleine looked at her gravely with saucer-sized eyes. "Do you think that's what dying feels like?"

167

Peaches thought yes, but said no. She felt death had green and blue and silver that didn't match how passing out felt.

Gram's face grew a thousand new worry lines when she spotted Peaches, held steady by Madeleine, coming down the long hallway towards her. Gram ran for the Cadillac. They drove like crazed blackhearted runaways towards the hospital.

In the emergency room, Gram studied Peaches' face. Thin black thread stitched the skin together. "Peaches, you're lucky you're gorgeous, though sometimes it seems you're determined to change that."

Peaches tried to speak through the numbing anesthesia, but her mouth didn't work. She wondered what kind of scar she'd have. Bloody told Peaches it would look cool once it healed, like a German dueling wound. Madeleine reached towards the bandaged cheek with her pinky finger, surprised when Peaches drew back. Peaches stilled herself and Madeleine traced a fingertip kiss across the rawness hidden beneath the dressing.

At home, Peaches fell into a dreamless sleep. She arrived at school late the next day, hearing the rumors that she was dead. For weeks afterwards, a taped bandage covered the nasty sewed-up split from her tumble.

When the stitches came off, something remained where nothing was before. Childhood skin healed easily and quickly, she remembered. Now she found that the wounds of adolescence were less pliant. The slight mark prohibited future beauty queen and modeling careers, but she didn't care. Those were never her dreams anyway.

Lady Unleashed

After the show, something bloomed inside Gram, late but strong. Her transformation seemed to make Peaches' woundful experience less painful, maybe even worthwhile.

"I had a dream, Peaches." Gram knelt down beside the huge bed where the triptych of Peaches, Madeleine, and Bloody lay. "Let's go after this gray city and drench it in color."

"That sounds good, Gram," said Peaches turning over to grab hold of sleep. "G'night."

"Girls, get dressed and get in the car. There's good work to be done." Gram prodded and poked each body. One by one, they sleepily rolled out of the mothership bed.

Gram loaded them up with bottles of spray paint while pushing them out the door. Madeleine led in a state of fully-bloomed, perky consciousness, while the others dragged after her.

Gram dropped into the driver's seat and backed the car down the drive. She duly trimmed the hedge near the mailbox, the sound of branches combing` the side of the car. They sailed through green lights, stopping for red at an avenue named after the explorer who didn't find youth, but did find Florida. They saw a pale workingwoman dressed in shiny white crossing the street on the arm of a woman in gold. It was dirty art made flesh, and Peaches pulled out her camera to snap it before closing her eyes again.

Through the open windows seeped in air that was sweetly soaked with the sticky, sugary smell of frying dough. Gram spun the wheel to turn into the all-night doughnut shop. "Who needs coffee?"

The backseat passengers grunted affirmations. Madeleine tagged along after Gram inside where the scent of the dough blistering up brown in hot fat was intense and intoxicating. The counters and walls gleamed against a backdrop of chrome.

Gram placed the order, and glanced back at the dozing girls in the car outside, their tilted heads illuminated by the red glow of the "Hot Doughnuts" sign. Gram saw Peaches take a picture of the backseat without opening her eyes, accidentally triggering the camera at the end of an outstretched arm.

Madeleine struck up a conversation with the slight young man standing behind them in line. He returned to the car with Gram and Madeleine, carrying their doughnuts and coffee like a hired porter. Madeleine reached in the backseat to prod the tired lumps of blood and humanity spread across it. "Move over, kids."

It was only after her first slug of caffeinated hot water and a bite of delicious, piping hot fatbread that Peaches realized there was a newbie in the car.

His neck was extravagantly tattooed with dark blue-green scrawls. A blue rope was knotted in tight spirals from his wrist to his elbow. He turned to Peaches, as if she looked like she held answers. His voice was as quiet as a baby rabbit when he spoke. "Can I smoke?"

Peaches nodded, and Bloody's hand was in front of his face, holding a small box of wooden matches. He dug a slim black case from his pocket and took out a cigarette, striking a match, before handing the box to

Peaches. His thick fingers stumbled over her slim ones. "Thanks. Y'all can call me Patch, if you like."

Peaches added packet after packet of sugar, sipping it until the concoction was perfectly tainted. She thought the world was a beautiful place when it was all sweet coffee and even sweeter doughnuts.

In the rearview mirror, Gram watched the backseat like a lady hawk. As the space between peoples grew thinner and Bloody moved nearly atop Peaches' lap, Gram decided the bridge ahead would do as well as any. She tucked the car into a barely lit space in a half-chained lot.

The group walked to Gram's target, and she showed Patch the rough design she had drawn when her imaginings had kept her from sleeping. Gram sent Madeleine up one side of the street as Bloody climbed a tree in the opposite direction, stationing both as lookouts. Peaches documented the night drama with her camera: Gram and Patch posed for her in front of the evolving masterpiece.

When done, it was splendid, in its color, in its topic, in its bold imposition on an urban wall. Gram's creation was a glimpse into a world that had never existed. Men, women, and children dressed in post-World War II apparel walked the city's main avenue smiling at each passerby. They were of every shade and kind. It was truly an impossible exchange for that time.

The painters put up their tools. The watchers left their posts. Madeleine's hand went over her mouth, as if to keep her heart down. "That's beautiful, Gram."

Bloody added her own honest touch to the commentary. "False, but yes, truly beautiful."

Patch looked up from straightening their exhausted art supplies. "Ma'am, until tonight, I thought Atlanta was no place for an artist."

Gram patted the boy on the shoulder and was about to reply when headlights appeared far at the top of the hill. Bloody whistled and they all trotted to the car around the corner. A police cruiser pulled alongside the painted bridge and shone its spotlight there. The motley vandals held their breath until the squad car drove away.

Madeleine searched through her bag for something to play on the return trip.

Patch put a gift in her hand. "I've got something."

Madeleine popped the young man's album in the stereo. "Who loves Patch?" she said.

The music pulsed and grew inside the car. It seemed to engineer the sunrise as the great ball of fire emerged low and orange in the east, shimmering off the earth around them.

Gram turned to see Patch touching the scar on Peaches' cheek. She swerved the car to a stop, smiling and sweetly declaring: "So, can we drop you here, Patch dear?"

Madeleine clicked out his music from the player, holding it lovingly to herself before handing it over. Patch refused the album. "They're from Belgium. You can keep that. I have another copy." He looked straight at Gram as he climbed from the car, "I had a good time tonight, ma'am." Then he reached to shake Peaches and Bloody's outstretched hands. "Thank y'all for letting me be a part."

They left him at the curb, and all three girls hung from their windows, waving goodbye to the talisman of their night. They sought breakfast instead of sleep, with Gram taking her rightful place at the stove. Soon a buttery feast was spread across the kitchen table. The girls gorged. Gram munched bacon quietly and considered future places around her city where she could effect an honorable change.

Here, There, Anywhere

On the day of her birth, Peaches had been prophesied to be a traveler. The prophecy didn't mention world-eater. Already, she and Bloody had encountered fresh trout in Tennessee, fried green tomatoes in Alabama, and seafood in the Low country of South Carolina. There had been saffron-hued barbecue with rice in the Piedmont, auburn barbecue with white bread toast along the Georgia coast.

Madeleine was jealous of her friends' freedom, their ability to leave and their invisibility from discipline. At first, it was enough to live vicariously through them, to listen and laugh at the stories they told. Her dreams, however, began to trouble her. They were getting run over in the street, struck down by her own indecision. She told her secret sisters she thought that the dreams meant something. "You can have one life, until the day you get hit by a bus. Or, you can have as many lives as you can, before the bus gets you. Y'all take me with you next time." They proved they would.

When Peaches and her friends were not vectoring around the southeast like a boomerang, Gram took them out and painted the town in recollections blurred with revelations. One night, near a subway station downtown, right off a central point where five major streets of the city met, Gram blended a scenic history, a panorama that begged forgiveness as it cleansed. Townspeople thrashed about, holding handfuls of flame as they burned a slave auction house to the ground. Mules were lined up in long rows, and newly scripted land deeds were tucked in boxes awaiting handout. The city was represented as green growth meeting blue sky, and the resulting image was surreal.

In another of Gram's paintings a breathtakingly elaborate American castle, the city's main train station, reemerged on the wall amidst the silhouettes of newer sports and entertainment complexes. Gram added the city's new array of art museums and galleries, as an afterthought.

Several blocks away, Gram painted an infamous restaurant and its segregationist owner who had closed the place down rather than admit blacks. This time, however, a little bit of everyone sat inside at the counter.

At one intersection to the north of the city, clustered with car dealerships, shopping centers, and a familiar fast-food landmark, Gram painted a crowd whose hate rose like heat. The men were a stark white and the women a dull gray, with every hand painted a blood red. A man hanged from a tree, as pale as his counterparts. His eyes were slack, as was his body, but his hands were clean.

They drove east to a small town that was the birthplace of one southern writer and home to another. On an overpass, Gram painted caricatures of both authors on each side of a bridge. Their fingers reached across the chasm, joining black and white.

One Sunday morning before breakfast, Peaches walked outside to retrieve the newspaper. She could read the front page's headline from the porch steps: "MYSTERY HISTORY: ATLANTA'S SECRET ARTIST".

Peaches ran back inside with the paper, shouting to Gram her news of the news. Photographs of the paintings peppered the pages, dwarfing news of world floods and city politics, as if the mysterious paintings were all that mattered. Gram glanced down at the paper as she cooked. She had inadvertently swung a big stick, it seemed.

The paper, formerly a voice of conviction, had gone dead in recent decades. Once, Atlanta and its daily had been a pair of powerhouses, two beacons on the South's landscape. Now, it covered the necessary, spoke demurely about things benign, and caused no trouble or notice. Gram read the article in the early afternoon and told Peaches how good it made her feel. "Peaches, it's quite wonderful to find that you do have a personality."

"You, Gram?" Peaches asked, cutting up another copy for her scrapbook.

"No, Peaches. Our municipal 'you'. The city." Gram grinned as she folded the newspaper, holding it on her lap like a child.

Gram's folk art was enhanced by the news coverage. At first, people assumed the murals were commissioned pieces from official sources. Once heralded by the media, however, they became an attraction for residents and visitors. Their content was hotly debated. Some questioned whether it was inherently racist to change the past as the pictures had sometimes done, while others regarded them as gestures of reparation.

Gram laughed at everything that was said, and she and her crew continued to paint in secret, though occasionally and more carefully. In her murals, she had touched and prodded and kneaded the city's substance, allowing it to find comfort in its own skin again.

Daughter of the Late New South

Hot, hot, hot! They sat on the porch eating steamed crabs, cracking them open, then sopping the white flakes of meat in melted butter and swallowing them down. Peaches sipped from a chilled glass of Pibb, laced with a chunk of lime that had been wrung from the fruit mercilessly, leaving clumps of pulp resting on cracked ice. Gram's drink was gin and tonic, clear and crisp in a short glass. It was pungent, cleaner than the usual sweet mustiness of Gram's bronze whiskey.

"Gram, what's with the gin?" asked Peaches.

Gram had mixed the drink purposefully, to plunge Peaches back in time.

"It's your father's birthday, Peaches. He was a gin and tonic man all year round."

Gram raised her glass to the heavens. She gazed towards the setting sun, as if something from the past was there. "It was truly a dreadful thing that happened to him. Those two were an extraordinary couple. Once your mother met him, she couldn't think of herself without him. He was the same way with her."

Peaches was silent as she lay her plate of crab flakes and butter on the ground for Beau to lick clean. She stared towards the horizon and her glowing glass city. "I wish I had known this was his birthday before now. I just never thought."

Gram shrugged and sipped the gin. "Peaches, a birthday is a death day, a cloudy day, or a sunny day, a spring day, or a winter day. It is your day or my day, or the best day, or the worst day. It's just one day."

177

"What was he like, Gram?" Peaches was sometimes unsettled by the philosophy.

"He was everything he left behind." Gram tossed the remnants of her glass over the porch railing, so she could fill it again. "You are the acorn that fell when the mighty oak came down. And you are whatever you do today, tomorrow, and the day after." Gram stood and went inside to the kitchen, returning with a fresh drink. "Everything he did before then, you are, and then some."

Peaches rocked slowly on the porch swing, and Gram smiled gently. "Peaches, your father had a wandering spirit, and there's one thing I always knew. When he left the house that morning, he was already happy, because it was a beautiful, sunny day. He was ecstatic when he heard you had arrived. Very few people get the luxury of absolute joy on the last day of their lives."

Peaches' tongue was thick and heavy, as if Gram had switched drinks on her. "But, Gram, he wouldn't have been crossing the train tracks if it wasn't for me."

Gram leaned close and took Peaches' hand. She held it between her own, as if she were warming frostbitten fingertips. "You didn't do that, Peaches. That wasn't yours."

Peaches' head hurt. Gram saw the pain and spoke consolation like a porch poet. "If you lit a candle for him on your birthday, he'd blow it out for you."

Then Gram looked down at her already empty glass and grimaced. "Peaches, what would you do if I didn't tell you about the past?"

"Assume things, I guess, Gram. Or not think about them at all." Peaches took a breath, and then asked: "What about…Brother's father?"

Gram turned chill. She gazed out into the yard, where a squirrel sniffed near her tulip bulbs. "You know those decisions that someone makes that seem impulsive and full of foreboding? Decisions that still make people cringe years later?"

Gram stood and opened the screen door. "I really can't talk about that one, Peaches. It's everything bad you can possibly think of, and probably even worse. I'm sure you know enough already."

Peaches was alone on the porch except for Beau, who lay sleeping next to Gram's rocking chair. She saw the buildings stand tall in a city that grew up too fast, saving itself from stagnation by dreaming far ahead.

Small-town News

Half a mile from the school campus Peaches was
wasting time in an ancient diner, waiting for Bloody to
finish an early test before they hopped a train and flew
away for the day. Jubilee was a cheap place, offering a
bottomless cup of coffee for under a dollar. Sometimes
during lulls, the old ladies would hitch up their lumpy
uniform jumpers and dance to the jukebox's song. When
the music stopped, they'd go back to wiping down
counters and booths, as if there had never been any
dancing at all.

"Peaches, how're you, girl?" A laughing music
man named Sam sat down in her booth across from her.

Peaches knew him through Madeleine, whose
playing drew him in. He had watched Madeleine on her
guitar from a payphone in a gas station as she played and
filled her tank. Madeleine invited him to Gram's house:
Peaches had liked him. Gram had too, sending him
home after dinner with a sack of boiled peanuts, half a
fried chicken, and a slice of Carolina peach pie.

Peaches was glad to see him today. His mood
was happy and often contagious. "Still kicking, Sam,"
she replied. "How about you?"

The waitress interrupted their rapport with
coffee and a slice of warm pecan pie. Sam handed the
woman a handful of quarters. A moment later, music
burst from the jukebox as the wait staff began to dance.

"Aw, y'know. All good, Peaches."

Peaches watched him take a bite of pie, then
drain half his coffee cup as he rolled a cigarette the size

of a small cigar. Sam puffed, and Peaches thought he looked like a character from a comic book.

"I've been meaning to ask you, Peaches, what town did you say you were from?"

"I didn't, Sam."

"C'mon, I know you're from outside of Atlanta. I can hear it in your voice. It's like background music." Sam scooped heaping spoonfuls of pie, plowing through the crust and scraping the goodness from it.

Peaches turned short with him. "No, you can't, Sam. Why do you want to know anyway?"

Sam grinned as he pushed his empty pie plate away. He downed the bit of coffee left in the cup. "Because I met a kid who's up visiting schools here. He asked if I've ever come across a girl named Peaches. I told him only one."

Sam raised a finger, and the waitress came to refill his coffee cup from a piping hot pot. "Y'all friends?"

Peaches nodded, her mind tangling as the old breached the border of the new. Sam reached across the table to pat her hand warmly. "Well, then, next time I see him, I'll send him by your Gram's house."

A smile broke across Peaches' face, as though she carried new life within her. "That would be really great, Sam. Thanks. Now, I've got a question for you."

He puffed on his fat cigarette, opening his arms wide to show he had nothing to hide. "All right, Peaches, fair enough."

Peaches threw his question back like a spitball. "So, Sam, what town did you say you were from?"

Sam laughed heartily, as if she had called him a chicken. "Aw, Peaches, I'm from Chicago."

"So, how do people get along in Chicago?" Peaches used Sam to sound out her theory that Southern cities were one thing and Northern cities quite another.

Sam trilled smoke from his nostrils as he contemplated her question. "Y'know, Peaches, I don't think I really talked to anyone that didn't look like me until I came down here. In Chicago, people that look like you live on the north side, and people that look like me live on the south side. Plus, if your car breaks down, no one stops up there. Here, someone always pulls over to help you."

Peaches held in a smile. The clock above the grill caught her eye, and she pulled some bills from her shirt pocket. Sam handed them back to her. "Peaches, I'll pay a couple bucks for a good conversation with you any day."

Peaches reached to hug him goodbye. "Thank you kindly, Sam. Tell Kahlil to come see me. And Gram says come around for dinner sometime soon." She stopped at the jukebox on the way out to toss in quarters and start up the old ladies' dance.

Boy-Man

A few evenings later, Peaches stopped suddenly, a round, pink peanut inches from her mouth as she stared at the apparition.

"Who is that, Peaches?" Madeleine asked.

Peaches stood to stumble down the steps. She turned to her friends, her face blanchings. "My brother."

She approached the figure straight and tall. His name pricked her tongue. "Kahlil."

The boy's smile broke open and lit up the world, a full moon shining like sun in the shadows. Kahlil reached towards her with arms open wide. "Peaches."

On the porch, Bloody whispered to Madeleine, her eyes glued to the pair. "That's her brother?"

Madeleine studied the boy whose skin was tanned by birth and whose looks were blessed by God. "I know. He's hot."

Peaches and Kahlil hugged tightly. They stepped back to look at each other, to see what had changed. He gripped her wrists, and his smile gleamed. "You've grown, girl."

"You too, boy," she said.

The boy in front of Peaches was nearly a man. She wondered how she had ever left Kahlil behind.

Kahlil pointed with a lazy hand towards the two girls on the porch swing, who watched the reunion with widening eyes. "Who's that up there?" he asked.

Peaches waved them down, and her two friends were instantly at her side. "Kahlil, meet Madeleine and Bloody."

Kahlil stuck out his hand and shook all around. "Hey, y'all. Peaches, I met your grandmother out on the street. She's a mighty nice lady. Kinda like your mama."

Peaches hesitated, offering the briefest of responses to a statement that was potent with question. "Yeah, I guess."

Kahlil gave her a look, then he glanced at the eager faces of Madeleine and Bloody, both desperate to learn more about him. "C'mon, tell me, Peaches, how is she?" he pressed.

Peaches smacked a look of cool, stony stubbornness on her face. "Mama's fine, Kahlil."

Bloody sputtered like a ghost was sighted in the yard. "Peaches, you have a mother?"

Peaches took her sights off Kahlil to set them on Bloody. "Yes, Bloody, everyone does."

Madeleine broke in, paving the bumps with sweet intentions. "How long are you in Atlanta, Kahlil?"

Kahlil put his arm around Peaches and hugged her close again. "I'm on a train out tonight. I'll be back full-time next fall. The schools here seem to want me."

Gram came up behind him, done with her curbside duties for the day. "Well, I think that calls for a celebration. Kahlil, you'll stay for dinner. I'll whip something up quick."

Kahlil spoke politely, like the sweet Southern son he was. "Ma'am, I'd be pleased. Thank you so much."

Gram scooted inside, and before the long hand was another turn around the clock, a neat little beef roast lay hot and delicious on a platter. Buttery red potatoes were soft and salted in a green bowl, pole beans steamed with bacon in a yellow bowl, and mint ice cream softened in its box on the counter.

After dinner, Kahlil helped Peaches with the dishes. Madeleine and Bloody left for home. "Peaches, I'm sorry but I'm going to ask again. How is your mother?"

Peaches dumped silverware in the sink, and it sounded like a land mine. "Kahlil, I'm sorry, but I don't know."

Gram walked in, infatuated by the oboe that had just snuck into the song emitting from the speakers. "Peaches, sweetie, marry someone like an oboe. You'll know it when you find it. Kahlil, dear, do you need a ride to the train station?"

Kahlil shook his wet hands over the sink, and then checked his watch. "Yes, ma'am, please."

Gram herded them into the Cadillac. First, they picked up his luggage at one of the university dorms in the west end. At the station, Kahlil hugged Peaches goodbye, laughing as he spoke. "Peaches, the town thinks you're running wild in the city. That's what they think happens to everybody in the city."

Peaches threatened him with a poke and a smile. "You'd better come see me when you come back, my friend."

On the ride home, Peaches finally voiced the deepest of desires. "Gram, can I go see Mama?"

Gram nodded, wondering why it had taken so blessed long for Peaches to ask. She didn't know Peaches came close to asking every night.

Lasting Impressions

After landing in Charleston, Peaches was a twitching mess during the plane's slow roll towards the gate. She watched out her window as another plane, a massive skyship, headed overseas. It coasted the runway and lifted its nose, sniffing the air as it headed far away. When her plane released its passengers, Peaches walked among those she shared air with for the past hour, pushing through the transient bodies towards the outside.

Peaches breathed in the coastal air as she petitioned a taxi driver to take her to the station. Her mother's hospital was located at the other end of the city's quaint old rail line. Soon, Peaches' face leaned against the hard metal of the train's window frame. She popped a piece of gum into her mouth, tucking it in the corner of her cheek like a chipmunk and letting the sweet taste drain down her throat.

The train passed rows of like houses. At one, a young girl sat on the steps. Her honey-colored hair was unkempt and uncombed, and she chewed a cookie held in both hands. Peaches watched her stand and crumble the cookie with her fingers until it was dust. The train moved past, and Peaches tucked the image away, wondering what came next.

The answer was her mother's new home. Peaches hated it, even more when she went inside. The air smelled numb and sorrowed, like a sudden death underwater. The ground floor of the hospital was overflowing with unmoving human shells. Their attendants smoked cigarettes at the doorway, exhaling a stream outside and watching their patients with lazy distraction.

Peaches rode an elevator that strained on its cables going up to her mother's floor. The walls were painted the color of prison, and bad fluorescent lighting stripped Peaches' eyes, blessedly saving her from shedding tears.

Peaches looked in and saw the woman she once thought of as an Amazon. Mama sat small in the closed room. The white stripes of hair, like long bangs, were braided and pulled back, suggesting that someone else fixed her hair now. The familiar face turned towards her, and something strange creaked inside Peaches. She saw the eyes she knew, and her chi burst into wet fire, nearly melting her down to invisible nothing.

Mama's head jerked as she gestured towards the curtains, holding up a hand as if in warning. "I saw sunshine just yesterday," she said.

Peaches wondered if the broken always spoke in alien subtext. "Yeah, so did I, Mama."

Mama gestured politely to a chair. Peaches sat down, not knowing what to say or do. In front of her was a sullied and wrecked Mama, a nattily wrapped gift with nothing inside. "How are you, Mama?"

Mama busied her hands, wringing and tugging loosely on the thin digits. "Well enough, Peaches. How are you?"

"I'm okay, Mama. Gram's good, too." Peaches tried to catch hold of the eyes boring a hole behind her, as if there was a secret passageway in the wall.

"Why are you still here, Mama?"

Mama sighed, a tornado of breath. "I can't be out there anymore, Peaches."

"I wish you would think about it, Mama."

"I think about you every day, Peaches, how I want you safe."

"It's just fear, Mama. Don't let it win."

Mama's voice turned cold, as if the girl's presence was a personal affront. "It's not fear, Peaches. I just don't think anything bad can find me here."

"No, Mama. I guess not."

A nurse entered with cupfuls of pills on a tray, and Peaches rose to leave. She kissed Mama goodbye with chaste care, so as to not startle the woman with human touch. Mama pulled Peaches back into an embrace and cupped her daughter's face with slow, soft fingers. It took a moment for the cerulean orbs to lock into place, before the pupils shifted again and her grip loosened.

Peaches let her mother touch her face as if it were a healed scar. Mama spoke in the same voice that she had once used for bedtime stories. "Don't you miss your father, Peaches?"

"I never met him, Mama. I miss you."

The exchange seared, as if this moment of all moments replaced every other memory she had of her mother. Peaches walked out in misery.

Waiting for the train, thinking that the Charleston evenings were strangely and uncomfortably cool for a Georgia girl, she saw an old man in a dark brown cloak and a brown beret. He gently took her hands in his. Warm blood eased through her joints as he massaged her fingers gently with his own. Then he disappeared.

The train came, and she bought a cookie in the dining car in memory of that little girl. By the time the train pulled into the station on the edge of the exquisite city center, the sky's light was dimming. Bedtime in the Holy City of the South. Peaches stood outside an inn, drinking the Charleston night. Aching recollections flooded her, bringing back storybook tales from her childhood years.

The Factor Called Humanity

"Tell me something about your mother, Madeleine," said Peaches.

Madeleine plucked an odd note from her guitar and flashed a crooked grin. "You've met my mother, Peaches."

"I don't really feel like I know anything about her though."

Madeleine bounced notes quickly on the guitar. She smirked through eyes that were glossy and hard. "Oh, Peaches, I don't think I do either. Except maybe from the speech she gives me every year on my birthday."

Peaches readied herself. "Do tell, Bean."

Madeleine stood like the porch was her stage. She stole the syrupy sweet, crawling drawl of a magnolia-crusted plantation yesterday. "'That day, that damned day, my sweet Madeleine, there was an angry sun that throbbed with heat.'"

Madeleine put a genteel hand to her throat, winding thin fingers around an invisible pearl necklace. "'The sun was not nearly as loud as the wretched screaming from the newborn mother-to-be. Your birth, my dear Madeleine, was a cacophony of pain, but I never blamed you. Your aching to escape was my dream, too.'"

Peaches watched her friend recite, disturbed how well the white-gloved voice fit. "'And like a brilliant explosion, you burst forth. My womb slumped in its emptiness. I had never before felt so comforted by loss.'"

Madeleine blotted her eyes with a pretend tissue. "'I had felt so ugly in my cloak of expectant motherhood, but I got my figure back almost immediately. And I was proud to be a soldier of childbirth, as my mother was, as her mother was, and as one day, you will be, Madeleine, my sweetheart.'"

Madeleine switched back to her own voice. "Sometimes I think I don't want to be my mother."

Peaches remembered the dead soul in the dark room. "Amen, sister."

Gram burst onto the porch, carrying a reference volume: a thousand pages of mental disorders bound in a thick red cover. "I bought this book, so I could learn what afflicted my daughter. War veterans have their diagnosis, along with petty thieves, compulsive eaters, and even the truly batty."

Gram looked old. "I've seen so many women fall down, just decades and decades of housewives whisked away for extended stays in Milledgeville. They'd come back broken. Sad. Sad."

Gram slammed the book closed. "I raised my little girl differently, but it didn't matter, because the damn world hadn't changed. My daughter's condition is nothing unique. Just psychological collapse. This same thing ruining lives, the world over. Sometimes I think it's just called humanity."

Gram whirled back through the screen door. Madeleine watched the door slam shut, her face fragile, and the color of gunsmoke. Peaches knew what her friend felt. It was the same inside her, the incurable condition known as girl.

Inside Outsiders

"Bean, why does your mother hate this truck?"

"She says it's not ladylike." Madeleine downshifted, as they rolled in the bumping barrel down a tree-lined avenue. "But it's really fun."

Peaches tried again. "You have jewelry on, and makeup, and the required restrictive clothing. Plus, your hair looks nice. What else does she want from you?"

Madeleine shrugged as she pumped the clutch with a heeled shoe. "Mine is a life where laughing and playing in the sunshine are soon called skin damage."

"So, are you going to be how you were made, or how you were raised?"

Madeleine smiled like a recovering alcoholic on her third day of clean. "You're not immune, Peaches, just because you don't want to play at it. It's a game, and it's the world's game."

"But look at the game, Bean. Their rules say this big ol' truck is ugly. I think it's really cool. Doubting the status quo is the only way to go."

Stopping at a traffic light, Madeleine closed her eyes. "Peaches, I don't believe in my façade anymore. If I did, I wouldn't be sitting here with you. But I'm twice cursed, all right? I straddle two lives, and straddling works right now. But I can't do that forever. I'll fall on my face."

They pulled up to Bloody's house. At the front door, chimes donged their arrival. Peaches made her a promise. "Madeleine, I'll catch you if you fall. Even if you fall on the wrong side of the line."

Madeleine smiled, brilliantly as always. Peaches smiled at her in return.

Bloody's mother peered through the door tentatively, as if masked bandits lay in wait. She breathed heavily when she saw who it was. "Oh, girls, you scare me."

They waited for their friend in the house's front hallway. A photograph of Bloody as a toddler was blown up life-size in a wood and metal frame. The setting was a dusty riverbank in South Korea, and Bloody's mother held the dirty little angel by her fat belly. Bloody was swaddled in a cloth diaper and wore a necklace of coppery beads that draped to her knees: it glittered in the sunshine. Brown baby eyes burned like burled coconuts from her bronzed face. Her black hair hung wild and uncombed, loops of it tied with bits of blue ribbon and colored string. It had been Bloody's sole visit to Korea. She didn't remember it anymore than she recalled her birth in an Atlanta hospital.

Madeleine turned to Bloody's mother, and, always gracious in the presence of authority, declared: "Bloody was a beautiful baby, ma'am."

Bloody's mother smiled demurely, then turned to scream up the stairs, like a lady born of banshee and dragon. "Bloody!"

Bloody sauntered down the stairs, and her mother rejected Madeleine's compliment. "Bloody is ugly girl now. Look at those boots, those big boots."

The woman spoke crossly, hands on her hips, as if she held a storm in place. She turned back to Madeleine, spreading her arms wide as if she was about to wrap her in a giant hug. "Mad-lin', you good girl, you pretty girl. Bloody, why can't you be like Mad-lin', not naughty girl with big boots like you a boy."

Peaches braced herself as the woman whirled in her direction. "Peaches, you bad girl, too. Big boots not for pretty girl like you. What's wrong with you girls? Why you so bad?"

She circled back to Madeleine with a glowing smile. "Mad-lin', you such a good girl. Why you with evil girls like Bloody and Peaches?"

Bloody stepped in front of her mother, wearing a silent stare. "Bean has good taste, Mom. Let's go, kids."

Bloody's mother closed the door behind them. She opened it again to deliver last words as they climbed into the truck. "Bloody, you still bad girl! You naughty, evil girl to your mama."

They rode the few miles to the little township housing and the campus of Lambskin, a college originally created to graduate Presbyterian girls to lives as good wives. The school was now firmly dedicated to overeducating smart girls from wildly diverse backgrounds. Madeleine had enrolled on Saturdays for advance credit, and her friends were checking it out.

As they walked across the university grounds, Peaches nearly skipped with excitement, anticipating what a class made up of only the brilliant was like. That sandcastle was about to crumble. Meaningless twaddle dribbled from the gap-toothed teacher, a stump lady who wore a frown all the way to her eyes. Bloody doodled on a pad of paper, unmoved by any propaganda regardless of the setting or the source. Peaches nudged Madeleine, who sat next to her with a listening look planted firmly on her face. "Madeleine, is the whole school like this?"

Madeleine smiled, whispering from the corner of her mouth where a slight dimple prettily pockmarked her cheek. "I've heard this teacher is the most rigid."

Peaches was relieved. She found the woman's bias extreme, yet some of the students absorbed it like honey butter. The teacher had taken points off for Madeleine's correct spelling of particular words. Madeleine was amused, hoping for just that reaction when she brought her friend to class. "I used 'oppressive' spelling, Peaches."

Peaches raised her hand high. The teacher buzzed towards Peaches like a fat, purple bee. Peaches stood to meet her, holding the assignment by her fingertips, as if it were soaked in hot paraffin. "You took points off a paper, because 'woman' was spelled with 'm-a-n'?"

"It is important that wymyn are empowered to believe they are not just part of man, the rib from Adam, that myth of Judeo-Christian patriarchy, for instance."

The class nodded like a dreamy cult, worse than the kids at Peerless. Something lit hotly inside her head. "Ma'am, my understanding is that the origins of both woman and man are benign. Wouldn't it be better to concentrate on useful change? Like equal pay, or the fact that little girls around the world still get their whoo-hoos cut off. Why waste time on useless symbolism when there's real work to be done?"

The class jerked out of their moonie stares. Madeleine struggled to swallow a giggle, Bloody kept drawing.

"Maybe you're too young to understand the oppression that wymyn face today," said the professor.

"Without pioneer wymyn's sacrifices, we wouldn't even be able to vote."

"Good Lord, that happened forever ago. You're forcing my friend here to conform to your belief system by penalizing her. I would think that you would want to empower her to think and act on her own."

The professor froze. "Time for presentations, ladies. Who wants to go first?"

The topic was "Wymyn in Religion," and showed a noticeable imbalance towards biblical harlots and Wiccan spirits. Peaches was especially irked when the class tittered in awed respect as they each tried on a corset, mistaking an obvious symbol of repression for some kind of cultural adornment.

Madeleine presented on, "Mary, the Mother of God." It was an eye-opening presentation for Peaches, who had conceded that one fact about the Church was unassailable: it was the only faith that awarded superhero status to a woman.

Madeleine passed around rosaries, explaining their use in prayer. One girl tried to fit it over her head, thinking the religious beads were nothing more than an old Celtic symbol strung on a rope. "Where would one buy a rosary then?" the girl asked.

Madeleine flashed with irritation. Peaches broke in quickly. "Look, it would offend my Catholic grandmother and about a billion other people on the planet if you wore it as jewelry, ok? Show a little respect, please."

As the class ended, chattering students left the room and Bloody and Peaches waited for Madeleine to gather her things. The teacher swooped in on Peaches, a beaked owl slicing through the neck of the living. "I hope you enjoyed my class, and I also hope you return. I think you could learn some things."

Peaches shook her head slowly, feeling maliciously indifferent. "You know, ma'am, there's a big difference between being righteous and being right."

Then they headed west.

City of Everlasting Night

It was dark when they crossed the Mississippi border into Louisiana, and Madeleine from the wheel squinted at the highway signs, hoping to sight an establishment providing both potties and coffee. Bloody dozed against the passenger window of the truck and Peaches rode between. All three glistened from the heat and humidity.

They caught the sweet-sour scent of the bayou drifting in through the window, and Peaches thought she was tasting the water of the Mississippi. One day, she thought, she would tell where she was in the world just by aspiration.

Parking the truck illegally on a lonely residential street in the Crescent City, they jumped a trolley and rode along ancient avenues lined by old houses and weathered retail. The girls had only a short skerrick of hours to roam and chase their id. When the sun rose, like vampires, they would be beckoned home.

Stepping off the trolley, they made their way to a crowded street named after liquid fire, a not quite ended Gomorrah. Bright neon turned night into day, illuminating the swirls of tourists and highlighting the faces of the three sprites, who gawked and laughed as they bunched up in the crowd. Bloody made liberal use of her elbows as they maneuvered. "Does this street run with beer or what?" said Peaches.

She copied Bloody's elbow defense and kept an eye on a dreamy Madeleine, who stared at the new world like a big-eyed child at a freak show. Eight dollar beer beckoned from a neon-colored glass.

Bloody pulled Peaches and Madeleine towards a sign bearing the starry sun and moon on the doorway of a tarot reader. Madeleine took the lead as tin bells sang them in.

An older woman came through the double doors, her face encircled with black twists of hair that touched the funny-colored jewels roped around her throat. She studied the girls, and hesitated. One face told her secrets of healed scars painted in childhood. Another was tinged with a stigmata of controlled anger. The last girl worried her the most. Her young soul hung delicately above the chakra of her head, thin strings holding it fast, as if a defect of birth kept it from being tied securely by skin and bone.

The visionary spoke in a voice that scratched like nails. "Girls, I will tell you one thing for free. A prophet once said as deep as sorrow can carve into your being, the more joy you can contain."

She picked up a dark red book of wooden matches and lit a candle, translucent and white like a baptismal sconce. "In the mêlée of surviving, some things must die. My husband died violently. My son is not dead, but gone. Some of us carry the burden, some of us break under it, and some of us go on in life as firsthand witnesses to it."

The sibyl then stood to walk them towards the door, whispering final words to each girl in turn. Peaches' skin prickled as the woman touched her hand and traced a vein. "You have a roar so loud, city walls tremble and dead flowers bloom," she whispered.

Tin bells clanged and the girls fell out into the cool night air. Bloody seemed melted and soft, as if her edges were blunted by the woman's gift of brutal certainty. "What did she say to y'all?"

Madeleine shone as if a star had fallen into her hand. "She said to live my life as if it were the eyeblink of a petulant god."

Bloody spoke hers. "She said that only when my pain moves above the surface, will my gifts be used as they should."

Madeleine took Peaches' hand in her own. "She told you good things, too, didn't she, Peaches?" Peaches avoided the question and Bloody lit a cigarette, her face silver and gold in the fire's light.

Walking again among the streaming rivers of people, the girls found a vast restaurant advertising hot coffee and greasy carbohydrates. Peaches eyed the slices of pastry under glass as Madeleine ordered bread pudding to split.

Dawn edged the horizon, and they were back outside, walking along a grassy median as they waited for a trolley car. Without warning, Peaches' world shaded black as liquid discomfort soaked her insides. The girl's head throbbed as blood drained from her skull like a valve had shut. She felt the old, familiar embrace of her deadening friend.

"I've been here a million times," she uttered, then wavered like a treetop in high wind before keeling over, clutching the air as if it could hold her upright. She crumpled to the grass as her head cracked in a silent whiplash against a rounded chunk of streetcar rail.

A solid beam of slow-moving light from an approaching trolley car clanged and rattled towards them. Cars shot through the intersection, trying to beat the speeding trolley across the median. Peaches tried to stand, but her face turned ashen green, and she fell crooked and slack against her friends.

Her eyes were hooded darkly as she battled to win gravity back. She concentrated on the task of walking steady and straight. Bloody and Madeleine stood on either side of her and they all headed slowly up the street.

At a street corner, Bloody stopped abruptly. A graveyard rose from the ground, beautiful and old, full of dreams long dead. Stone crypts and mausoleums settled next to tombstones and burial plots, a peaceful place within the haunted city. Bloody spoke her paranoia and superstition, as if either were ever useful. "Hey, I think we should go the long way around."

Peaches ignored her own wish to collapse on the cool sidewalk and spoke thickly through her fog. "What for, Bloody?"

"You're covered in blood, we're in front of a cemetery, and this is New Orleans." Bloody hedged as she subtly backed away. "Vampires!"

Madeleine held Peaches by the arm, steadying the rocking boat as best she could. She reached for Bloody in the hopes of patting her way to a quick compromise, but Bloody budged not at all.

Peaches' face dripped blood down to her shirt collar, and her words were breathless grunts. "Look, I'm covered in blood, and I feel like the undead. No worries for you. They'd come after the easy meal, and that's me."

The logic took hold, and Bloody grasped Peaches' other arm, pulling her in a brisk, confident walk alongside the burial ground. Madeleine giggled when she heard the whooshing gasp emerge from Bloody. They had reached the final fencepost of the graveyard.

A juke joint beckoned. At the doorway, a dirty, black dog lapped from an overturned Frisbee brimming with beer. He delicately nosed the air as the girls passed, and pushed his head into Peaches' palm, licking her hand clean.

Bloody whispered in Peaches' ear. "Do you think he's a vampire?"

Peaches tried to move past the canine panting beside her. "No, Bloody. He's a dog."

The dog's owner, an old leather-vested greaser, looked at the opening on Peaches' head. "Who won the fight, sister?"

"I don't know, bro'. I left the other one on the ground." Peaches' smirk turned to a wince as her face wound shifted with her moving mouth.

Madeleine led her towards the restroom, leaving her there.

Peaches stood in front of the sink and mirror, wet down the toilet paper and sopped up the blood. Her eyes, sunken and shadowed, glowed green.

A tall, porcelain girl entered the tight space, laughing loudly. She wore a long, leopard coat and was dressed in the vivid drama of a bunged movie star. She stumbled towards Peaches, slurring through a wicked, red-white smile. "Hey there, tiger. Say, y'know you're bleeding?"

Peaches watched the girl's pale fingers stretch towards her and stroke her long, black fingernails gently across her brow. Peaches quickly seized the woman's hand and brought it under the flowing tap, cleansing the blood flecks from her fingertips.

The girl's eyes stayed solidly on Peaches, piercing through her like a spindle. Peaches pushed their joined hands out of the water and into a joined fist, tight like the secret handshake of blood sisters. The phantasmal girl grinned, then retreated back through the door, where a slight hubbub ensued.

"Cool hair!" said a waiting girl as the phantasm slid past. "Hey, you bit me!"

Peaches jumped to lock the bathroom door, doffed her skirt, pulled on her warm hoodie, then leapt through the short hallway back to the booth, her heart still beating from the close call. Bloody yanked at Peaches' sleeve; "Did you see that girl bite the other one? I bet you, for sure, she is a…"

Peaches already knew. "Shut up, Bloody."

Madeleine interjected with a smooth subject change, her favored weapon in most social situations. "What's your real name, Bloody?"

"You don't know, Bean?" Bloody stirred her drink with a pinky finger, feigning nonchalance.

"C'mon, Bloody." Peaches sipped from the cider, drenching her internal self with cold sweetness.

"What about you, Peaches?" Bloody countered.

"It's the name on my birth certificate, Bloody."

Madeleine sat back in astonishment, "Really? It's Peaches?"

"Mama had a rough day. C'mon, what's yours, dearest Bloody?"

Bloody remained as quiet as a jailed capo, downed her drink and lit a smoke, stalling for time. Finally, she sighed. "Look, someone told my parents it was a popular name in English-speaking countries."

Peaches sputtered with laughter, then grasped the tabletop with both hands to keep from falling out of the booth. "Good Lord, someone lied!"

Bloody glared ferociously at her friends.

They walked to an outdoor café and drank café au lait in broad cups. They gorged themselves on hot beignets, the French doughnut of wet bread dropped in sizzling fat to puff up and be powdered with hot confectioner's sugar like a Creole courtesan. At midnight they tossed money on the table before heading through the city square to the trolley tracks. Youthful tap dancers, card players, and aged psychics worked the mostly tourist crowd. They had to drag Madeleine away from the musicians, who raised rent money and fed their habits with the coins and bills she dropped into the cups in front of them.

Back in the truck, Madeleine took the wheel. Bloody curled up like a cat in the far passenger seat. Peaches again tucked herself in between the pair. Through the foggy haze, they saw rain clouds overtake the city's sky. Bloody murmured sleepily as she arranged her tired body against the door. "New Orleans is an ashtray of rainbow-colored cigarettes."

Peaches laughed and thought there might be more to say. "I think these folks are just like their jambalaya."

It took nearly seven hours and stops at three state borders to get back home, but Madeleine handled driving duty like a professional trucker. She grew tired only when the truck finally shot down one of the many hub highways that curved through Atlanta. The panoramic view of the sovereign city's skyline hit them like a jolt. By that time, all three were already cracked on coffee bought at various breakfast franchises, each cup the liquid equal of a half-bottle of gas station speed. They ended the trip by bouncing the truck over the curb into Gram's drive. This truck was made for such things.

Gram waited on the porch, Beau beside her. The old lady smelled sin on their breath as they spoke lies about a school retreat and the serenity of an ersatz shore of the supposed site on a North Georgia lake. Gram fingered the torn slit near Peaches' hairline.

"I ran into a tree branch last night when we were on a meditative walk in the woods."

Madeleine stopped the interrogation by kissing Gram goodnight. The two other girls did the same, and upstairs they fled.

Peaches left the lights in her room off and they lit candles instead. Bloody fell on the green bed and was asleep before she took another breath. Peaches yanked memories of the day out of her pockets, and then reached under her bed to pull out her father's album. She flipped to the first blank page and tucked it inside the otherwise ordinary throwaways that her own participation made into souvenirs. Madeleine scooted to the end of the bed to rest on her elbows, looking down at the album illuminated by the candlelight. Peaches tried to close it, but Madeleine tucked a finger between the final pages and flipped it back open. Madeleine finally closed the album and climbed into bed. Peaches shoved the book back into its hiding place, then blew out the candles. The room clicked to pitch-black.

It was late when Gram slipped into Peaches' bedroom with a penlight to pull out the scrapbook. "New Orleans," she whispered as she saw the souvenirs.

She closed the book and pushed it back under the bed, then saw Madeleine awake and grinning through the dark. Gram walked to the closet for another blanket and covered the girl, holding a finger to her lips as she tucked her in. Madeleine smiled and blinked one eye in a conspiratorial wink. "Goodnight…Bean," said Gram.

Going down the stairs, Peaches' grandmother decided once again to let that spigot drip slowly against the coming ice of this night. Climbing into bed, she prayed to God for Peaches' protection, following with a prayer to the Virgin Mary that the girl might also live free. She repeated her keenly felt words on behalf of the other two girls and fell asleep. Beau snored from the foot of her bed and dreamed of his own ghosts.

Sun Shade: Pale

Every year, summer hit Atlanta like a tomahawk, and the tree-lined city struggled to cool itself with only random success. The closest coast was hours to the east, towards the islands where plantation owners had once left slaves alone and in charge for entire seasons while they partied in cooler climes. Now, to ensure its citizens' survival, Atlanta had become an oasis of air conditioning and swimming pools. Though moderate weather ruled much of the year, true summer heat usually came with a fury after Independence Day, when tens of thousands of visitors and locals marked the day chasing each other down Peachtree Street shortly after dawn, from deep in Buckhead to a point past Piedmont Park. Onlookers crowded the restaurants, churches, and greenspace along the route of the amiable foot race.

Summer sometimes brought a paralyzing drought upon the city. Trees curled and plants baked beneath the yellow sun. The air turned amber. Even when there was rain, Atlanta's bounty was less than its due. Man had erected fierce heat domes over the city, the creations of asphalt and concrete, smog and pollution, sliding the thunderheads and water to other sections of town.

Sometimes the storms broke through the domes of air and brought the city to its knees, toppling trees and power lines and flooding the streets. At other times, there was only a brief spattering of such sweet likkour across the parched landscape. Peaches thought summer's gentle rain was the best kind, a warm and sloppy kiss from the heavens. Waking up to it washed old nightmares away. The world turned green in the gray haze of raindrops stretching from sky to ground.

After one such August day, Peaches dragged Gram to yet another new experience: a free nighttime show in a downtown park. The plaza had been built over abandoned acreage, bricked anew and spread with trees, statues, and dancing fountains, then tainted one fearsome night. Nails crammed in a packed pipe exploded, eternally separating a mother's body from her soul, the surprise gift of a madman named for the jolliest of reindeers. His previous contributions to the universal exchange of ideas had consisted of violent blasts vented upon citizens of surrounding states. Why, Peaches wondered, did he not simply turn his anger on himself?

This night, the scene loomed improbably delightful. The city stood on display from midtown to downtown, and commercial monoliths rose impressively across the horizon. In the park itself, corporate Atlanta appeared as a covert sponsor, its presence rather like a snack machine in church. Yet Peaches still thought of the show as special, different, and good. Through the chatter at beer tents and the cries of vendors, music played across the park, a god-like noise, violent and soothing, brilliant and mournful both.

Inebriated kids and smashed adults, careless crackers dressed up and dressed down, black-eyed, insolent teens, and normatives of all ages and sizes applied their minds to the deafening unsilence, braced by the surrounding skyline.

Gram marveled at the night's depth and listened to the city's heartbeat. It brought a tear to her eye, recalling a time long gone of moonlit nights, convertibles, and drive-in restaurants, before city life dried up and moved to the suburbs.

It was enough to see the verve again for a moment, because it meant her old city could rise again. For a flicker in time, Atlanta, no longer ashamed, planted new life proudly with seeds born from flashing music. A city all dressed up, steepling and shining across the blue-black night. "Peaches, my dear, I think mine is the generation that marks the end. Y'all seem to be coming up with a replacement."

Peaches took her grandmother's hand and pulled her towards the stage, where Madeleine and Bloody stood near the speakers. It was Madeleine's favorite spot, the closeness letting the music seal itself within her skull, so she could take the band home in her head and keep them overnight as part of her dreams. She had borrowed this band before, the night when Peaches took a face-damaging tumble. That was right before Gram began to drench the town in paint and pictures.

The concert was over all too soon and Peaches thought that was too bad. The glass of the skyscrapers had not yet shattered, and no riots had broken out.

To Gram's house a mile of city blocks north, the four of them proceeded. Meanwhile, herds of listeners packed the underground rail, and double and triple lines of cars probed at the streets for the highways home.

Somewhere in the middle of the city, Peaches picked up a small rock and put it in her pocket. Gram laughed at her granddaughter's taking a little chunk of pavement. Peaches shrugged it off. That's what her city was made of.

Some Kind of Understanding

The wanderers saw New York, as everyone must. They heard music there, as they did everywhere. And Peaches found differences that became even deeper in her return-flight dreams.

Her fall was hard and deep this time into the dream world, first into a packed stadium brimming over like an old lady's jar of hard candy. A nightmare that could only be born in New York.

A confusing sport played itself out on the field below, with a horde of folk running through long, mean poles and fiery netting. Giant screens around the stadium blew the audience up to monster-sized proportions with dot-like pixels, a painting in pointillism. The camera panned a brittle-faced woman holding her child in the air. She cheered in celebration as nearby faces screamed and shook. The players on the field heard the crowd's roar and revved up their violence, tossing wet things into the stands that were batted and bounced around. The crowd's hungry exhilaration somehow felt wrong to Peaches, pronged with something bestial and uncivilized. She felt empathy for the underdog, though she still couldn't figure out who the underdog was.

Suddenly, a flicker of horror burbled as an evil chapter from the real intruded: a game of rope, blood, and death. Peaches could join in, watch, or run away; it was now close enough for her to touch and see. She stood at her seat, and the spotlight shone on her as the invisible dream master muted the crowd. Peaches' voice echoed through the stadium like a priestess of old Rome. "What kind of people are y'all?"

The giant screens around the stadium flipped to capital letters, as high and wide as the screen itself. The crowd chanted the prompted cheer in unison. "YOUR PEOPLE! YOUR PEOPLE! YOUR PEOPLE!"

Rows above Peaches, a little girl on her daddy's shoulders clutched a rubber toy figurine, then threw it at Peaches' head. It spiraled through the air, and Peaches ducked as she caught it: a doll-sized plastic Jesus. Her hands filled with the blood that poured from open wounds on the doll's wrists, palms, ankles, and feet. An impossible amount of blood.

Below her on the field, the only human not wearing a mask stared at her. Peaches tried to speak, to tell him it was beyond her control and outside her understanding. Before she could take another breath, the Jesus doll exploded like a high-speed collision, shredding Peaches' face like a bomb-rigged Halloween mask.

Peaches awoke. Terrified, she tried to shake off the dream. She spent the rest of the flight scribbling messy poetry to sound out the tangles in her head. The poetry traced her bloodline, all of the dead and wounded that had fallen during her lifetime. New South. Old South. The child Brother, stunted at the edge of manhood. Why? A woman broken at the cusp, her son's future erased; her daughter's past replaced. Something from a prophecy?

Her genealogy had no real past. No proof that she possessed the old in any part. No gun from a Klan uncle. Very little mention of the old war, except a stunted dog bearing the name of a dead general.

211

On the way home from the airport, a pouring rain fell and Peaches knew that she was marked by the ancient stain. Her birth, her subtle accent, and her coloring were her insignia before the world.

As the three girls moved from the underground to walk the streets towards Gram's house, Peaches took Madeleine and Bloody aside to deliver to them something she wanted desperately for herself. Beneath the shadows of skyscrapers, Peaches pulled leaves from dogwood trees and poured droplets on herself and each of her friends. "Look, from now on, let's go forth and be who we are, not who we were."

Bloody remained solemn, as if Peaches' words were an oath. Madeleine pulled away from the sidewalk to spin in circles on the soaking, green grass. Then Bloody grabbed Peaches' hand, and they joined Madeleine, twirling each other around in a spinning circle. They were the city's silver daughters, rising while cold ashes and rain blew down from the silver-gray sky, and only they understood why.

The Roar of Twilight

The school year was ending, and summertime joy lingered teased just out of view. The usual antipathy that shadowed the students of Peerless lightened during the last sweet, warm weeks of school. Even when the spring-summer clouds poured down, it was merely a vigorous dewing, drawing silver and aqua halos wetly around all living things. The last days sounded out bright and ripe. The sun rose. Pollen fell.

Every year the school took leave from its structured syllabi to celebrate the patron of its founding order, as if he had been a great prince, not a mere priest. The Protestant students were distracted by the name of the saint: fashion plus perfume equals sainthood? Oh, Lord, these Catholics! The almost-holiday began with Mass, followed by a field day. The entire student body streamed into the sunshine, glowing like glistening beanpoles at day's first light. Boys and girls milled about with easy familiarity as they amused themselves with sports and food until early afternoon. Then a stage was set up on a grassy knoll of green space at the edge of campus. A few makeshift bands played short sets of noisy sound to a crowd of friends, before Madeleine, the day's headliner, took to the stage.

Since her experiences elsewhere, Madeleine was a girl on fire, a she-dragon molting her old skin. Each breath she took was a freedom-song loud enough to hear, and Peaches and Bloody were all ears. They had always loved her, but now she was becoming great before their eyes.

As her status grew, her mother's patience had lessened. Mrs. Bennett tightened the reins, stalking Madeleine like a phantom. Her mother forbade her, punished her, and came close to beating her, anything to keep her off the stage. Madeleine stood sturdy and strong, determined to have one last stand.

On this saint's day, students milled close to hear one of their own. Lean living bodies filled the lawn, and Peaches and Bloody found a vantage spot front and center. They were joined by Gram, whose invitation to the performance came from the artist herself. The drummer, a boy with chocolate hair and cocoa eyes, joined Madeleine's ephedrine ditty midway through. She plucked. He kicked. Together they ran full speed through the last verse. The crowd roared.

"Hey, y'all, thanks for coming by," Madeleine said. "How's the life, huh?" More roar.

She called a boy up on stage, who watched the crowd below him with wide, worried eyes. He brought a harmonica to his lips, sounding the intro. Drum and cymbals followed. Mad Bean's strings and throat fused. The guitarist bled notes over them. The drum men slid through the verses like heavy rain rolling off a roof. The audience learned the new song and pounded it back at Madeleine's beckoning. As the band lopped back through the final chorus, the blonde teen on electric guitar got a verse of his own for his fingers to sing.

Afterwards, when the boy with the harmonica had fled back into the crowd, Madeleine and her band flew through the next few songs without pause, flipping them to the crowd like a blackjack dealer with a charity of aces. Madeleine was careful to avoid pop songs in her playlist. She made the crowd's blood move fast and their appendages faster.

A girl violinist ascended. The crowd leapt again to its feet as a downhome tune echoed from the makeshift band. Madeleine played like the rest of her life was just a delusion. She bounced around stage like a boxed-in jumping bean. Madeleine was Elvis with a Dolly twist, God with Mary's eyes, a fired stone. She ate the noise she made as if there was a long journey ahead, and she might get hungry on the way.

Like their Moms and Dads years before when rock and roll was young, they danced and sang. When the song ended, the entire school—teachers, students, presbyters and ancient sages—filled the square, overflowing to the campus boundary, where ordinary citizens stood transfixed in their passing by.

The encore was her charisma made visible, and Madeleine swallowed her audience's energy whole, returning it tenfold.

A funny-faced boy with a trumpet climbed on stage. Jangly notes suddenly sprang from Madeleine's guitar. The kid on trumpet battled for control, breaking loudly through the old skat song. Madeleine gambled and pulled her voice low, darkening the melody as if haints were in the audience and she was paid to show them a party. It was her finale, and when it ended, all the instruments stopped. It was as if every guitar string broke, the skins of the drum collapsed, and there was no air left on which to sound the horn.

Madeleine's three favorite followers toasted her with sunlit green glasses holding eight ounces of carbonated, sugary dreams. Everything broke open as Madeleine squeezed a final, sweet-sour note to the dripping end. The crowd took a gasping breath, refilling dry, empty lungs in unison, as the music stopped and the lights went out in Georgia. Madeleine coolly dropped off the stage, and the people grasped at and touched her like Evita.

The show was over, but the day's celebration was not yet done. At Gram's bidding, some of the audience made its way to her house for an evening barbecue. Word of mouth had her yard packed by twilight with a beautiful collision of student strangers who chatted as friends. Pink slabs of pork blackened on the grill.

They carried massive amounts of potato salad and devilled eggs out to the picnic tables and found a place on the porch where Madeleine's native clique had staked a place with their boyfriends, staring at Madeleine as if she were a three-carat diamond found in a flower bed.

A girl with a skullcap of blackish roots hidden beneath Miss Piggy golden locks opened her large, round mouth to pronounce: "I don't think the 'I Have A Dream' speech is really relevant anymore. Children play together now. It's not like it was."

Peaches shook her head. "Look at your life. Where is this dream taking place?"

"It's happening out there." A hand languished in the air, waving at the city around them.

"Just not in your world," Peaches replied.

The girl tossed her hair, gleaming like a doll under glass. "Honestly, Peaches, you're a waste of a good education."

"Maybe we both are."

Madeleine listened. "Why can't y'all just get along? You're not so different. Each of you is more yourself because of the other."

Peaches and her nemesis were momentarily unified in horror. Gram stuck her head out the screen door. "Peaches, this is not what I've taught you." She was a bit spent from chaperoning the young crew.

Peaches stared at her shoes. "No, ma'am, it's not." She tried to push past Gram into the house, but Madeleine's fingers caught hold of her shoulder. Peaches sighed and faced her foe, sticking out her hand as she fitted a congenial smile upon her face. "Look, girl, cheers to you and yours."

With a nudge from Madeleine, the adversary smiled and shook Peaches' outstretched hand. Gram stepped back into the kitchen with a smile.

Coals turned to ash and a round moon lifted high. The sated crowd departed for home. Madeleine stood outside, watching her disciples leave. Soon enough, Bloody and Peaches joined her as Gram came from the kitchen. They pulled together on the porch in a perfectly tied knot.

"Today was the best day I've ever had," Madeleine told them, her voice low, straining to explain. "Now I'm scared to go home."

She turned her back to lean over the porch railing. Her words came out slow. It was as if for the first time since childhood, Madeleine was now comfortable with her country girl drawl. "I remember being young and falling, and how much it hurt to leave skin behind on the pavement." Madeleine touched her elbows, and felt the healed-over contusion of furrowed skin. She continued, "I remember a camping trip when I was little, and getting lost in the woods. I was hungry, and I wanted a hamburger so bad that I saw white tile and black counters in the trees. It got dark, and I was still lost."

"We're a mutt race," she concluded. "There hasn't been a pure lineage since the apes lost their edge. And I'm just white-gold trash trained to think."

She stopped speaking. Then: "Gram, will you please play with me?"

Peaches was on her feet in a flash, passing through the screen door. "Gram, I'll get your violin!"

Gram stuttered a futile refusal. "I haven't played in decades, girls. Since before your mothers were born. These strings will probably snap."

Madeleine knelt in front of the rocker. "I bet it missed you, Gram. And I bet you missed it."

Peaches returned with the old case, and from inside emerged an even older violin.

Gram took the violin like an infant, blowing away the dust as she tested the strings. She held the bow high like a magic wand, stretching her fingers to nimble up the old joints. The three girls sat quietly, waiting until she was ready. They held their breath when the bow touched down, scraping sweetness from the dry strings, like one flower blooming, then another, and another.

Gram was inside it, her eyes unseeing as the girls trembled from her light touch. She played like she had found a love lost for decades. Her cigarette burned in the ashtray unnoticed. A slow orange river of fire crawled up the thin paper in waves as the smoke twisted and curled, rising towards a jamboree of clouds in the sky.

Madeleine locked her fingers around her guitar and followed Gram's lead. They moved through the music together, in a dance. The beauty grew, and it seemed the whole city watched the little house and listened.

Peaches clicked her camera in photo after photo, unnoticed by the players who slowed as the song ended, wistful about leaving it behind. The porch turned quiet, except for a chorus of birds calling to each other, their din rippling through the air like applause. Gram and Madeleine each stared off into space, mystified. Gram's feelings knotted. Tears squeezed through clouded eyes as she wept for the lost years, for the blessed privilege of being a wife and mother, and the loss of girlhood dreams. Peaches wondered what her grandmother might have turned out to be in a world that really let her play.

Madeleine reached out and touched Gram's shoulder. The woman was calm and together. Gram tucked the violin back on her shoulder and began to fiddle like a house on fire. The girls clapped and whistled. The old lady burned the bow back and forth with the spirit of a hundred years. Madeleine matched Gram's grin, slipping quickly into a crude song full of naughty innuendo, like Cupid stealing music from the devil's collection.

When it was over, Madeleine packed up her things solemnly and hugged each of her friends close. Silence announced the night hour, and the four marched towards the British sedan known as mother's. Bloody jumped in the front seat, hitching a ride to the train station up the street, while Gram and Peaches stood on the pavement under the curving streetlights.

Madeleine cranked the starter, and music shot from the speakers. With uncommon patience, she twisted knobs until she found a track that really mattered. From her place in the driver's seat, Madeleine smiled at Peaches and Gram, then turned to the task at hand of edging the car backwards into the street.

Madeleine shifted gears to point the car east towards Peachtree Street. Two girls' hands rose from the sunroof to wave goodbye as brake lights flickered, then disappeared. Gram turned to head back inside, where a mountain range of dirty dishes awaited. Peaches didn't move. Her attention was caught by the funny, hypercolor flash of the license plate in the streetlight. Hot red flashed across her vision, as purple skimmed through the surface of her mind. She heard tires scream and brakes clamp down.

Madeleine's car returned to full view, skidding and sliding, a hurtling yellow cab pushing it in a violent boomerang, back to where it started out. The car's brake lights screamed scarlet, and the night broke open in awful song. Peaches lifted her arm and reached to halt the world's turning. Her hand hung limply in the air, impotent. Metal punched and glass exploded, singing together sorrowfully as Madeleine's car flipped and rolled along the street in front of Gram's house.

From the cab, a bear of a man flew through the cab's windshield, to bump and collide with the pavement. Yards from where Gram and Peaches stood, he lay prone and violently vomited out the remains of his last several hours, spraying a mist of bile and blood.

Peaches stood still in the cool night air, trying to forget the sight of the crumpled car until she found herself still there. The wreckage was a metal egg that cradled and trapped what it contained. Peaches looked inside at the fragile human bodies, and her mind blinked black, trying to hide the awful vision.

She sprawled herself across the hood as a sparkling layer of snowy glass crunched beneath her, then shoved her arm through an opening in the crinkled windshield and grasped for her friends. Bloody moaned when Peaches touched skin that was slick, ripped, and warm. With her other hand, Peaches reached for Madeleine, but the girl's fingers were pliable and rubbery. Peaches squeezed them, hoping the blood would touch brain and lungs and the girl's chest would move again.

Amid the wailing of sirens that broke the night, a giant machine came to cut the girls out of the mangled metal. Peaches held Bloody's hand as the rescue workers lashed the unconscious girl tightly to a stretcher. Nearby, a sheet covered the body of a Southern belle, dead on Southern ground.

Police told the cab driver he was going to jail. The man rubbed his beer-soaked head and began to cry, wiping his face with a wrinkled shirt stained with blood. Peaches hurtled like a savage past the two police officers to try and tidal-wave the man. She slapped his face with a backhand fist, and his head whipped back as she tackled him to the ground. She slammed his head again and again against the pavement.

It was a phantasm, that fight. It didn't happen. Peaches only played with that in her head later that night, waiting with Gram for word of Bloody at the downtown hospital famous for its attention to wrecked bones and gunshot wounds. In her attempt, she had made it past the police officers, but the man was already safe in the back seat of a squad car. Peaches slapped her fists against the window, until the cops pulled her back. Peaches spit at the window. The man's eyes met hers through wet glass. She wanted him to spit back, but he broke down instead, and greasy tears washed some of the blood from his face.

The police car pulled away, and Gram brought Peaches inside. They made coffee for the remaining crew cleaning the street. It wasn't until everyone had left that Gram pulled Peaches to the front porch. Together, they smashed Gram's violin on the railing Madeleine had held as she spoke her final piece. The strings severed and the wood shattered, making a noise that mimed the accident an hour before. Then feet stomped the pieces of the broken violin. Then grandchild and grandmother broke down and wept at the loss of one of their own.

G'bye

The morning began wet and cold. Before the altar, a closed casket concealed the child. No stories were told, just ancient songs and a brief sermon, a somber celebration of a vibrant life.

Gram's white Cadillac flicked on its headlights to join the procession of dark cars trailing the black hearse. At the cemetery the mahogany treasure chest was offloaded from the hearse by eight boys from Peerless. All of their faces showed the first deep pain of their fresh lives as they strove to bring their infinitely cool Madeleine to the broken earth that lay at the edge of the green canopy shielding her family from a winter sun.

Peaches stood behind the seated mourners, Gram at her right and Bloody on her left. Bloody held tightly onto Peaches. She was still weak and broken from the wreck that took her friend away. Peaches stared at the glistening wood casket, thinking that for all that Madeleine was, the beautiful wood and brass didn't suffice.

Fake turf draped the pile of red clay. Flowers from friends lay around the coffin that hung cradled over the hole on a simple pulley. A priest in white began the farewell ritual of words and water as the crowd wept, "May the angels greet you…." Peaches still couldn't feel Madeleine in any of it.

She focused on a delicate white butterfly that landed on a rainbow of starched pom-pom flowers. Tears plunked down her face as the butterfly's wings fluttered above the blooms. When the carved, wooden box began its descent, the butterfly flitted in revelry above it, dancing like a tiny tongue of white-hot flame. The coffin creaked until it thudded into place, and the first chunk of red soil rained down upon it.

The tiny ghost dancer swooped low, and a few in the audience gasped as it narrowly avoided the clods of shoveled clay. It flew higher, flittering on the breeze of relief. The clay fell. The butterfly danced. With the final shovelful, the butterfly soared over the heads of the crowd. It hovered over Peaches, Bloody, and Gram, then followed a zigzag path towards the sky.

Gram's eyes were bright as they walked towards the car. "I'd be proud if my life had just one day like that last one she had."

For a moment, memory brought a beautiful bit of lovely. The eye of a petulant god blinked shut.

The Last Reckoning

Beau was next. As his little body was laid to rest in the yard beneath the old oak tree, Peaches wondered what kind of bully God was, to take a poor, crippled dog from the people who loved and cared for him.

Gram and Peaches were now alone in the big house, except for the great silence that had taken over every room. The stereo remained off, and even the ghosts stayed out of sight. Peaches felt pushed down. What was inherently Gram became muted and numb. Both lived each day in quiet fear, as if an army waited at the city gates to burn and bludgeon all the citizens left standing.

On Juneteenth's eve, Peaches sat on the porch, pretending to plan an overseas journey before she started college in the fall. Instead, she settled for simply staring at the place where Madeleine had breathed her last. Gram peddled her peanuts and tomatoes, crossing herself every time she stepped over the sacred spot where the young soul had been stolen away.

This night, Peaches started as her grandmother stumbled and folded like a napkin, collapsing in the gutter beside the car of a man holding an outstretched dollar through his open window. Peaches leapt from the porch as the man jumped from the driver's seat and scooped Gram into his arms. Peaches raced across the yard towards her grandmother, while people leapt from their cars with cell phones to their ears, calling for help.

Tree branches bent and loose soil scattered as a helicopter descended a few minutes later in the big side yard. It soon rose, taking away a stretcher holding Gram, with Peaches beside her. At the hospital, Gram's eyes opened during the last rites. "Fix me up, Father. Enough so I can die at home," she told the priest, who told the doctors.

Peaches had once thought her grandmother could never leave her. Now, Gram returned to lie in bed next to her husband's slight impression, which still glowed at its edges like the cracks in the doorway to heaven. Her face was as pale as the moon, and her hair was loose and flowing like a young girl's. Peaches knew the light that came from somewhere would soon cut Gram's soul loose from her body.

When the city had turned dark and somewhat quiet, Peaches, acting on orders, drove the Cadillac and her grandmother through town. Gram, bundled up in the backseat, poked her in the shoulder as they passed the Krispy Kreme. Two minutes later, Peaches watched worriedly as Gram sipped a cup of sweet, creamed coffee. "Are you sure this is good for you, Gram?"

Gram downed a slug as she swallowed the last bite of a glob of sugary dough. She relished the simple pleasure, along with the flickering thought that there would be no coroner in her future. "I need the kick, Peaches. Otherwise, I'll never get the job done."

On the wall bridging the school property, near the spot where Madeleine had often charmed the world, Gram painted a miniature of the little singer's last show. Peaches had to hold her grandmother up, supporting the frail body and bracing her arm as it gently moved the paintbrush across the rough surface. Gram worked turtle-slow, fearing if she stopped she might not be able to start again.

Gram drew and colored everything she remembered, from bouncing teen socialites to neckties in the office buildings. She painted in herself, and Peaches, and Bloody, and even Beau. She threw in heroes from around the way, sons and daughters of the past. She drew roads that became highways, around train tracks that became an airport. Gram painted a theatre that had burned, next to a hotel that had burned, inside a city that had burned—all of them in fact. Finally, she painted a phoenix rising from their ashes.

When Gram finished, it was only because there was no more space. The two stood back to look, and found it good. Across the bottom, Gram signed both of her last names: her father's and her husband's . It was her life's logo.

When they returned home, the old soul and her successor sat on the front porch staring at their city. Peaches turned to Gram to speak her thoughts, but her mouth quickly shut closed. Her grandmother sat gleaming, star-lit, her eyes locked on the moving sky.

Gram reached out to lightly chuck Peaches under the chin, the beads of a rosary hanging from her fingers. "I read your scrapbook, Peaches. I know you went to all those places."

Peaches' stomach rolled. "I'm sorry for deceiving you, Gram."

Gram took her granddaughter's young hands and squeezed them with her own, warming them with the heat of a near century. "Peaches, I know you had such a time."

Something inside Peaches cracked like an iceberg. "Such a time, Gram."

Gram eyed her granddaughter. She smiled at her Cracker Jack prize. "I want you to take my ashes around the world. Keep some here in Atlanta, but I want the rest to go everywhere you think I might have gone. There's money…."

Peaches split in half. One side tilted in a grin, while the other fought back a frown and opened up a waterfall of tears. "Gram…."

Gram leapt quickly into her next request. "Another thing, Peaches. I want you to feel free to sell this house."

Peaches walked to the railing, staring out into the darkness. She tried to imagine an office building atop this place. "Sell? That's different than everything you've ever told me."

"What I've said, Peaches, is only my telling." Gram sighed.

Peaches stumbled inside the house and returned with a book of matches. She struck one, holding the lick of fire out to her grandmother. "Gram, I'll douse the place with gasoline right now if you want. But you have to set the fire."

Gram leaned forward and blew the flame out with one quick birthday breath. "Your choice, Peaches."

Peaches smiled. "Yes ma'am. Now it is."

Gram had her own smile as she sat back, one arm reaching down to pet now-gone Beau. She took her hand back. The house phones rang, a triplet of bells. The stern, abrupt tone of an old rotary dial hanging on the kitchen wall. The thin trilling of the answering machine in the den. The mouse-ding of the cordless phone that lay now in Peaches' lap. They had been a trinity of lifelines, in case her grandmother ever needed the world's help again.

Gram tilted her head upwards, as if she could read the caller's name on a display in the swollen clouds. "Answer it, Peaches, dear."

Peaches plunked her finger clumsily on the talk button. "Hey, Mama."

From the miles north, a voice from the past: "Peaches, sweetie. How is your Gram?"

Peaches handed the phone over to Gram, who patted her granddaughter's hand, as she arced her voice over the miles to stroke her daughter. "Honey, it's so good to hear from you."

At Gram's right side, Peaches heard her mother ask again the question.

Gram answered: "Honey, things are changing around here."

Peaches heard the tears in her mother's voice as she offered apologies for all the things she hadn't done. Gram stopped her. "My sweet daughter, the past doesn't matter as much as what you choose to do now. I love you, honey."

It was altogether too much for Peaches, the fast approaching end of her grandmother and the ever-present lack of her mother. She refused the phone. Gram then spoke a final goodbye to her daughter from across phone lines. "I'll tell Peaches to come see you. Take care of yourself, daughter."

The voice in Charleston was lost again as Gram severed their connection. Gram stared until Peaches looked up to meet her gaze.

"I failed at some things, Peaches. You still need to learn to make biscuits and fried chicken."

Peaches' face broke into a sharp smile. "I know how to make biscuits and fried chicken, Gram. I watched."

Gram raised an eyebrow sternly as she straightened in her seat. "You help your mother, Peaches."

Her light was disappearing like the sun at dusk. "And you live your life as if you learned from our mistakes, mine and your mother's. Paint your city, sing your song, Peaches. Roar so loud that all the ghosts will hear."

Peaches knelt at her feet, as if the old woman spoke words that were God's. "I love you, Gram, for everything."

The sky clouded. Rain began. Gram's face relaxed. Darkness crowded the porch, closing in on the old lady whose lips curved into a final, gentle smile. She slumped in the rocking chair, her lips painted rose, her dress ironed and straight, and her hair gleaming silver in the dark night. Crickets chirped, the highway hummed, and Atlanta was a blur of red and yellow light against black, black sky.

Much later, Peaches struggled to decide whom to call. She went into the house, wiping tearful wetness on the wall of the hallway she held on to, unable to stand upright for long. She made it to Gram's kitchen, then kept walking out the screen door and off the back porch, towards the shed far in the back of the yard.

On dusty shelves, Peaches found a baker's dozen of baby rosebushes. She loaded up a red wagon, adding a shovel and a bag of black topsoil, before pulling her load around to the front of the house. Peaches dug deep into wet clay, ripping holes along the front fence and then tussling the runtling flower bushes into the sodden ground. Each planting, every new cut into the wet dirt felt like thuggery to her, but she pierced the seamless patches of green grass without pause.

By the time Peaches finished, thirteen baby bushes sat in the ground, dripping from the rain.

The Wake

When Peaches awoke on the porch hours later, the world was dim and dew-soaked. A truck passed by on the street, tooting its horn in morning greeting. Birds chirped a dawn chant to their creator. Peaches stole a cigarette from her grandmother's pack. The old woman's eyes lay open to witness the girl's sin. Peaches closed them and found the match Gram had defiantly blown out, burnt carbon topping paper-thin wood. She tossed it on the ground, as if daring it now to light. It didn't, and Peaches took a seat at the top of the steps to smoke the American tobacco, thinking she was in a tabloid photograph of a front-porch death she had somehow found herself in.

Peaches realized it was Sunday morning: the few cars that passed held passengers dressed in churchly fashion. She went inside to peel off her muddy clothes. The shower, usually comforting, was unfamiliar. She watched caked clay run in red stripes down towards the drain. When the stripes turned clear, she knew she was clean.

Peaches dressed herself in dark blue, her version of black. She went downstairs to Gram's kitchen and brewed a pot of coffee to wake her brain. As it trickled and dripped, Peaches stood before the massive stove, saying prayers that her genes were sufficient to the task. There was a standing invitation to the masses of people for Sunday breakfast, no matter who cooked.

Soon, the old stovetop steamed with food, and Peaches tasted what she had made. She found her biscuits were white and fluffy, her bacon balanced, and her grits smooth and creamy. Smells of butter and grease filled the kitchen, and it was as sweet to her as wild honeysuckle.

Kahlil, now a rising sophomore at Profitt, arrived to help with breakfast. The sight of his face at the back door was a reminder to Peaches of what she had left out front. He came through the screen door, but didn't look at Peaches until he stood right in front of her. "Peaches, I'm sorry. I'm so sorry to tell you this, but I think your Gram is dead."

Peaches nodded, then shook her head slowly. She dropped it against his chest, staining his college shirt with her tears. He patted and smoothed her as she shook in his arms. She remembered old days and young ways, and thought history cycled in and out, that there were no new experiences, just different eyes.

Kahlil picked up the phone to make the call for Peaches. She went outside and sat next to her Gram, as the breakfast folk lined up to pay their respects. The funeral home hearse pulled into the drive behind Gram's Cadillac, and Peaches went inside to turn on the stereo as they carried Gram away. "Atlantaland" by Jerry Rose and His Roseland Crackers played from an old '78 recording as the transitory pallbearers lifted their burden and bore it down the sidewalk. The street characters saluted in their various fashions. Some of the women blew a kiss. The older men with hats tugged them free of their heads.

Peaches watched Gram's pallet roll away, her mind swimming through old thoughts. Kahlil nudged her, and she turned to stare at her friend with confused eyes. He touched her shoulder gently, the way he did that first night at the pool. "Are you all right, Peaches?"

233

Peaches' misery collided with the airy elation of the soft, morning sun. She stared at him, a lightning rod that had deflected the force of some of her life's worst blows. "How come you're always around when I lose a mother, Kahlil?"

He breathed in deeply, his own sadness filling his mouth and throat. He didn't answer, but took her inside and sat her down at the phone. Kahlil scrambled mountains of eggs, while Peaches called the local paper to read out stumbling words she hoped were appropriate for Gram's obituary. The voice on the other end of the phone smiled when told of Gram's avocations. He stopped her, and spoke in the lilt of a Southern boy grown old. "Miss, your grandmother was the mystery artist?"

Peaches attempted nonchalance as something like joy flowered inside her. "Yes sir, my Gram is the Atlanta Mystery History Artist."

The man put her on hold until an editor took the line. He passed along condolences, then sent a reporter to the house to take notes and beg photos of the urban murals. Noonday newswires shot word of the charming artist's death across the nation as a teaser for the following day's feature story. When the New York Post called later for quotes, Peaches nearly laughed out loud at what her grandmother had done.

By early afternoon, Peaches was spent, and slept through the day and night on Gram's bed. Kahlil spent the night on the sofa, flipping through television channels and dozing until the real estate agents, alerted to the possibility of prime property by the newspaper story, began knocking on the door shortly after dawn. He shooed them away. By noon, the incoming tide bore later-rising developers, hungry like vultures for square footage with potential.

When Peaches awoke, Kahlil told her of the visitors. She dialed a realtor, one from the Yellow Pages who had not casually dropped a card at the door. Peaches was still indecisive about the future of the house, but she knew this realtor's fresh sign in the yard was enough to divert the buzzards his way.

Across town, Bloody soaked her mother's neck and shirt collar with warm tears. She thought how terribly she would miss Madeleine and now Gram, but she missed Peaches most of all because she was still close by. Her heart hurt in wonder at how Peaches could take another heaping loss so soon.

Finished with the tears, she snagged car keys from her mother, and rolled down the main thoroughfare beneath the buildings that great businesses had built. Where her alma mater brushed up against the cityscape, Bloody suddenly saw Gram's last work. She yanked the emergency brake, nearly bursting to free herself from the seatbelt. She ran up and stared at the wall, her mouth agape at the last reckoning. She pressed her thumb by Gram's signature and imposed her print on the still-damp painting.

When she pulled in Gram's drive, the first thing she saw was the For Sale sign. Burning her roots to the ground, she thought.

Pausing in the car, Bloody opened a newspaper she had bought, flipped through the pages, and read the quotes from people who knew Gram from her peanut stand and her Sunday breakfasts. A number of local figures who never knew Gram spoke of her paintings as contributions to art and history; a few others derided them. An editor who had lamented the city's erosion of culture for years wrote a column that lay next to a color collage of Gram's midnight paintings. "We didn't recognize it as art, because we hadn't seen anything like it in so long."

For the moment at least, Gram, dead, was now playing the prophet, igniting an uproar of public discourse, the old white woman who painted commentaries across public and private property in the dead of night. She had raised silver flowers from a caked, muddy past and dared the city to encounter the beauty of the possible.

Bloody stared at the real-estate sign. She poured peanuts into the glass bottle of Atlanta juice, wishing for a shotgun. Then she tucked her thumb tightly across the bottle and shook it, removing her painted thumb to spew liquid and salt across the sign in a peanuty stew.

Kahlil answered the door and joined her on the front porch, letting Bloody weep for Gram and for Gram's house. Peaches had left an hour before on her bike, he said: beside herself, worn out, the skin around her eyes pulled tight after another spilling of tears.

Peaches had ridden quickly. She cut down a street that was the unspoken dividing line between gays and everyone else, bumping off the cracked sidewalk as untamed shrubbery and crazy cement forced her and the bicycle in and out of the street.

She came to the front of the Romanesque church next to Peerless. She wasn't privy to whether God was really inside, but she figured it wasn't an unlikely place for an omnipotent being like Him to be. A separate world of marble and stained glass, where the faint smell of incense mingled with the scent of warm beeswax.

The church felt sweet and cool as Peaches entered. She cautiously genuflected at the last pew, then walked up a side aisle, gazing at stained-glass windows hung above alcoves dedicated to saints, both famous and obscure.

She ducked into a side chapel, the marble walls a deep, jade green that highlighted an elaborate mosaic encrusted with sparkling gold in its center. Peaches had been in the chapel once before during school, when she went in search of Madeleine, whom she had found kneeling prayerfully in front of the icon. Madeleine had turned when she heard her friend approach. Peaches had apologized for interrupting another's spiritual dialogue. "Sorry, Bean."

Peaches remembered Madeleine smiling as if caught in mischief, then sitting back in the pew as Peaches joined her. She whispered even though they were the only ones there, "This is the chapel of St. Pelagia, Peaches. They say she was once a dancer who changed her life when a bishop preached about a dancer who created beauty but never created good."

Peaches teased her friend with an easy grin. "Is this like the adult section of the church, Bean?"

Madeleine rolled her eyes, and then continued her telling. "No, Peaches. Actually, Pelagia converted. She confessed her sins, and then began a new life outside Jerusalem as a hermit." Madeleine mused, thoughtful in her consideration of renamings. "There weren't too many female hermits back then."

"Yeah, like there are now!" Peaches cracked, poking at her friend.

"She wore men's clothes, so no one would bother her. A lot of people were surprised she was female when she died. That's one story anyway." Madeleine stood and pointed out a detail in the picture. "But look at this, what do you see? No dancers here."

Peaches joined her at the wall, and studied the corner of the mosaic. "It looks like a girl jumping off the roof into the ocean."

Madeleine's smile melted into a crooked smirk. "Pelagia of Antioch. A young girl thrown from the roof of her home for refusing to let pagan soldiers have their way with her."

Peaches beat Madeleine to her next point. "I'm guessing that the church likes the martyred virgin story better than the Greta Garbo one."

Madeleine nodded. "I like this mosaic, because it gives both stories a chance."

Now, overwrought with thoughts of Gram, Peaches sat in the same chapel, her eyes locked on the enchanting and pious woman emblazoned in blue, white, and gold. She rubbed her hand across the finish on the ornate, richly carved pew, then leaned to find a place on the velvet-padded kneeler. Peaches now knelt where someone she had loved had knelt before.

Suddenly, the church echoed with sound. The organist was opening his pipes to an etude in the gallery above and behind her. Finishing her prayers, Peaches walked to the gilt box for offerings, and dropped coins in the slot. She picked up a needle-thin stick and set it afire. She lit one votive candle for Madeleine and another for Gram. Then, she remembered and lit one for Beau. She watched the flame stick to the white wick as each votive candle erupted in a growing teardrop of hot red. Peaches donated more coins, lighting candles for her father, her mother, her brother, and one for both Bloody and Kahlil. The final candle was for anyone, anywhere who had no one to pray for them.

Peaches stood to leave, pondering a final prayer for courage or comfort, or at how to begin a successful search for that. The organist began to play an improvisation on an old hymn that Peaches recognized, though she cold not recall the words. It crept along her skin, then broke her heart, leaving inside something that glowed warmly, as if a new heart now grew. She sweated and shivered and felt beholden.

Leaving the dim alcove and the candles burning there, like bright little boats anchored in a dark port, she strode through the high-ceilinged arches of imported stone, breathing the scented air as if it were a plucked flower. She pushed open the heavy, arched doors leading to marble steps dropping down to the street, where tile ended the city sidewalk.

The world outside was green, beautiful, and bright. To Peaches, it was God. Each leaf on every tree reflected and absorbed the sunlight, turning almost translucent with a white shadow shine. The heat enveloped her. In front of her was Gram's final art wall, exactly as they had left it, and Peaches shivered again.

Now, Peaches was blown back into the present and knew what she must do. Her bike slipped on the slick stone as she whizzed away, down the streets of her newest mother, the one that poisoned her children with dirty air and water.

Peaches dropped her bike in the front yard of Gram's house, one wheel spinning in the air. Kahlil and

Bloody watched as she tore down the realtor's sign, now sticky from Bloody's spray. All three smiled boldly.

They sat together on the porch, eating handfuls of salty, cold boiled peanuts. Peaches tasted her grandmother in the soft buds of pink protein she plucked easily from their knobbed coatings.

The setting sun bled red and orange as the sky began to darken. Kahlil departed, leaving the girls alone to clink glasses filled with secret liquid and chunks of ice and lime. Peaches told stories, and Bloody responded with secrets and treasures.

Bloody was subdued, almost faint, as if she were a hundred years old in her head. "What are you going to do now, Peaches?"

"I don't know, Bloody. Clean things up, and then run away. To prove that I exist, even without the things that used to define my existence.

Bloody laughed like the girl Peaches had always known. "You're the tree falling in the forest, Peaches."

Peaches chucked brown-husked shells into the bushes, hoping peanut vines might magically grow. "But Bloody, I will be heard."

For the next few weeks, Bloody and Kahlil were around her daily as Peaches struggled to determine a course of action for the new part of her life. She was exhausted and shredded, nearly bleeding from marathon crying jags that overtook her without warning. She didn't feel lost, just on the border between two states of mind. She teetered on a line yet uncrossed, marking limbo or purgatory, a life without breath. Peaches felt a naked, bony, vulgar reality, where it seemed that everyone she loved was destined to disappear.

She returned to the church every day, first for the funeral Mass where Gram's urn sat on a little white-clothed table before the altar; Then once or twice a day just to keep the candles burning. On the evening of the thirteenth day, Peaches donated blood, warm and red, not in reparation or regret, but because she had it to give. The needle-puncher distracted Peaches from the moment of dull pain, but the rope-like bandage around her wound made her feel like a tied-off junkie. After, she sat eating peanut butter cookies and drinking juice, thinking thoughts of kindergarten and biting people.

Gram's Sunday breakfasts became special ceremonies, an inheritance that Peaches gladly accepted. One Sunday morning, Peaches led the breakfast masses through the city streets towards the cemetery that was home to Atlanta's first heroes. In recent years, very few had been given the privilege of being allowed to rest within its crumbling brick walls.

The night that Peaches received the small urn of Gram's ashes, she stood on the front porch and asked her city for permission to leave her grandmother there. The skyline flickered in response, and it was enough for Peaches to assume it accepted Gram's entry into the lasting record of Atlanta's past.

Among the graves of the city's oldest elite, the mourners prayed and sang as Peaches released part of her grandmother into the air. The gray ash, cradled momentarily by the breeze, scattered across the earth, while visiting tourists watched curiously. Soon enough, the ashes disappeared, the group dispersed and the cool, strange wind ceased to blow. Peaches walked back home with Kahlil and Bloody, praying her own reconstruction could now begin.

Resurging (Again)

Each night when darkness draped the sky and the city gleamed, music from inside the house competed with Peaches' thoughts. Often, too often. Peaches lit a cigarette, a deadly habit that provided fire, and Peaches was a dragon in her cave, guarding the gold before taking wing.

The plane was a big one, the kind she had always wanted to ride. After an ocean of sleep, a flight attendant nudged her awake. Peaches ate airplane food that tasted real, and then slept again.

It was the next morning when she arrived across the water. She took a funny old black cab to a modest hotel and fell back asleep. Bloody arrived that night on an open ticket slipped inside the front door of her house, bought by Peaches with loose cash as yet unbanked from around the house.

On the ground floor of the hotel, a band played, and the girls went downstairs to sit at the bar and listen. They tipped pints, and Peaches found the foreign cider sweet and smooth. Bloody drank black beer until her eyes nearly shut. In their room she collapsed into sleep, while Peaches sat on the rooftop, facing rows of Dickensian chimneys. She drank room-brewed coffee and made plans.

Awakened by a riotous morning sun, they started their visitations, leaving ashes first on the palace grounds. Peaches threw ashes into the wind blowing across the jade green fields of Eire, around a few choice graves in Pere-Lachaise cemetery in Paris, and along both sides of the old Berlin Wall. The two girls climbed to the top of a Salzburg mountain, and other places that Gram had not visited--until now.

On the isle of Crete, Peaches finally began to really eat again. She swallowed pastries and sea creatures, and tasted fruits and fresh vegetables as if for the first time. The stripes of purple on calamari and the scarlet of tomatoes colored the backdrop of her dreams.

On her last night in a hostel room outside Athens lined with more bunk beds than a labor camp, Peaches fell asleep to soft singing from a sweet Slavic boy drunk on ouzo. The dream gods brought her home to walk the streets of Atlanta. Peaches marveled at the smooth, paved stones that were the sidewalks of midtown, before crossing the border into downtown, where gnarled, cracked cement birthed weeds and shards of glass. She grew angry as she walked, sensing the architectural hemorrhage amid the useless developments piled atop the ghost forms of old buildings and dead dream trees.

In the past, her city had been known for its open arms, its welcoming spirit unhindered by the old. Time and again, city leaders had bluffed the opposition, on one occasion to become the state capital when only a one-horse town. They had cajoled professional sports teams southward without a stadium to house them in, and winked and smiled to lure Olympic deities. That was then. Now, the city seemed to have lost its bravado, its "we will be what we dream" spirit.

Peaches' dream led her down the city's greatest street. Not one block contained a single tree of that charming name. A hard, tough city had chosen as its symbol a fruit of unsurpassed softness, lushness, and

243

fragrance that did not exist within its precincts. That was the core truth of Atlanta.

Suddenly, the dream became a night terror. Airplanes targeted buildings, and explosions rocked the towers. Peaches ran for cover along the wide sidewalks she had once biked. Rubble rained down in rock-sized hail. She raced to reach a girl in the shadows, who pointed her towards a building standing sturdy amidst the debris.

Ducking inside the entrance, looking back once to ensure the girl was following. Peaches saw her still outside on the sidewalk; arms raised high as if wings might sprout from her back, causing her to rise above the collapsing skyline. A telephone pole began a toppling next to where the girl stood. Peaches watched the heavy, wooden pole drop to the ground, passing harmlessly through the figure, as sparks from loosened wires danced across the sidewalk.

Peaches gasped awake and sat up in bed, perspiration soaking her skin. The sweet air of the Mediterranean blew through the open window. The last moment of the dream imprinted itself on the black wall of the dark room: Madeleine, rising, turned to bestow a wink upon Peaches as Atlanta burned to the ground for the third time.

Peaches stared out a blue-curtained window at the waxing moon. The ghosts were beckoning. It was time to go home.

Making Change

In hopscotch fashion, Peaches left Athens for London, then took a plane to Charleston, the city of Mama. She hoped Bloody had found the scribbled note that she had left, detailing her itinerary and apologizing for her hasty departure.

Peaches sat on the same train as years before, watching the window change colors as the world blurred by. She knew it wasn't much longer to the hospital once she passed the cookie girl's house. The girl was not there, and Peaches wished she had taken a photograph of her. She knew now that anything could happen to little girls in just a few years.

The train stopped. Inside the hospital, it was as before, every day passing like a Tuesday colored gray. Peaches paused at Mama's door. Her mother was in the same position she had left her: sitting, watching. Speaking softly to the shadow in her doorway, like a woman underwater, Mama said: "I saw sunshine just yesterday."

Peaches' fingernails etched into her hands as she ventured into the room. Peaches tossed it back to the little ghost, quick and hard like a basketball off her mother's head. "No, you didn't, Mama."

Mama turned from her sinkpool of shadows. "Peaches, honey, you've grown…"

"Aw, Mama, I'm huge now." Peaches grabbed at the curtain strings and yanked hard. The fabric swished to either side as blinding sunlight poured in like a river through a dam.

Mama's mouth opened in a silent scream as color and light overtook the heavy darkness of the room. Outside, the world was brilliantly real, grass glowing green as the sky blazed blue-violet, a vibrant painting by an artist in a moment of ecstasy.

Peaches spoke slowly and sweetly from her place at the window. "The sunshine won't hurt you, Mama. I miss you, and I think it's about time you thought of coming home."

Peaches reached to undo the window, but found it triple-latched. She pulled her shirtsleeve down over her arm, and then used her elbow to smash a hole through the windowpane. The glass shattered, and an alarm began to wail. Cold, fresh air slid into the room as Mama jerked, her eyes glowing with a blue light unseen for years.

Peaches bellowed as loudly as her loose, ethereal smile. "Isn't life grand, mama?"

Mama gazed at Peaches. There was something both startling and familiar in her daughter's yelp. She stood and reached for her little girl. Peaches let herself be pulled in close, smiling fondly into the blue cells of her childhood mother. "Live, Mama, or die. Enough of this in-between. It's your choice, but look outside because you're missing it."

The dark-haired lady stared at the light-haired girl. Peaches kissed her Mama goodbye, then walked out, skirting panicky nurses who were heading to the source of the alarm.

Mama moved closer to the window as two nurses whirled into the room. She stepped up and down on popping shards of glass, creating a happy sound. The nurses howled and tried to hold her back, but Mama smiled into the sunshine, letting a cool breeze move her hair. She wondered what the beach was like this time of year, and whether the sea air would do Brother good.

Turning away from the window, she saw what Peaches had left for her. The old leather photo album lay on the chair. Mama sat down and pulled it to her lap. She flipped it open, and her breath caught: the first page a photo of her good husband, taken one winter's day. He was holding the dead fisherman's spear over the sea. Mama saw her daughter in his face, and wondered if it was the spear that made them look so much alike.

While the staff cleaned up, Mama turned the pages of her daughter's life, viewing the chapters she had missed. The train ticket to Atlanta with a date long gone. Matchbooks, train tickets, gas receipts, and bus transfers from towns across the Southernscape. Plane tickets, souvenir scraps, and pictures of Peaches, intertwined with photographs of Gram's oil-painted graffiti on walls and buildings throughout Atlanta. Mama saw Peaches' photos of Sunday breakfasts and sweet moments on the porch. A whole sheaf of pages was dedicated to a young girl's song, followed by the inevitable obituary that brought tears to Mama's eyes.

She read the newspaper accounts of her mother's life and traced her fingers across photos of her mother's last artwork, reveling in what Gram had become. On the final pages were freshly pasted scraps of Peaches' journey overseas. The last page held a stark black and white photo of Mama's children, when they were young and hers.

Mama shut the book, and watched the milling nurses as they swept up the broken glass. She stood and moved to the window, staring over the trees at her daughter's silhouette: Peaches, hurrying along the path down to the train.

Peaches looked back towards her mother's building just once, to make a wish that what she had done made a difference. Then she found her way to the Charleston airport.

Looking out onto the tarmac, Peaches concluded that no more romantic movies could be made with loved ones bidding adieu from the windows of planes. National security hade ended that. She wondered if it might spell a comeback for trains. First, though, there would need to be a comeback of romance, she concluded.

As the jet raised into the sky, Peaches dozed. In Atlanta, the ground whacked inside her as the plane touched and bumped against the runway. Peaches walked quickly through the airport, dropping coins into a payphone to alert Kahlil of her impending home-coming. Kahlil waited for her on the porch. Later, a white moon rose and darkness fell and Peaches went walking alone. After she passed the spot where the ghost of Madeleine had stood in her overseas dream, Peaches paused to breathe, sitting on a bus-stop bench. She thought of Madeleine and death by cab drivers.

A petite woman wearing hat and gloves and smelling sweetly of jasmine took the empty spot on the bench next to Peaches. They sat together, as quiet as the cluster of skyline that scanned the silent city with sleepy eyes. "Things have certainly changed here," the woman said in a soft voice.

Peaches tilted her head and looked around, the old city still visible and breathing through the concrete staidness of the new. "I guess that depends on when you were here last, ma'am."

The woman reached to pat Peaches on the knee, like an old lady. "Way before yesterday, my dear."

Peaches nodded, remembering her recent wander through the world. "It's been a little while for me, too, ma'am."

The last bus of the night chugged to a stop in front of their bench. Its exhaust besooted the air, adding to the smog that vacationed in Atlanta every summer. The woman looked expectantly at Peaches, matching the question on the broad face of the driver. "Are you waiting for this bus, dear?"

Peaches shook her head, and waved the bus on. Its doors shut as it sped north up the show street. "I wish Atlanta had cable cars," she said.

The woman smiled and mused, weaving poetry from plain words. "Cable cars create a city that people see. And they can hear its heartbeat in the clack of the tracks."

Peaches saw eye to eye with the friendly stranger. "I think people like a bit of yesterday sometime."

The woman removed one of her gloves, as if the humid night permitted this slight informality. "It seems much that was here is now gone. Is it quiet enough at night to still hear the heartbeat?"

Peaches nodded, then shook her head, not wanting to tell the woman how few listened at all any more. "Yes ma'am. Well, sometimes."

Peaches painted a picture in words for her: new city streets awake and swelling with stretch SUVs, limos, and—she paused, mindful of death—honking cabs. The scene swelled up. Young people strolling along sidewalks in a world that was loud, bright, and badly lit.

Peaches stuck out a foot from the bench in her imagined scene to trip a group of white cap males following young women who pranced and preened. "My peers think there is beauty in flash."

The woman grimaced at the sight. "The new generations. Please tell me there's more to Atlanta than this."

Peaches thought of a white marble tomb set in water and nestled at the edge of downtown. "We birthed a prophet. Maybe we will again."

Nearly grown youth chattered and jabbered as they ambled past the bench. The woman's face crinkled, perceiving a stranger in her house. "These children live as if they exist in only one world. Turn them off, dear."

Peaches waved her hand across the scene, and it disappeared. They were alone again in the quiet dark, home to millions scattered and sequestered among hills and around mills and traces, and linked by broad creeks and ferries.

The woman turned to Peaches curiously, trying to determine what else might have changed. "I remember Jim Crow."

Peaches considered an answer, wanting it to be neat and clean, but the world wasn't there yet. "It's still here. It's just changed names, ma'am. It's all over the country. Maybe the world."

The woman seemed disappointed. "It was always like that. It's never been a unique situation. We just happened to catch hell for it here." She posed another question, "Are there still beautiful houses in the West End?"

"Yes ma'am, just different owners." Peaches answered, then whispered with urgency as if there were listeners in the shadows. "But, shh, not so loud. The griffins are aloft. They might hear us."

"Griffins?" the woman asked. "I knew a family named Griffin."

"Flying griffins," said Peaches. "The natural enemy of phoenixes."

The woman stood, taking a moment to put her gloves back on. "Will you walk me towards my place, dear? I've missed the bus." She stared down the dark street and grew contemplative. "I actually hate this particular house. It's certainly not mine anymore. It never was really. I just want to see how they've done it up."

The woman and girl strolled up the street where a solitary little house stood, an anomaly amidst the skyscrapers, restaurants, and bars. While Gram's house was truly old, this structure was a kind of a grown-up's dollhouse, a meticulously crafted replica of pre-fabled history. Its shingles and shutters were a thick, dull brown; its red bricks were about as historic as a day-old newspaper. A solid sheet of uniform grass covered every inch of ground. The property was surrounded by a fence of black iron that caged the lawn and kept marking dogs and playing children from scarring the shrine.

Peaches turned to speak to the woman. "You know, this house has burned to the ground twice. Each time they put another one up, it just looks dumber and about as historic as me."

The woman sighed. "My dear, I've come to realize that people never tire of playing Scarlett and rebuilding Tara."

"Ma'am, that has to inspire you at least a little bit."

The older woman smiled gently, her eyes bright in the reflection of the streetlights. Her Irish was up, and cool anger tinged her words. "The wannabes never have inspired me, dear. They never understood me, or even really liked me. Some people in this city did, though. And I certainly loved many of them." She looked with disdain at the house. "This thing is barely breathing," she said.

The words hung like smoke, and Peaches suddenly stood alone, staring at the sky. Only a handful of stars. She searched for the brightest one, as if she could steal its strength, then store its energy deep inside, slowly treading home.

Too early, the telephone awakened her. Peaches hung it back up without answering. It rang again. Still in sloth mode, Peaches imagined cooking underway in the kitchen until the voice on the other end of the line bled the fantasy dry. It was Bloody at the airport, seeking a ride.

Peaches took a quick shower of wonderful, blasting hot water in a bathroom where water always ran with a rush and towels wrapped you up like a baby. She eased the Caddy out onto the street and turned onto the highway, the stereo's song loud enough to be heard through the cracked windows. Peaches brought Bloody back to the house, wanting to use her formidable brain to critically examine the new plan.

The orphan girl Peaches was now a landowner, a country girl with a city estate. The house was lined with cash from the peanut and tomato venture and from her grandfather's not insubstantial estate. The insurance paperwork was complete. Peaches' worth was sufficient to make the house a permanent outpost of human sense. No griffins need apply.

Birth Day

Peaches awoke early on her birthday to find Madeleine and Gram had again visited her in a dream. They were spirits shimmering through the stages of their lives as she watched. Gram as a young girl, a wife, a mother, and then an old woman. All in a moment. Madeleine as a toddler, a teenager, then the quick shadow of the young woman she would never become.

Peaches begged them to stay, but they laughed. Heaven really was an Elysian field. Who could leave? Gram disclosed barbecue and salty boiled peanuts, crusted fruit pies, flowing waters of various potencies. It was peopled by little children who were actually your ancestors, or vice versa.

Madeleine, for her part, found heaven's music divine ("What else?"), and revealed to Peaches that she joined daily in raising noise with some of the souls represented in the posters on her bedroom walls.

Awakened fully, Peaches slammed her eyes shut as it hit her, the familiar flash of dizziness that burned slowly from her center out to her skin. The old fainting nemesis, weakened somewhat from age, but still battling her defending army of angels and spirits arrayed around her. It soon passed.

On the front porch, as the sun rose and the clouds spread, she sipped coffee from a blue mug, watching early risers move out of the shadows, hungry for their Sunday breakfast. Bloody joined her on the porch, half-awake, her hair tufted and twisted like a rooster's crown.

Children from the reviving neighborhood gathered in the park, slipping from chill beds in search of each other's warmth.

As they watched them play, Bloody leaned over to seize Peaches' elbow. Her voice was hoarse and mixed with gravel as if she still lay asleep. "Peaches, I had a dream…".

Peaches grinned, a birthday smile planted firmly on her face. "I did, too, Bloody."

Then they saw Peaches' mother walking up the sidewalk, dressed in her Sunday best, back straight, shoulders squared, and her mind alive after a morning walk. Brother, who occasionally responded quite brightly to his new surroundings in Atlanta, today remained in his room. A breeze pushed waves of newly planted dogwoods and oaks to mix with the sharp, hot scent of morning coffee.

Mama climbed the porch steps and hugged her daughter, kissing one cheek and then the other. "Happy birthday, Peaches."

Bloody jumped to her feet, exuberant: "Come see your present, Peaches."

They led Peaches around the side of the house. Planted like flowers across the park were giant mirror balls shimmering in the morning sun, each encrusted with living butterflies.

Bloody clapped her hands to her mouth as she laughed aloud in delight. "Peaches, it took half the night to roll these things out here." She stared at the fluttering colors teeming around the shining orbs. "Oh, my, it was worth it."

Mama put her arm around Peaches and pulled her close. "You know, honey, some people believe that butterflies are spirits. If that's true, it seems quite a few souls have come to see Peaches today."

Something welled up inside Peaches, and she struggled to push it back down. "Thank you. It's beautiful."

Mama, twinkling in the sunlight, led Peaches and Bloody into the house where they would prepare the breakfast feast. Kahlil entered, accompanying him a team of peers and a large, spiral-cut ham. He greeted Peaches with a birthday kiss.

Peaches stood stirring the pudding of corn and butter, her face red from the stove's heat. "Sunday breakfast. My, my."

Bloody smiled from her place at the counter, popping out perfect circles of biscuit from a flattened sheet of dough. "It's a goddamned tradition," she declared.

Mama whisked a dozen eggs around the edge of a giant black skillet. "Peaches, I can't believe your Gram used to do this alone."

Peaches grinned, pausing from her duty at the stove to pluck a piece of biscuit dough from the side of Bloody's rolling pin. "Mama, I can't believe I had to do all the dishes."

From speakers inside the house and on the porch, an anthem of twang and remembering played. Fiddling, rap, country boys meeting city boys to make music in the middle. Female tones shone through, wrapping the song up in a nap of sweetness. The crystal bell of Gram's tinkled, and the Sunday crowd moved towards the tables nestled on the grounds. Mama, Kahlil, Bloody, and Peaches watched from the cool shadows of the porch, a knotting-together of pasts too many to count. Mama said grace.

Peaches thought of a house, the one she grew up in. Her mind traveled across the grass, past her father's peach tree, and over to the side of the house under the bedroom window that was once hers. She pictured the garden hose below it, yellow and long and coiled like a snake. In her mind's eye, she reached for the spigot imbedded in the brick wall of that house in the little town. She grasped the metal handle carved like a flower, and turned it gently. The spigot opened and water flowed, shooting forth upon the green grass. It sputtered as it gushed warmly to the ground, washing away caked red clay hardened by the shining sun on that town far away.

Peaches thought that over time she had developed a tolerance for those beautiful birds that rise again after their fires burn and their ashes blow away. A tolerance for phoenixes. She had found a tolerance, too, for penitents returned to the fold, and for those who acknowledged and celebrated every rebirth as if it were their own. A tolerance as well, for herself and all the things she had become.

Peaches, staring out at the city, was still her father's daughter and mother's child. She heard a whir of tires and the flat slap of the Sunday newspaper strike the pavement as a young delivery girl bicycled by. Peaches walked toward the wedge of news, smiling, no longer fearful of what it or the day contained, knowing that every day was just another day for those blessed enough to hear the whispered secrets of time and eternity hidden in the sound of the wind.

Peaches
A Southern girl grows up

Atlanta, Georgia,
and
Auckland, New Zealand

Caroline Seton Ledlie
13 March 2005

Made in the USA
Middletown, DE
30 October 2015